WAYNE STINNETT

ENDURING CHARITY

A CHARITY STYLES NOVEL

Caribbean Thriller Series
Volume 4

DOWN ISLAND PRESS

2018

Copyright © 2018
Published by DOWN ISLAND PRESS, LLC, 2018
Beaufort, SC
Copyright © 2018 by Wayne Stinnett

Library of Congress cataloging-in-publication Data
Stinnett, Wayne
Enduring Charity/Wayne Stinnett
p. cm. - (A Charity Styles novel)
ISBN-13: 978-1-7322360-0-4 (Down Island Press)
ISBN-10: 1-7322360-0-3

Cover photograph by Aragami
Graphics by Wicked Good Book Covers
Edited by Larks & Katydids
Final Proofreading by Donna Rich
Interior Design by Ampersand Book Interiors

This is a work of fiction. Names, characters, and incidents are either the product of the author's imagination or are used fictitiously. Any resemblance to actual persons, living or dead, businesses, companies, events, or locales is entirely coincidental. Most of the locations herein are also fictional or are used fictitiously. However, I take great pains to depict the location and description of the many well-known islands, locales, beaches, reefs, bars, and restaurants throughout the Florida Keys and the Caribbean, to the best of my ability.

FOREWORD

When I first started this series, I had no idea how difficult it would be to write from a woman's point of view. With the first Charity book, I found her to be a little angular. Over the course of the next two books, Charity softened a little, became more fleshed out. In this book, I wanted Charity to see her past and recognize herself as an emotional person. She also needs to face her future and come to terms with both.

My wife, Greta, is a constant source of ideas and my best sounding board—particularly when writing these Charity books. Not that I seek out her advice on how women think or feel. I believe we're basically the same in that respect. We all feel the same emotions at varying levels; different emotions are more pronounced in some people than in others. But just observing and following my wife's decision-making process, whether big decisions or small, has provided a lot of fodder for how Charity is evolving.

Speaking of evolution, my beta reading group has become a huge help in picking apart all the little details of my books. They help fine-tune the story so the reader has a much more pleasant experience.

Many thanks to Alan Fader, Dana Vihlen, Marc Lowe, Katy McKnight, Drew Mutch, Tom Crisp, Mike Ramsey,

Debbie Kocol, Dave Parsons, Charles Hofbauer, Karl Schulte, Ron Ramey, Dr. John Trainer, and Glen Hibbert. And a special thanks to Captain Dan Horn of Pyrate Radio. The recommendations these folks offer are always insightful and on point. Thank you for all your help.

DEDICATION

*Dedicated to the memory of Anna Louise Cooper Stinnett,
known simply as Mom by myself and my three siblings.
Mom was the rock that held the Stinnett clan together. At
4'-11" tall, she was a giant of endurance and fortitude, who
allowed three rambunctious sons to explore the hillsides of
St. Albans, West Virginia and the many waterways around
Eau Gallie, Florida. She was a woman who could make
pinto beans and cornbread seem a gourmet meal. Indeed,
I was a young man before I realized our special meal was
the staple of poor people all through Appalachia. Thanks
for making me tough, Mom.*

"Writing is sweat and drudgery most of the time. And
you have to love it in order to endure the solitude and
the discipline."
- **Peter Benchley**

If you'd like to receive my twice a month newsletter for specials, book recommendations, and updates on coming books, please sign up on my website:

WWW.WAYNESTINNETT.COM

THE CHARITY STYLES CARIBBEAN THRILLER SERIES

Merciless Charity
Ruthless Charity
Reckless Charity
Enduring Charity

THE JESSE MCDERMITT CARIBBEAN ADVENTURE SERIES

Fallen Out
Fallen Palm
Fallen Hunter
Fallen Pride
Fallen Mangrove
Fallen King
Fallen Honor
Fallen Tide
Fallen Hero
Rising Storm
Rising Fury
Rising Force (Fall, 2018)

The Gaspar's Revenge Ship's Store is now open. There you can purchase all kinds of swag related to my books.
WWW.GASPARS-REVENGE.COM

MAPS

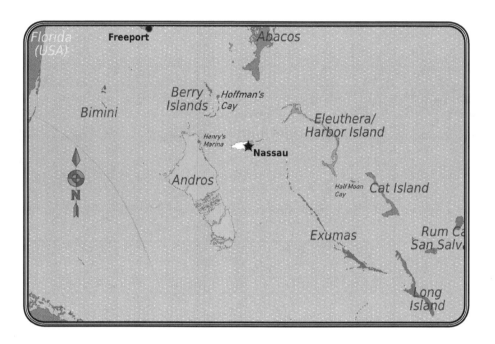

Florida (USA) Freeport Abacos

Bimini Berry Islands Hoffman's Cay Eleuthera/ Harbor Island

Henry's Marina Nassau

N

Andros Half Moon Cay Cat Island

Exumas Rum Ca San Salv

Long Island

ENDURING CHARITY

CHAPTER ONE:

A light wind gently rocked the old boat. It was a warm easterly breeze carrying the aroma of the sea, mixed with the faint echoes of exotic scents from distant lands. It was this same wind that carried the first Europeans across the ocean. Between the twenty-third and twenty-fifth latitudes, the wind came straight out of the east this time of year in the western Atlantic, unfaltering for half the reach of the ocean. Approaching the coast of Europe and Africa, the winds bent east-northeast. Tracing these trade winds in reverse, there was very little but open ocean to impede their progress, all the way back to the coasts of Morocco, Portugal, Spain, and beyond there, into the very cradle of exploration, the Mediterranean Sea. Air so fresh is seldom found anywhere on shore.

An occasional soft *thunk* from the halyard against the wooden mast and the subtle creaking of the seventy-six-year-old wooden boat's hull were the most prominent sounds. The water was so tranquil that even those were

few. Quietly floating a hundred yards from the white sand beach, the boat itself was the only thing around that wasn't natural; though not seeing a boat in such an idyllic setting might seem more so.

From the trees along the shoreline, an occasional wading bird would call to its mate. The slight movement the sea and wind imparted on the boat caused the hammock below the boom to casually swing back and forth. To the west the sun hung low, just a few degrees above a clear horizon.

Charity Styles had sailed *Wind Dancer* to Hoffman's Cay to dive the blue hole. Yesterday, she'd anchored on the lee side of the uninhabited island, part of the Berry Islands of the northern Bahamas. It held the distinction of having one of the few inland blue holes in the island nation, and she found them fascinating.

Lying in the hammock, watching the sun perform its evening dance of color and light, Charity thought about her life to this point. In ten days, she'd reach her thirtieth birthday. To her, it would be just another day; no cause for jubilation. Her generation barely recognized thirty as a milestone.

Today, however, was different. Most Americans her age would be out with friends, in rowdy celebration of the coming new year. It was said that whatever one was doing at the stroke of midnight on New Year's Eve was the activity they would be involved in for most of the coming year. This was why couples kissed at midnight.

Charity was alone on her boat. She'd been alone before, and it never bothered her. Besides, Victor wasn't far away and would be joining her soon. They'd been sailing and island-hopping together for nearly four months, explor-

ing the hundreds of tiny islands, shoals, and anchorages from the Virgin Islands up through the Bahamas. For most of that time, the two had anchored in secluded coves with nobody else around, allowing them ample time to explore each other, as well.

They'd left Hawksbill Cay three days earlier, having spent a week anchored off a small, isolated cove with a white sand beach. They hadn't even seen another boat during that whole week. Their plan had been to reach Hoffman's Cay in two days, stopping for the night and to reprovision in Nassau. Then they would spend the last few days of the year diving and exploring the blue hole.

The first leg of the ninety-mile journey went very well. The wind was steady, the seas fair, and the skies clear. On the second leg, after a day-long layover to replenish their food, water, and fuel in Nassau, Victor hit a floating log just two hours out of port and began taking on water. He didn't find a hull breach, but water was coming in around the propeller shaft seal.

Charity had followed him back to the marina, and rather than risk running his engine, she anchored and towed him in with her dinghy. It took a couple of hours before they could get his boat out of the water, but the bilge pumps didn't have any trouble keeping up with the leak.

Rather than both being stuck in Nassau, Victor had urged her to sail the forty-five miles to the anchorage; he would join her once he had *Salty Dog* on the hard and inspected for damage. There were quite a few go-fast boats around the capital and commercial hub of the Bahamas, any one of which he could hire to bring him across in less than an hour. He'd called her earlier in the afternoon to say he'd be another night in Nassau.

Charity watched the sunset from her hammock, a half-full glass of wine on the cabin top beside her. In truth, she was glad for the temporary solitude. Life is permanently temporary; it's here for a little while. So one has to take advantage of the quiet moments to reflect.

She cared deeply for Victor, but the only period she had any alone time was when they were under sail. Last night had been the first night she'd been completely alone for quite a while, and she had enjoyed it.

Lifting the wine glass to her lips, she thought again about the life she'd left behind. For the better part of two years, *Wind Dancer* had left a trail of death and destruction in her wake. So far, there had been no pursuers, nobody looking for her in retribution for what she'd done or to silence her from talking about it. She'd contacted one or two trusted friends, and it seemed as if everything she'd been told was true: Her past was indeed gone and buried.

She placed the glass back on the cabin top as the last of the sun slipped silently below the horizon. There wasn't a cloud anywhere, so only a small portion of the south-western sky glowed a rusty red, and that only lasted a few seconds before it too was gone. Twilight didn't last long on the water.

The Florida Keys – and what had once been home – lay almost two full days of sailing in the very same direction the sun had gone. She hadn't had a real home since before college, before her father died. The Army had been home for a while. But she'd never felt as needed and had such a sense of belonging as she did when she worked for the American government in the Keys.

Drifting off to sleep, Charity lay unmoving, wearing only shorts and a tank top. Anchored far enough from shore that the bugs couldn't find her and the night air was tempered by the warm, shallow water, she was more than comfortable and slept peacefully.

Until a strange sound woke her.

She sprang from the hammock, fully awake and alert, standing on the side deck. Charity could tell by the position of the stars that she'd been asleep for only a couple of hours. The sound of an engine could be heard on the other side of the island, moving slowly toward the south. She followed it in her mind, her ears telling her where the boat was located. It slowly passed the tip of Hoffman's Cay and turned into the deep cut between it and the two smaller islands to the south, White Cay and Fowl Cay.

The natural channel was tricky during daylight hours; it made several turns before clearing the islands. Either the person at the helm was nuts or they knew the waters very well.

Charity was anchored on the west side of Hoffman's Cay, just north of a point of land jutting out into the shallow water. Beyond the spit of land, she could see the lights of the boat as it cleared the southern tip of Hoffman's and turned north. The pilot picked his way through the shallows, slowly approaching the point. Finally, Charity heard a large splash. They were anchoring in the next cove to the south of the point.

The engine shut off, and it was quiet again. Occasionally, she heard someone talking — either a woman, or a man with a high voice. Charity couldn't make out anything that was said, just the tone of the speech. She wasn't even sure if it was English.

Patience was something Charity had in spades. She waited and watched the other boat until it became quiet again. Over the headland, she could see the lights from the boat, a trawler, but she couldn't make out any detail. The inside lights were soon doused, leaving only their mast light shining.

Charity looked up at the top of her mast. *Wind Dancer's* mast light was on, but nothing more, so she didn't know if the other boat was aware of her presence or not. She assumed they were, since hers was the preferred anchorage.

Maybe they just don't want to crowd, Charity thought, gathering her things. Most cruisers she'd met really valued their privacy and appreciated solitary vistas, still mornings, and quiet evenings.

She went aft to the cockpit and double-checked that the dinghy's painter was secure. She opened a small console next to the helm and took out one of her handguns, wrapped in oilcloth. There were other hiding places for items of value all over the boat. Most cruisers were also pirates in some small way, smuggling untaxed alcohol, cash, recreational drugs, and weapons into and out of island nations. Boats had dozens of places where a little crafty carpentry work could hide a lot, and few customs inspectors dug really deep into a boat's bilge area unless they were certain what they were looking for.

Charity was no different. *Wind Dancer* had a dozen stash spots built into her interior woodwork during a complete refit, paid for by the United States government. She had half a dozen firearms, some explosives, military-grade electronic and surveillance equipment, and a considerable sum of cash on board. Even some untaxed alcohol.

The helm console hiding spot was only used when underway, for quick access. When she was in port, Charity hid the big Colt 1911 in another, more secure spot down in the cabin.

She stuck the Colt, which had once belonged to her father, into the big cargo pocket of her shorts and sat down on the starboard bench. From there, she could easily watch the other boat and the approach around the spit. Putting her feet up, she got comfortable and watched the sky for a while. A half-moon hung directly overhead and provided plenty of light to see her surroundings. After nearly an hour, not seeing any movement or hearing any sound from the other boat, she finally rose and went to the cabin hatch.

Below, she closed and secured the hatch. Increasingly often, this was something she hadn't bothered with. She and Victor had almost always been alone in an anchorage. But with another boat so close by, it was prudent to take precautions. She opened the aft portholes on either side of the salon, then rinsed her glass and put it away. The moonlight streaming through the overhead port light was more than enough to see by. Besides, Charity knew every nook and cranny of her old boat, like it was part of her.

Going forward to the vee berth, she opened the over-head hatch just enough to let the breeze fill the tiny cabin. Placing the Colt on the shelf near her head, she stripped down to just her panties and crawled onto the bunk. In minutes, she was again fast asleep, secure in the knowl-edge that she'd hear anything that came even remotely close to her boat.

CHAPTER TWO:

Victor Pitt watched the sun going down from the cockpit of his boat. Normally, this was something he very much enjoyed. Especially lately. He and Charity had been together for four months, anchored primarily in isolated coves for days on end. She rarely wore anything if they were alone and it was warm enough. The diffuse light of the setting sun on her body always got his blood pumping.

But tonight, his view of the sunset was sandwiched between an old Chris-Craft Commander that looked like it hadn't been in the water since the millennium and a hulking warehouse building. The *Dog* was on the hard, waiting for parts to arrive from Florida. And Victor was alone.

It was only the second time *Salty Dog* had been out of the water since he'd bought her eight years earlier. Victor detested having his boat up on blocks on the hard, he hated being this close to so many people, he hated the noise, and he hated being away from Charity. In short, Victor wasn't really in the mood for the loud New Year festivities.

Yet the celebration was beginning to crank up all around him, in the many bars and restaurants all around Brown Boat Basin. A band was playing at the *Green Parrot*, half a mile across Nassau Harbor at Hurricane Hole. It was competing, and winning, against jukeboxes and other bands in nearby bars all along the waterfront.

The log that *Salty Dog* had collided with the day before had been partially submerged, so he hadn't seen it. Another day or two and it would have been so waterlogged that it would have begun to sink, as all things eventually do in the ocean. The hull was fine, but the log had somehow turned and impacted the prop and rudder, knocking the stuffing box loose and allowing water to come in. He hoped the prop-shaft was okay, but they wouldn't know until they pulled the shaft and tested it. Since the new prop would be at least three days in arriving, the mechanic had opted to wait until it arrived before starting any work.

It was New Year's Eve, and Victor was stuck in one of the biggest tourist traps in the Caribbean — Nassau, capital city of the Bahamas. He had a boat arranged for the morning, to take him north to join Charity on Hoffman's Cay. Then the two of them could sail back to Nassau once the work on *Salty Dog* was finished. But he was stuck there one more night.

Reaching down, he opened the cooler at his feet and took out his last beer. They'd just reprovisioned two days ago, right here in Nassau, but since they were only planning to be on Hoffman's Cay for a week, they'd loaded only Charity's boat with groceries. Her refrigerator worked better than his, so he had most of the dry goods.

The last of the sun disappeared, along with the last of Victor's beer. Taking the cooler back down to the galley, he cleaned it and put it away. Reclining on the settee, he picked up a paperback from the table, intent on finding out what the Key Largo fly fisherman, Thorn, was up to these days — but after a few minutes of trying to read, he knew it was pointless. As was any chance of getting any sleep until the parties died down.

If you can't beat 'em, he thought, rising and going to his stateroom at the back of the big Formosa ketch. From his hanging locker, he took a pair of jeans and a clean button-down shirt and changed out of his shorts and tee-shirt. Slipping a pair of worn Topsiders on his feet and his *Salty Dog* cap over his unruly hair, he went forward to the engine room and opened the hatch. He had to lay on his side next to the engine to be able to feel around under it. Reaching deeper, he felt the panel and moved his hand along the top to find the groove. He pulled the panel out and reached in again. He felt the familiar watertight box and pulled it out. Opening it, he took out two hundred dollars, then put the box back and went back up the ladder, locking the hatch behind him.

Exiting the marina's storage yard, Victor turned left on Bay Street and followed the sound of celebration. It wasn't a long walk; just a hundred yards up the street he found a place called *Celebrity Status* and went inside.

The clientele seemed to be an even mix of locals and cruisers, but tourists outnumbered both. A cruise ship must be at the terminal for the night. Victor took a stool at the end of the bar and ordered a Kalik. The three-piece band wasn't all that bad. Two black men played steel drums and bongos, and a young white man with dreads played guitar.

After another beer, Victor began to relax. He decided that being in a big city wasn't really all that bad. With so many tourists around, he melted easily into the background.

Two young women, one blond and one brunette, took seats at the bar next to him. They were dressed for a night on the town, wearing clingy dresses that barely reached their thighs. He guessed they were in their mid-twenties, and pretended to ignore them and their incessant chatter about having the *real* Bahamian experience.

Yeah, he thought, *like you're really gonna find that in a tourist bar.*

"There's a place on Mackey Street that's supposed to be authentic," the blonde said.

"Where's that?" the brunette asked.

The blonde looked toward the bartender, who had his back turned. "I don't know," she said, glancing around. Her eyes fell on Victor. "Excuse me." She touched his shoulder. "Do you know where Mackey Street is?"

Victor looked at the two women. They were both attractive; the brunette had chocolate-brown eyes that looked almost black, and the blonde's eyes were a dazzling shade of green. They also seemed to have started their celebration earlier than prudent. Obviously off a cruise ship.

"From Paradise Island," he replied, "cross the bridge and instead of turning left to get here, stay straight. That's Mackey."

"You've been to the *Jump Up and Shout*?" she asked.

"Never heard of it," he replied, motioning the bartender for another beer. "But you don't want to go too far up Mackey. Once you're over the hill, it's not safe."

After learning that Victor wasn't from their cruise ship, the blonde began telling him about the different ports the *Delta Star* had visited that week. Most of the ports she mentioned had been on his and Charity's list of places to avoid.

The blonde was the more outgoing of the two and did most of the talking. She ordered three shots of rum and offered one to Victor. The two women tossed the shots down, grimacing, then got up to dance. Victor accepted the shot with a nod, swallowed the rum in one gulp, and ordered another beer.

The brunette seemed the quiet type, following along with whatever the other woman wanted to do. The two danced together, and the band, seeing the pretty tourists, changed to a slower, more seductive beat. The two women had no trouble getting into the groove, dancing even more provocatively.

Victor was starting to feel a bit woozy. He knew that the liquor in these kinds of places wasn't top shelf and was watered down, so he doubted it was the rum shot. He'd only had four beers, but lately he and Charity hadn't been drinking much, so maybe his tolerance was lower. At any rate, he was having a hard time focusing on anything but the mesmerizing movements of the bodies of the two women.

Victor learned that the blonde's name was Rayna. She tried to pull him up to join them. There wasn't really a dance floor, so the women were just dancing next to their seats at the bar. The song ended, and the women stopped their gyrations — to the obvious disappointment of many of the men in the bar.

Rayna sat next to Victor and turned toward him. She crossed her long legs, letting her calf barely caress Victor's leg. The brunette, whose name Victor had finally learned was Fiona, stood next to her friend, one arm draped across the back of Victor's barstool as she leaned against the blonde.

"How dangerous is it?" Fiona asked, leaning in close to Victor, giving him an ample view of her cleavage. "Mackey Street, I mean."

"If tourists go over the hill after dark," Victor said, beginning to slur his words, "they're pretty much gonna get robbed."

"He's right, Miss," the bartender said, leaning over the bar. "Far be it fuh me to say someting bad bout me own island, but crime be almost certain on di udduh side of di hill."

"Besides," Victor said, feeling even more light-headed, "this isn't the real Bahamas." He swept his arm toward the street and the bay beyond it, nearly falling off his stool. "That's out there."

Rayna and Fiona both leaned in close to Victor, each placing a hand on one of his thighs. Fiona pulled his shoulder and head around, practically burying his face in their abundant bosoms.

The touch of their hands through his Dockers sent a jolt of electricity through Victor's nervous system. Rayna put her hand on his head and slowly pulled his cheek to her chest, igniting a fire and waking every cell of his libido. As their hands slowly massaged their way up his thighs, Victor no longer cared what their names were.

Rayna's words tickled his ear. "Maybe you could walk a couple of girls back to the ship?"

Together, the three of them left the bar and went up Bay Street toward the bridge. A small part of Victor's mind knew that what he was doing was wrong. Hell, it was insanity. A flicker of consciousness told him that he'd been drugged. But whatever it was that Blondie had slipped in his rum shot was making him feel far too excited to do anything about it. Nor even want to.

They walked down the street with Victor sandwiched between them. The women had their arms around his waist and his arms over their shoulders, helping him walk. To further drive him over the edge, both women held his wrists so that his open hands were held firmly against their breasts.

The two women turned Victor into an alley and suddenly there were three young men standing in front of them. They stopped. Victor was only vaguely aware that anyone else was around and continued to fondle the women's breasts through and under their satiny dresses. He decided he liked the brunette best; she had actually encouraged him to go for second base, pushing his hand under the top of her skimpy dress as they walked.

CHAPTER THREE:

The sound of a small outboard woke Charity. A shaft
of sunlight from a porthole fell on the bulkhead
at her feet, the angle telling her it was just past dawn.
Sitting up in her bunk, fully aware of her surroundings,
she quickly retrieved the Colt from the shelf next to the
bunk where she'd left it. She came up onto her knees,
pushing the overhead hatch completely open. Rising to
a low crouch, she lifted her head through the opening
to peek out over the starboard deck. The upper half of
the other boat was in view on the other side of the spit.
The classic lines of the trawler looked familiar, but she
couldn't place it.

Charity rose higher, bringing her shoulders and arms
up through the hatch, ready for a fight even if she was clad
only in blue bikini panties. Looking all around, she saw
that there weren't any other boats in sight.

The outboard sound was approaching the point and a
moment later, a dinghy came into view. Charity crouched,

watching with just her head above the deck. There were two people aboard; a woman and a girl.

The dinghy turned and headed toward *Wind Dancer*. The woman on the tiller slowed the engine and the little boat settled into the water as it grew nearer. Charity smiled. The woman driving the boat lifted a hand from the gunwale and waved. Charity waved back and motioned her to come over.

Withdrawing from the hatch, Charity opened a drawer at the foot of the bunk. She stripped off her panties and put on a bikini, then pulled a tank top and shorts on over it. She felt the inflatable dinghy bump the side of her boat, as she exited the stateroom.

"Ahoy, *Wind Dancer*," a woman's voice called out, as Charity hurried aft and opened the main hatch.

Climbing quickly to the cockpit, Charity smiled down at the mother and daughter. "Savannah Richmond, right?"

"You have a good memory, Gabby. We didn't expect to find anyone else here this time of year, especially someone we knew."

"Would you like to come aboard?" Charity asked. "I just woke up and don't have coffee on yet, but I can make some."

Savannah lifted a large thermos. "I have plenty, thanks. Plus a few sausage biscuits and a big bowl of sliced mango. We're going to the blue hole. Want to join us?"

"Let me grab a few things," Charity said. "I'll meet you at the beach."

Savannah pushed off and yanked on the starter cord. The little outboard started instantly and she turned the boat toward shore, bringing it up on plane in seconds.

Charity went below and put a few things in a small beach bag, which she called her excursion bag. Besides a change of clothes, it had everything necessary to survive a day ashore on an island that might not be very hospitable. She shoved her Colt into the bottom, it being a usual accessory for the excursion bags. Just as she was about to leave, she stopped at the navigation desk and switched on the radar. It took a moment to warm up, but with the radar antenna mounted high on the mast, it could look over the surrounding low islands. No echoes appeared within eight miles other than the islands themselves.

Though there wasn't anyone around, she locked the hatch anyway. That was an unbendable rule. The boat was never left unsecured for any length of time. Untying the line to the dinghy, she pulled it up alongside *Wind Dancer*, tied it off to the rail, and stepped down into it. The outboard started with just two pulls and she waited a moment to make sure it was running smoothly before untying and shoving off. In seconds, the small dinghy was skimming across the surface toward the little horseshoe-shaped beach.

Savannah and her daughter were waiting on the sandy shore by their boat. Charity stopped the engine in the shallows, raised it out of the water, and waited for the bottom to touch the sand. She stepped out into calf-deep water and pulled her dinghy up onto the sand alongside Savannah's.

"You liked it here so much, you never went back?" Savannah asked.

Charity looked at her, puzzled.

"You were picking up friends in Key Biscayne when we met," Savannah reminded her. "You said you were going to cruise the Bahamas for a few weeks."

Savannah started picking things up from her dinghy and Charity took the cooler from her. "Oh, yes. No, I've been back to Florida since then. And a lot of other places."

"Flo," Savannah said to her daughter, "do you remember Miss Gabby?"

The young girl extended her hand. She'd grown since Charity had first met her. Her sparkling blue eyes were filled with the wisdom of an old soul. When Charity took the girl's hand, she got that same *déjà vu* feeling she had the first time they'd met. It seemed as if she knew the girl from somewhere else. Maybe another life.

"Very nice to see you again," Flo said.

Charity smiled at the girl. "Likewise, I'm sure."

"How long's it been?" Savannah asked. "Two years?"

"I don't think that long," Charity replied, though she knew exactly what the date was. "It was summer before last, wasn't it?"

Charity had met Savannah and her daughter on the first night after leaving her former co-workers and departing on her first mission to Mexico. The date was indelibly stamped in her mind.

"You're right." Savannah followed Flo toward the little path that led the way to the blue hole. "You've been here before?"

"No, this is my first time," Charity replied. "I arrived yesterday and spent most of the day diving in the hole."

"You scuba dive?"

"Yes," she replied. "My boyfriend has a compressor on his boat, but he's stuck in Nassau for repairs, and I've already used the three tanks I have on board."

"I have a compressor," Savannah said, "and four full tanks. It takes a while for it to fill a tank, but if you like,

I can fill yours when we get back and the three of us can dive this afternoon, using mine."

"Your daughter dives? How old is she?"

Savannah laughed, as they trudged along the sandy trail. "Flo's only eight, but her first shoes were fins. I don't let her go past ten feet yet, though."

The trail wound through a thicket of dense candle-wood, banyan trees, and yellow elder, the latter covered with bright yellow flowers. The trail opened onto higher ground, where the constant easterly breeze bent inva-sive Australian pine trees, so they grew to look like great, breaking waves frozen in time with gnarled roots and trunks for foam. The hole soon opened ahead of them; the chalky, white limestone cliffs surrounding the water measured a couple of football fields across, with the water some twenty feet below.

"Can I jump, Mom?"

"Look first," Savannah warned, as she lowered the basket and blanket to the ground in a rocky clearing near the edge of the cliff.

To Charity's amazement, the girl barely hesitated. She glanced over the edge then leapt into the abyss, shrieking with a child's abandon.

"She's fine," Savannah said, appearing to read Charity's anxious look. "We've spent weeks here on many occasions. It's Flo's favorite place. She's jumped off that cliff at least a thousand times. So, how've you been? You mentioned a boyfriend."

"I've been well, thank you." Charity helped Savannah spread a large blanket over the rock and sand. "His name is Rene," she said, using Victor's alias. "Rene Cook. He works on boats and we've been traveling together for a few months. How have you two been?"

Savannah's eyes drifted away for a moment. "Oh, we're getting by just fine."

As the two women sat down on the blanket, Flo came scrambling up a trail in the cliff face to their right. Charity had been up and down it several times, carrying her scuba gear, and thought that a mountain goat would look twice before scaling it.

"You mentioned coffee," Charity said, sitting down next to Savannah, as Flo threw herself off the cliff again. Her shrieks, echoing off the surrounding cliff, were punctuated by a large splash.

"Oh, yes." Savannah dragged the basket closer and handed Charity a plastic mug from inside. She took out another and filled them both from a large thermos.

Charity sipped the coffee. "Mmm," she said. "This is very good."

"Thanks," Savannah said. "It's from a little farm in Costa Rica. A friend in the Keys gave me some a few weeks ago. I'm afraid this is the last, then it's back to whatever the next marina has in stock."

"You're a full-time cruiser?"

"We'll take a slip now and then," Savannah replied, "but not for very long. We prefer anchoring in out of the way places like this. You said you'd been traveling with your boyfriend for several months. Are you and he full-time? Cruisers, I mean."

"Pretty much," Charity replied, as Flo came scrambling up the trail again. "On both counts."

"Mom, look what I found!" The girl approached, carrying a dark brown bottle in her hand.

"Is there a note inside?" Savannah asked, as Flo knelt in front of her and handed her the bottle.

"I don't think so. I held it up to the sun; it looks empty."

Savannah turned the bottle over and inspected the bottom. "It's old, maybe the sixteenth century. Probably a rum bottle left by a pirate. It'll make a fine addition to your collection."

The girl beamed as she rose. "I knew it was a pirate's."

"Where did you find it?" Charity asked.

Flo stopped at the edge of the cliff. "Near the top of the trail. It was stuck in the side of the wall. Only the tip was sticking out."

"Could be treasure buried under it."

Flo grinned, as she once more leapt off the cliff, screaming, "I bet it's Anne Bonny's."

Savannah grinned and shook her head. "You never know."

"If she found it at the top of the trail, why didn't she just walk back down to look for the treasure?"

Savannah laughed. "Several years ago — I guess Flo was about five or six — she wanted to walk down. She ended up falling and tumbling over some rocks before going over the cliff. She was scraped up a little, nothing serious, but she now has a rule against walking down the trail when she can just jump and walk up it."

Charity smiled. "Well, a girl has to have her rules."

Savannah stood and took her shirt off. "Let's go see what she found."

Charity rose as Savannah trotted to the edge of the cliff and looked down. She removed her shoes and wiggled out of her shorts, tossing them on the ground.

"You're jumping?" Charity asked, pulling her tank top off.

"Last one in!" Savannah shouted as she threw herself over the edge.

Charity heard the splash just as she reached the edge. She pulled her shoes and shorts off, leaving them with Savannah's things. Taking a few tentative steps closer to the edge, she saw Savannah and Flo swimming out away from the sheer rock wall.

In two steps, Charity was standing at the edge of the crumbling limestone. All through her teens and twenties, she'd been a competitive swimmer, culminating with a bronze medal in the Sydney Olympics at the age of nineteen. She'd tried diving, but much preferred the adrenaline rush when the competition was right beside her in the next lane.

Charity leapt, pushing up and out with her powerful legs. She extended her arms out to her sides and arched her back in a strikingly graceful pose. Her body hurtled toward the water, slowly tumbling forward. At the last moment, just before she became perpendicular to the water, she stretched her arms over her head, interlocking her thumbs.

Though only about twenty feet, the fall seemed to take a long time. Her entry wasn't perfect; she didn't quite rotate to fully perpendicular. But she hadn't meant to. As she entered the water, the slight angle helped propel her away from the rocky wall beneath the surface.

Diving at least ten feet below the surface, Charity arched her back to turn upward. She opened her eyes and kicked toward the surface amid a thousand tiny bubbles.

"That was awesome!" Flo shouted when Charity surfaced face first, allowing her hair to stream down her back. "Can you show me?"

"If it's okay with your mom." Charity swam toward them. "Just not from way up there at first, okay? If you mess up, you'd be surprised at how quickly a swan dive turns into a belly flop."

All three laughed.

It felt good to laugh. Charity hadn't laughed a lot in the last two years. When she was with Victor, he was very subdued, always looking over his shoulder. Even when they made love, he took it too seriously. He tried so hard to concentrate only on her that it seemed like a performance.

"Where'd you learn to dive like that?" Savannah asked as the three of them swam slowly toward a large cavern with a sand beach. Water and wave action had cut the rock away beneath the overhanging cliff, creating a cavern.

"I was once a competitive swimmer. Mostly high school and college."

They reached the wall, and Flo scampered up onto the beach. Savannah and Charity moved a bit slower, stepping up into the large alcove using several rocks sticking out from the wall below the surface.

"This is an amazing place," Charity said, looking out over the calm surface of the water. "Kinda spooky, too."

Savannah looked at her quizzically. "You had an accent when we first met. Cuban, if I remember correctly. And black hair."

Dammit, Charity thought, *I'm slipping.*

What the heck? That part of her life was over now. And she felt pretty certain that Victor was just being paranoid and there wasn't anyone after him, either.

"I should apologize," Charity said.

Savannah lowered herself cross-legged to the sand, arms wrapped around her knees. "Apologize for what?"

Sitting next to her, Charity thought about what she could say. "For lying," she began. "When we met before, I was working undercover for the government. My real name is Charity Styles."

There was a shriek and a blur, then Flo hit the water twenty feet out. She surfaced and swam toward them, again scaling the rocks at the edge like a mountain goat.

"There wasn't anything under the bottle," Flo said. "I dug and dug. Just rock."

"Well, it's still a nice bottle," Charity said. "And Anne Bonny spent a lot of time in these waters."

"I'm gonna go jump again," Flo said, then disappeared up the trail.

"Undercover as what?" Savannah asked.

Charity looked across the water to the opposite wall. Covered with vines and brush, it towered twenty feet high all around. "I worked for Homeland Security until just a few months ago."

"What kind of work did you do?"

Charity didn't want to tell her that she had been a government assassin. She liked the woman and didn't have many whom she could call friend.

"I don't work for them anymore," she said, choosing her words carefully. "At the time, I worked for an anti-terrorist group within Homeland Security, helping to keep our southern waters safe."

"There's a terrorist threat in Florida?"

"Throughout the Caribbean," Charity replied. "You're a cruiser. You know how easy it is to move in and out of

Florida by water. I worked to help expose and eliminate any threats."

"I see," Savannah said. "But you're no longer working for them?"

"Our unit was dismantled a few months ago," Charity replied, now actually believing it was true. "I had some money set aside and decided to just drop out for a while."

"I can certainly understand that," Savannah said. "I moved aboard because I was on the run from an abusive ex, then shortly after, an escaped homicidal maniac. That was nine years ago. The ex is no longer in the picture, and the escaped murderer is dead. But Florence and I have enjoyed the lifestyle so much, we've just never gone back."

"Flo's father?"

"Well..." Savannah started.

"I'm sorry. It's none of my business."

"Oh, it's okay. I left my husband before I became pregnant. Legal separation and all. After a couple of months, we decided to reconcile. But it didn't last long. We split up for good before I knew I was pregnant. The truth is, he might not be Flo's father."

"Ooh, the plot thickens," Charity said, grinning. She decided that she liked this woman. Though they'd only met once, the fact that she had a secret made her more human, which in turn made Charity feel more human, as well.

Savannah laughed. "Yeah, well, nobody's going to write a story about my life." She looked out over the deep, mysterious water for a moment. "When my husband and I first separated, I went to the Keys with my sister. We took our dad's yacht, and even hired an experienced captain so we could just enjoy ourselves. My sister died last month."

"Oh, I'm so sorry," Charity said.

Savannah seemed to shake off the sudden melancholy and grinned at Charity. "Anyway, I met a guy while we were in the Keys, and we had a short affair. Then my ex and I decided to give our marriage one more try. There's a chance that the guy in the Keys might be Flo's father."

"Does he know?"

Savannah looked seriously at Charity, arching an eyebrow. "If you were uncertain, would you tell a guy whom you'd had a short fling with that he might be a father?"

"Probably not," Charity replied after considering it a moment. "So *you* don't even know."

Savannah again looked off across the water and sighed. "No, I don't. Everyone just assumed that Flo was Derrick's daughter. He's my ex. I've only told one other person that he might not be."

Charity laughed lightly as she stood up and offered her new friend a hand. "Well, your secret's safe with me. It's doubtful either of us has any friends in common, anyway."

Savannah smiled and took Charity's hand. "I mean, is there any rule that says a kid has to have two parents?" she asked, rising to stand next to Charity. "Can't a woman fill both roles? *I* am Flo's parents."

"Absolutely," Charity agreed, liking this self-assured woman even more. "Speaking of Flo, she's about a minute past due for her next jump, isn't she?"

"She's okay," Savannah said, turning toward the trail. "Probably digging for Anne Bonny's treasure."

Just then, they heard a man's voice, which froze them both in place. It seemed to come from all around as it echoed off the cliffs surrounding the hole. "Hey! You down there! Better get up here!"

"What the hell?" Charity said, instinctively looking around for anything that could be used as a weapon.

Savannah moved quickly to the trailhead. Scrambling up the rocky incline, she sent several rocks toppling into the water.

Charity hurriedly caught up to her. "Wait," she said, grabbing her elbow.

Savannah turned sharply. There was a fire in her eyes unlike any Charity had seen before. "Someone's up there with my little girl!"

When Savannah turned and started back up the trail, it was all Charity could do to keep up with her. The two of them quickly reached the top and found three men clustered around their blanket. A fourth was standing near the edge of the cliff, holding Flo. One of the men at their blanket was rifling through Savannah's basket.

"Well, well," the man holding Flo said. "Would you look at what we got here."

All four men's eyes roved over the two women's bodies, clad only in their swimsuits. Charity's eyes quickly assessed the men. The one holding Flo wasn't very big, but the leader was usually the one in charge and he was holding the girl. He had a meanness in his hard-set eyes which Charity had seen before in other men. He was the leader. He had long brown hair and a scraggly beard. His friends looked about the same, only bigger. Boat bums.

"Let go of my child!" Savannah shrieked, taking a step forward as Charity slowly side-stepped away from her. A bald man by the blanket lurched forward, arms spread like he was trying to herd a chicken into a pen. It was enough to stop Savannah from taking another step.

"Shut the hell up!" the man holding Flo said. "I'm giving the orders here, not you."

"Where's your men?" asked the guy going through the basket.

"Asleep," Charity lied, getting five feet of space between her and Savannah. "On the boat. But one yell, and all three will be here in minutes. And they have guns."

Charity knew she couldn't predict how Savannah would react when Charity moved against these men. She might crumble in fear, or maybe even get in the way with some sort of desperate attack.

But Charity knew how the men would react. In the first microsecond, they'd dismiss her advance as their number, size, and sex gave them a false sense of superiority. That would change to confusion when the first man went down, and the others would come at her, thinking it a lucky kick or punch. The last two would then become enraged when a second man fell.

Men's emotions made them easy to manipulate. They were either on or off.

The man holding Flo quickly shoved her to the ground beside him and pulled a revolver from his waistband. He pointed it at the two women. "Lying bitch!" he yelled at Charity. "We checked the boat first. Nothin' but a mutt. Where are the men?"

A blur caught Charity's eyes. Out of nowhere a large dog charged straight through the group of men by the blanket, knocking one of them to the ground. Still a good ten feet from the gunman, the huge beast leapt. The man didn't even have time to aim before the animal was on him. The impact carried them both over the edge of the cliff, just as the gun went off wildly into the air.

Florence ran to her mother, who shielded the child behind her.

The man who had been knocked aside as the charging dog attacked the gunman got quickly to his feet. He pulled a long knife from a sheath at his belt and held it menacingly. He was shirtless, dark-tanned, and muscular, with his blond hair twisted and matted into dreads.

"Fuckin' bitch," he hissed. "You killed Kenny! Now I'm gonna carve all three of you up."

Charity would have laughed at his declaration if it hadn't been for the seriousness of the situation. Dread Head and the other two men started forward, spreading out. Charity's mind worked swiftly. So far, the only weapon these three had brandished was the hunting knife. There was no doubt in her mind that she could take all of them, unarmed. But the man with the knife would have to be first. And the other two men were bigger than him.

When they came within ten feet, just as Charity was about to make her move against the dreadlocked man, Savannah took a sudden step forward. In a flash, she spun on her bare left foot, leaping high into the air like a pirouetting ballerina. Her right leg whipped out as she spun around backward. The impact of the sole of her foot on the side of the first man's head sent him tumbling sideways. He collided with the man in the middle and they both went down.

While the knife wielding man was temporarily distracted, Charity moved. With lightning-fast precision, she stepped forward with her left foot, then brought her right foot up in a snapping front kick, striking the man's elbow and causing him to drop the knife. She then stepped in close before he could recover from the stinging pain in his elbow, and hammered him with a vicious right upper-cut just below the sternum. Air whooshed from the man's lungs as he doubled over.

Without waiting, Charity grabbed the man's hair on both sides of his head, forcing him down even faster as she brought her right knee up into his face. She followed through, arching her back and driving her knee higher. She didn't have to wait to see if he was going to go down. She knew the strike was true.

She turned to face the two bigger men. The one Savannah had kicked was moving slowly, but the larger, bald man was already on his feet.

Without warning, Charity attacked. She simply opened that part of her mind that held all the demons and turned them loose on the bigger man. She executed a shoulder roll that culminated in a crouching whip kick designed to sweep the man's feet out from under him. When she heard the sharp crack from the man's knee, she knew he was finished, and turned her attention to the man Savannah had kicked.

To Charity's surprise, Savannah was already on him, landing blow after blow to his face and head. Not slaps or backhands, but solid, powerful punches, meant to incapacitate at the very least. He never regained his feet.

The man with the dislocated knee was screaming in pain. Charity calmly stepped over and kicked him in the head, ending the noise.

Flo ran to Savannah, who held her close, pulling her face to her and wrapping her arms around the girl's head, so she couldn't see the men.

Savannah snapped her head around, her blond hair whipping across her shoulders. "Woden!"

Charity watched as the huge Rottweiler charged up from the path as if answering to Savannah's summons, stopping at the top. His lips pulled back menacingly, exposing two-inch canines. The dog moved swiftly to Savannah's side, placing himself between Charity and those he was obviously trained to protect at any cost. The dog stared at Charity, its lips quivering as a low rumble emanated from deep in his massive chest. Charity harbored no doubt that the dog would attack instantly, with just one word from his master.

Savannah quieted the dog with a touch on his muscular flank. "She's with us, Woden."

Charity went quickly to the ledge and looked down. The man with the gun floated face-down in the water, just a few feet from the rocky wall. The water around his head was tinged pink, and there was a large red stain on a jagged outcrop at the edge.

Charity ran to her bag and pulled the Colt out as Savannah reassured her daughter. "Come on," she urged them. "They might not be alone. There could be more."

Leaving their belongings, Charity led Savannah and Flo down the trail toward the beach. The dog passed her and led the way to the dinghies.

Another boat was anchored near *Sea Biscuit*. It was a derelict-looking sloop about thirty-five feet long that appeared to be in complete disarray. The sailboat's hull was dingy, and there were water stains below the scuppers. The starboard hand rail was missing halfway to the bow, and the sails looked in poor shape, just piled up on the foredeck and hanging across the boom. There didn't appear to be anyone aboard. Charity doubted more than four would travel together in such a small craft. On the beach sat a third dinghy, looking much like its mothership. The inflatable had patches on patches, and bare wires were dangling from under the console and wrapped around the throttle control. It was obvious that it had been stolen.

Charity went to her dinghy and opened the little anchor locker. "Get back out to your boat," she said to Savannah. "Stay there until I get back."

"What are you going to do?" Savannah asked, as Charity pulled a long coil of anchor line from the bow of her dinghy. Attached to it was a fifteen-pound mushroom anchor.

Charity looked at Savannah, then down at Flo. "Go out to your boat. I have to clean this up."

Turning, Charity started back up the trail, throwing the coil of rope over her head and shoulder. Savannah took two quick steps and caught her arm.

Charity wheeled, the adrenaline still coursing through her veins.

"What are you going to do, Gabby?"

"My name is Charity," she stated flatly. "This is the kind of work I did for two years. Now go to your boat and look after your daughter."

Charity went up the trail at a sprint. When she got to the clearing, she heard Savannah's outboard start and move quickly away from the beach. Charity dropped the anchor and coiled rope, then surveyed the three men.

They were all lean and muscular, a good thing. Looking at the small anchor again, she realized that eventually they'd come back up to the surface as decomposition gasses built up inside their bodies. Then she spotted the knife the man had dropped and had an idea. She picked up the knife and hefted it. It had a heavy, eight-inch blade.

There were reputed to be no living things in the Hoffman's blue hole, except oysters, and that was all Charity saw on her dives into the hole. But it was over six hundred feet deep, and she felt certain there were deep-water crabs down there, waiting to catch the oysters that got dislodged, or any hapless animal that fell in and drowned. She inspected the knife's blade. It had a keen edge and a serrated spine. She looked again at the scum at her feet. An easy entry point for the crabs would also allow decomposition gas to escape.

From her excursion pack, she retrieved her suppressor and slowly threaded the long cylinder onto the barrel of the Colt. One of the men behind her moaned and began to stir. Devoid of emotion, Charity stepped over to the three men, sprawled on the ground.

One by one, she shot each man in the head.

CHAPTER FOUR:

"**Y**ou should have waited!" Leilani said, feigning irritation as her five friends filed into the little cabin.

Rayna flopped back on the double bed, her short dress riding up her thighs. "You weren't ready, and we had a deadline. You're always late."

"Did he cry like the last guy?"

"Not this one," Fiona said, sitting on the bed and bumping Rayna aside with her hip.

The blonde wiggled her butt over to make room, her dress riding up more. She made no move to pull it down. "A damned shame, that man."

"He fought back?" Leilani asked Brent.

Brent was the unofficial leader of the Gang of Six, as they liked to call themselves. At six-one, he was the tallest of the group of three men and three women. A ruggedly handsome young man, he'd grown up in orphanages and foster homes, much like the others.

"Oh, he tried." Doug sat in a chair and draped one leg over the armrest. "But he was real hard-pressed to do any kind of concentrating, on account of the X."

Rayna laughed uncontrollably. "You said he was real hard," she finally gasped out. "That's what I meant by it was a damned shame. He was huge."

Fiona giggled uneasily. "Yeah, he was," she agreed.

Like the others, Fiona lost her parents as a child and grew up in an orphanage. Ten years later, at fourteen, she ran away and lived off the streets. At sixteen, she was a high-demand prostitute in Dallas.

"Shoulda did that before you brought him to us," Doug said. "Not our fault."

"That's hardly fair," Rayna said. "When we go after a rich woman, you guys always get to have your way with her before Brent bashes their brains out. Girls have needs too, you know."

"Anyway," Brent said, pulling a sock from his pocket, and hefting the weight of the pool ball stuffed into the toe. "He wasn't any match for the old one-ball."

"Are you sure he was dead?" Leilani asked. The smallest of the Gang of Six, Leilani stood just under five feet tall and her weight was well below a hundred pounds. Lithe and athletic, she made up for her lack of stature with her ability to contort her body into places most people wouldn't even attempt.

"It's never taken more than one crack before," Brent said, stuffing the makeshift sap back into his pocket, "but this guy needed two. The one-ball is the hardest ball on the table; that's why it's always put in the front of the rack. Fuckin' caved in the side of his skull, man. He was dead; I checked."

There was a tapping on the door and all six of them tensed. Jeff came out of the bathroom and looked through the little peephole, then opened the door.

"How did we do?" a tall gentleman asked, striding confidently into the room with a beautiful redhead at his heels.

Mister and Missus Pence made a striking couple. In their late thirties or early forties, they could easily have passed for much younger. Clive Pence was a dashing British man, fit and tanned from the Caribbean sun. His wife, Yvette, was a few years younger and just drop-dead gorgeous, with long, wavy red hair, flawless skin, and a fit, curvy body.

"No credit cards," Brent said, emptying the contents of his pockets on the bed. "British passport says his name is Rene Cook. Not very much cash, a little under two hundred. Some sort of Spanish coin on a chain, a dive watch, keys, and a hat."

Yvette picked up the pendant. "Spanish doubloon," she said. "That's worth a good bit. Probably enough for tickets on the next couple of cruise ships. But not much more." She picked up the watch and examined it. "Cheap dive watch." She tossed it on the bed and picked up the key ring. It was on one of those buoy-shaped floats that boaters used. She read the inscription on the side of the float.

"*Salty Dog?*" she asked. "Do you remember the marina he came from?"

"Brent told me," Rayna replied. "Brown Boat Yard, just down the street from where we picked him up."

Yvette glanced over at the younger blond woman. "Pull your dress down, Rayna. You're not a slut anymore."

The younger woman was about to say something, but the look on Yvette's face gave her pause. The Pences didn't

tolerate insubordination. She wiggled up higher on the bed, pulling her dress down to cover her thighs.

"Leilani," Yvette said, tossing the key ring onto the bed in front of the diminutive Polynesian woman, "go to the boatyard and get aboard his boat. Make sure the gate guard notices you. You know the drill; search all the tiny crevices where these sailors like to hide stuff. He's got more than two hundred, and it's hidden somewhere on his boat."

Leilani picked up the key ring. It had a little wristband attached to it; she slipped it over her hand. "It might take a while."

"You have all night; the ship doesn't sail until nine o'clock. What did the guy look like?"

"Tall and hot," Fiona whispered.

"That's you, then," Yvette ordered, pointing to Brent.

"The guy had blond hair, though," Rayna said.

The redhead picked up the cap, looked at the logo and boat name on the front, and slapped it into Brent's chest. "Give her half an hour to get aboard. You know what to do; stumble into the boatyard like you're drunk and ask the dockmaster if your *date* has arrived yet. His mind will be too preoccupied with the visual image of you screwing your little island hottie's brains out to notice the hair color."

"You got everything off the body?" Clive asked.

"He had nothing on him when we left," Jeff replied. "Nothing but his clothes, that is."

The newest member of the group, Jeff came from a broken home like the others — except his parents hadn't died. At least not that he knew of. They were both crack addicts and had just abandoned him when he was seven years old. Nobody wanted a seven-year-old boy, so he was shuffled from one foster home to another.

"Stay on the boat tonight," Clive told Brent. "He'll be a John Doe in the morgue by morning and won't be missed by the boatyard until they want money. Wait until the guards change shifts in the morning before returning. And remember—"

"No fooling around," Brent said, rolling his eyes. "I know, I know."

Leilani could see the change in Clive's demeanor caused by the attitude in the younger man. He stepped across the room and, without warning, punched Brent in the stomach so hard the younger man went to his knees, retching.

"No sex!" Clive said, looking around the room at them. "It's a simple rule. It matters not whether you like our rules. You'll do as we say." He looked down at Brent. "Do you fully understand me?"

Struggling to regain his feet, Brent croaked out a weak, "Yes, sir."

"I'm terribly sorry, Brent. Did you say something?"

"Yes, sir," Brent said, more forcefully. "No sex."

"Good," Clive said, turning toward Leilani. He casually pushed an errant strand of hair behind her ear, then cupped her chin in his hand, turning her face up to meet his gaze. "I trust you don't have a problem with rules, young lady?"

"No, sir," she replied, looking up at the man towering over her. "I like rules."

Clive turned her and smacked her on the butt. "Get going, then. Brent will be along shortly to act as lookout."

Gathering up her small purse and a light sweater, Leilani went to the door. "See you guys in the morning."

In the hallway, she made her way up to the main deck where the exits were located and left the cruise ship. There was a line of taxis waiting for possible fares, but she walked past them. It wasn't far, and she preferred walking.

Twenty minutes later, she approached the gate at the entrance to the boatyard. She removed her sweater and draped it across one arm. Pulling her skin-tight little blue dress down in front, she cupped her tiny breasts and pushed them up, exposing more of what little cleavage the gods had given her.

An old black man sat in a tiny little shack next to the gate. The window facing the street was open. Leilani could barely look over the countertop.

"Hi, there," she said with a warm smile. She showed the man the name of the boat on the key ring float attached to her wrist. "Rene asked me to meet him here. He should be along in a just a few minutes."

The man looked down at her from the window. Though he was at least twice her age, the old guy made no attempt to hide his eyes as they moved up and down her body. "Yuh not di same *friend* Cap'n Rene arrived with yesterday."

Clive had said the guy was alone on the boat. Was there a woman waiting for him? No, she decided. Clive had the guys watching all day. He'd chosen that particular man because his boat was expensive-looking and the guy was alone, waiting for repairs. Whomever he'd arrived with was no longer around.

"Well," she said, twisting a long strand of jet-black hair, "I'm his friend for tonight."

She knew exactly what she appeared to be in the man's eyes: a very expensive prostitute. She didn't care; it was part of the ruse, just another act in a long line of self-degradation. When Brent arrived later, the old man was only going to remember her.

"Dere be no noise," the old man said. "No loud music and no loud hanky-panky, yuh unnerstand?"

Leilani turned the smile — and her charm — up a notch. "Yes, we know. And we appreciate it, we really do." She cocked her head coyly. "It's New Year's Eve," she whined.

"Jest dis once," the old man relented, pushing a button that caused the gate lock to buzz. "But yuh be quiet, yuh unnerstand?"

Pushing the gate open, Leilani stepped through. "We'll be as quiet as we can," she said.

Leilani could feel the man's eyes undressing her as she sauntered seductively across the dimly lit yard. They didn't have to do much; all she was wearing was the dress and her flat sandals.

The guy's boat was easy to find. It was in the middle of the yard, sitting way up high on blocks, the name *Salty Dog* emblazoned across the back. A ladder leaned against the side, leading up to the back of the boat. She quickly climbed up and went to the door, looking around. The top was bare, just the cabin sticking up a little bit and two masts sticking up from there. The first key unlocked the padlock and she slid the upper part of the hatch forward, then opened the little bat-wing doors below it.

Steps led down to a small kitchen area. On one side was the stove, sink, and a small refrigerator, along with a row of cabinets. On the other side was a table with a couch around two sides. Another steering wheel was in front of the dining table. Leilani didn't know a lot about boats, but it didn't take a genius to figure out that the outside steering wheel was for good weather and the one on the inside was for bad.

There was a single light on, not very bright. She looked around, found two small brass lamps mounted on the walls and switched them on. Searching this room would be a waste of time, and she knew it. She quickly went down three more steps into a little living room. A switch on the wall turned on four small overhead lights. There was a long couch on the right and a TV and stereo system across from it. There were hatches in the floor, but experience told her she wouldn't find anything of value in those, so she continued forward.

Beyond the living room were two doors, each with intricate sailboat carvings in the wood. Opening the one on the left, she found a bathroom. The one on the right opened into what looked like an office, with a table built onto the wall. There was a computer on the desk, but they avoided stealing any kind of electronic stuff — too easy to trace. Cash and jewelry were primarily what they were after.

Another door at the end opened into a big closet and storage area, clothes hanging from rods down both sides, and a tool chest and bench in the very front, where it got narrow.

"That's it?" she said aloud, turning around. Surely the good stuff wouldn't be hidden there. "Where's the bedroom?"

Through the kitchen, she could see another opening to the back of the boat. It was beside the steps up to the outside. She must have missed it in the darkness. Returning the way she'd come, Leilani crossed the kitchen and

went down three steps to a narrow hallway. There was a workbench and a combination washer and dryer on one side with an open door ahead.

"Whoa," Leilani murmured as she stepped through the door. The outside lights poured in through three little windows in the back and more along the sides. The room was easily the biggest one on the boat, and the bed occupied most of it.

She stepped up to the edge of the bed, which was as high as her belly. The thing was huge, way bigger than king-sized. If it weren't for the Pences' rules, the whole Gang of Six could sleep together on it.

We could pile the Pences in, too, she thought, thinking of eight writhing bodies on that big bed.

Leilani had been with the group as long as anyone, but she'd almost always managed to be in the wrong place when the dirty work needed doing. She didn't have a problem seducing the men, or robbing them, but deep inside, she didn't want to see anyone hurt — something she'd shielded from the Pences all along.

Their rule against sex was just for the Gang of Six and didn't apply to the Pences, themselves. They spent a lot of time screwing each other, and now and then a passenger or two. Sometimes, Clive would even take one of the girls into his cabin and Leilani knew she was his favorite.

She was sure that the boys had bunked with Yvette on occasion, as well. They never talked about how she was, though. At least not with her or one of the other girls. But sex between any of the Gang of Six was strictly forbidden. At least, that was what the Pences thought.

This room will have to be searched, she decided.

But she doubted they would find the big score in there. These boaters liked to hide the really good stuff where the customs inspectors couldn't find it — or weren't willing to get dirty to find it. They almost always had cash and sometimes guns that were easily sold.

Leaving the bedroom, she opened a door across from the workbench. It was dark inside, but she smelled oil and fuel. She felt around inside the door and found a switch. When she turned it on, she knew she had the right place. The single overhead caged bulb revealed an orderly work room. The engine room extended up under the kitchen and dining area where the engines were located, but there wasn't a lot of headroom there, and it was dark. Just the small sort of space where she knew cruisers hid stuff.

Fortunately, Leilani didn't require very much in the way of headroom. The work room had a higher ceiling, but not by much. Leilani could move around without bumping her head, but most people would have had to duck. It was bright and clean, everything in its place. She'd search it, too. But her money was on the little nooks and crannies way back where the engines were.

The clank of the ladder startled her. Was Brent already here? If the search went as easily as she hoped it might, they'd find whatever valuables the man had on board in short order. He seemed to have been a neat freak, which was unusual for a single guy living on a boat. That made him easily predictable. A place for everything and every-thing in its place — including his cash. Finding it quickly would leave a lot of time with nothing for her and Brent to do.

What the Pences don't know won't hurt them, she thought, a wicked grin on her face. She licked her lips, already getting worked up at the idea of being with Brent. They'd come close twice but lacked the time and privacy they'd need to keep it from the Pences.

Closing the engine room door, Leilani went up the steps and met Brent just as he was coming down into the kitchen. "Find anything, yet?" he asked.

"I've only been here ten minutes," she replied, "but I know where to search first. Follow me."

"What do you mean you've only been here ten minutes?" Brent asked. "I waited half an hour after you left."

"I walked," she replied, leading Brent down the rear steps. He had to turn a little sideways to get his broad shoulders through the narrow door frame. Leilani stopped at the engine room door and pointed to the back. "That's his bedroom there. I'd say we have the second-best chance of finding anything in there. First best is in here, but you're too big."

Brent chuckled sophomorically. "That's what *she* said."

As he moved to get past her in the tight confines of the narrow hallway, she looked up at the man, standing more than a head above her. His body pressed hard against her as he tried to slide past where she was leaning against the closed door.

"You might notice the really big bed in there," she said, arching her back slightly to press her hips into his. "You search his bedroom and I'll look in here. If we get this done fast, we'll have a lot of time to kill."

"I thought you said you liked his dumbass rules."

"I said I like *rules*," she replied, playing coy. "My rules. My very strict rules. And I like punishing guys who break my very strict rules."

Brent grinned, his hands moving under her dress and grabbing her ass. He easily lifted her ninety-five-pound frame off the floor and pressed her against the door, so that she was face to face with him. "What rules are those?"

Leilani could already feel him becoming aroused, growing larger, as he held her against the door with his body weight, squeezing her butt with his big powerful hands.

Her knee jerked upward, fast and hard. She caught Brent right in the balls and completely by surprise. He fell back against the bench, his hands going to his groin as his knees buckled.

"My rules are simple," she said, as Brent fell to his knees, his face only inches from her crotch. Leilani couldn't resist herself. She grabbed Brent by the hair and pushed his face into her burning desire.

"Rule One," she said, grinding her pelvis against the man's face, "I get to do whatever I want to you, and you get to take it. I *will* be kicking and punching you in the balls again before this night's over; learn to enjoy it. Rule Two, I get off first and more frequently."

Pushing him back, she lifted his chin, so he could see her. She could see the desire in his eyes and knew he'd be putty in her hands.

"Rule Three, Brent. You get off when I'm ready to get you off, no sooner. If you don't like my rules, that means the little taste you just got is *all* you'll get tonight. Unless you count Rosy Palm helping you out. Do you like my rules?"

Though still in obvious pain, he nodded and reached for her dress again. She swatted his hands away. "We have work to do first. Now, go search that cabin."

Opening the engine room door, she stepped down into it and looked around. There was another light switch beside the first one and she flicked it on. Two rows of bright fluorescent overhead lights came on in the smaller space on either side of the engine. Another differently colored engine sat off to the side of the big one. She figured it was a backup engine, or maybe powered a generator or something.

Crouching slightly, she moved toward the front of the boat, past the main engine, careful not to let her pretty blue dress snag on anything or get smeared with grease. Searching the many drawers and cubbyholes along the wall, she found her worries to be unfounded; the engine room and equipment were spotless.

Yvette knew the natural skills and abilities of all the Gang of Six. That was why Leilani always got the boats. Not only was she small enough to make a more thorough search, but she had a knack for how these boat people thought.

At the end were a bunch of electrical gadgets, thousands of wires and hoses, switches, and other machines. Her search was methodical and thorough, as she worked her way down the opposite side. Things weren't always what they seemed. What might look like a solid panel could be hollow with a hoard of cash behind it.

Finding no such hiding place, she continued to the little shop area, where she went through every drawer and cabinet. The orderliness of everything was amazing, and she was impressed. She wasn't disappointed that she hadn't found anything. Leilani considered it a challenge. She just hadn't found the hiding places yet.

She saved the lowest part of the boat for last. At least this one looked clean, she thought when she opened the hatch in the floor. She squatted and looked closer. It was spotless, just like the rest of the boat. And it was also very tight. But not too tight.

She stood and pulled her dress up over her head, folding it and placing it on a clean bench, with the boat's key ring on top of it. She removed her sandals, then stepped down into the very bottom of the boat, completely naked. She'd need more flexibility, and there was bound to be some dirt down there.

She situated herself so she could crawl under the floor head-first, then started to snake her way through the bowels of the boat. Just ahead, there was light spilling in around the main engine, where the floor opened to the space above.

Finally, she found two hiding places, way back under the bigger engine, at what appeared at first to be a solid bulkhead. There wasn't much light, but she felt around until she found a groove in the top of both panels that allowed her to pull them out. Each one contained a sturdy-looking plastic box.

Pulling the first box out, she found it locked. "Dammit," she mumbled.

Then Leilani remembered the second key on the key ring. She lifted the box and shoved it through the opening next to the engine, then did the same with the second box. The opening on the other side of the engine was slightly wider and she was able to contort her body, turning like a snake, and climb up out of the bilge.

Retrieving the key ring, she squatted and tried it on the first box. The lock turned, and she opened it. A grin slowly spread across her face. Inside were neat stacks of bundled American currency. She closed the box and pulled the second one over.

Opening it, she gave out a low whistle. It had a bunch of different colored, small, leather binders. She recognized them as passports, each embossed with a different seal denoting the country of origin. On top of them was a big, shiny handgun.

Leilani sat back cross-legged on the rough planking and took out several of the document binders. She opened the first one, an American passport. The picture was of a handsome older man with sandy blond hair and very masculine features. His name was Rene Cook. The second one had the same man, pictured differently, and with a different name. The third had yet another name, but it was obviously the same guy in the picture.

Who the hell was this guy? Leilani wondered.

CHAPTER FIVE:

Unpleasant tasks were best done quickly, and with the brain set on auto-pilot. It wasn't difficult, as the cliff was slightly downhill from where the bodies lay. But it was time-consuming, rolling them off the edge at a spot that would be clear of the rocks the gunman had found.

There was a bit of a blood slick around the men's bodies as they floated close together in the water. It would dissipate quickly, and Charity had splashed water on the rocks to get rid of the blood where the gunman had bashed his brains out in the fall.

Charity stood and took one last look around. The men hadn't brought anything with them aside from the clothes they wore. Between all four, they barely had ten dollars in their pockets. She left that and everything else on the bodies, but kept the big hunting knife and leather sheath.

The anchor lay on the ground beside her. A very short rope connected it to all four of the men's ankles. She'd brought the line up from there, knotting it around the bodies at one-foot intervals, binding them together for all eternity. If there were crabs down there, she didn't want a body part coming loose and drifting away.

She nudged the anchor with her foot, and it toppled off the edge of the rock. It went down quickly, taking the men's bodies, feet first, on a six-hundred-foot descent to the bottom. A steady stream of pinkish air bubbles slowed after a few seconds, as water pressure squeezed the air out of the men's lungs through severed tracheas.

Charity knew that between that and the lateral incisions she'd made in each man's belly, most decomposition gasses would easily escape. If there were no crabs down there, eventually bacteria would leave nothing but their bones.

Leaving the grisly scene, Charity went up the steep trail to the clearing. She gathered up all of her and Savannah's belongings and was about to start down the trail when Savannah appeared.

"What did you do with the bodies?"

It didn't escape Charity's attention that she'd said *bodies*, not men. Three of the men had still been alive when Savannah and Flo left. And Savannah's attitude was now one of stone-cold indifference.

Charity nodded her head toward the cliff. "At the bottom."

Savannah stepped over to the edge and looked down. "They're six hundred feet closer to where they belong then."

"Is Flo okay?"

"She's on the boat with Woden."

Charity studied the woman's face. Her eyes, which earlier had been alive and sparkling, were now dull and inscrutable.

"You've experienced something like this before?" Charity asked, already knowing the answer. She herself had been set upon by scum a few times in the last two years — not since she'd been with Victor, though. It seemed that a woman alone on a boat was considered fair game to certain men. The four that Charity had killed were bent on doing harm to the two women, and maybe the girl. She harbored no qualms about ending their miserable lives.

"Once," Savannah replied. "Nearly twice." She looked toward the cliff. "I did what *I* had to do, as well."

"We probably ought to get out of here," Charity said, already wishing she were miles away.

Savannah turned and faced her. "Thanks," she said. "Normally, my guard's not down."

"Nor mine," Charity said, extending Savannah's basket to her.

"You handle yourself very well." Savannah took the basket and started down the trail.

"I spent some time in Israel," Charity said, following her. "I learned their military's fighting technique, Krav Maga."

"Well, thanks," Savannah said again.

"Turd fondlers like that deserve nothing less," Charity said. "That's what my friend Jesse calls them: turd fondlers. I think it's appropriate."

Savannah stopped dead in her tracks and turned around.

"What?" Charity asked.

"Jesse, from Marathon?"

"Well, an island near there," Charity replied. "You know—"

Savannah turned and started down the trail again, faster this time. Charity hurried after her, then suddenly stopped when she realized who it was that Savannah had had an affair with in the Keys all those years ago.

No wonder the kid seemed familiar, she thought, as she again hurried after her friend.

"Savannah, wait!" she called out, when she reached the beach and saw the woman already trying to push her dinghy into the water. The fallen tide had left the three little boats high and dry.

"I need to go," Savannah said nervously, shoving against the dinghy but making little headway.

"We'll need to help each other," Charity said. "Can we talk about this?"

"Talk about what?" Savannah asked, her breathing becoming labored as she strained to push the dinghy.

"Savannah!"

The woman stopped and sat on the starboard pontoon, exasperated.

"The guy in the Keys who you said might be Flo's father?" Charity asked. "Was it Jesse McDermitt?"

Savannah nodded, her hands clasped between her thighs. Her mood and expression had changed yet again. No longer did she look confident and happy, nor cold and calculating. She just looked hurt.

"You know him?" Savannah asked.

Charity thought about her answer carefully. For weeks, she and Jesse had chased a man all over the Caribbean. Charity had killed men before that trip, but it had been in battlefield situations against a known enemy. She and

Jesse, both civilians, had set out to find and kill a man. They'd discussed it daily during the hunt, his way of preparing her for what had to come. The man they were after had been responsible for the deaths of several people, including a man Charity had grown to care a great deal for. When the time came, Charity had killed Jason Smith with her own bare hands. And it felt good.

"We worked together a few times," she replied. "Jesse was a transportation contractor for the same group I worked with. I never got to know him very well, but he's one of the few people in the world I trust."

"Ha," Savannah said with a forced laugh. "You still probably know him better than I do."

"A woman could do a lot worse."

"Oh, don't I know it," Savannah said. "I've had a lot worse. More than once."

Charity sat on the side of her own dinghy. "Same here. More times than I care to admit. Look, I'm not going to say anything to anyone. In fact, I doubt I'll ever see him again. The Keys aren't real high on the list of places that Rene and I want to visit."

Savannah looked up the hill. "Those guys will float back up, you know."

"No, they won't."

"They will," Savannah insisted. "They'll get bloated and even an anchor won't—"

"They won't bloat. I took care of that."

"You mean you—"

"I provided a means for any gas buildup to escape," Charity interrupted matter-of-factly. "They'll never be seen again."

Savannah shuddered. "You said that was what you used to do?"

"Why don't we continue this later?" Charity asked. "We still have six hours of daylight. This anchorage is a little too crowded for my taste."

Rubbing her face vigorously, Savannah pushed her hair back over her head. Finally, she stood and looked at the ugly boat anchored near her own. "I agree," she said. "*Sea Biscuit* might catch something. What does your boat draw?"

"Five-and-a-half feet," Charity replied, standing and moving around to the other side of Savannah's dinghy.

"Bond Cay is out, then. But High Cay is only about an hour's run on the outside."

"Less than that, if the wind's good," Charity said, as the two women started to drag Savannah's boat to the water.

"What do we do about their boat and dinghy?" Savannah asked, once they got Charity's dinghy in the water.

"Leave them," Charity said. "There isn't anything on them that either of us could possibly need."

"Someone will find it, eventually."

They returned to Charity's little dinghy and started dragging it to the water.

"And what?" Charity asked. "How many stranded derelicts have you seen in your time on the water?"

"Point taken," Savannah said as she stepped into her dinghy and started the engine.

The wind was light, and five knots was all Charity could get out of *Wind Dancer* on the short hop to High Cay. Savannah's boat, being a trawler, wasn't dependent on wind and she slowly pulled ahead. When Charity finally entered the anchorage, *Sea Biscuit* was there, riding sedately at anchor.

Dropping the hook about a hundred yards astern of Savannah's boat in fifteen feet of water, Charity backed down hard, digging the anchor's flukes into the sandy bottom on the lee side of the island.

Another boat was anchored about half a mile farther south. Charity inspected it through her binoculars. It was a sailing catamaran. She could see kids jumping from the two stern platforms and playing in the water.

"Gabby!" Savannah shouted. Charity didn't bother to correct her. "I have wine."

CHAPTER SIX:

The morning broke with gray clouds and strong winds. Charity rose from her bunk and opened the overhead hatch to look outside. *Wind Dancer* was pointed the other way. The tide was rising, and the current had shifted. *Sea Biscuit* was now behind her, hidden by *Dancer's* dodger and Bimini top.

Last night, she'd stayed aboard *Sea Biscuit* until nearly midnight and drank far too much wine. Now her head hurt, but she'd felt that Savannah needed it after what they'd been through.

At first, nothing was said about what happened at the blue hole, nor had Jesse been mentioned, though Charity could tell that both things weighed heavily on Savannah's mind. Instead, they talked about other things: places they'd been and what they'd seen. The wine helped them both open more easily to the other.

Charity dressed while she thought back on all that Savannah had told her the night before. After Flo had gone to bed, Savannah suggested they go up and sit on the bridge. There, over another bottle of wine, Savannah told Charity about her trip to the Keys with her sister, and how she'd met Jesse when he intervened to help their captain fight off several would-be kidnappers.

"Yeah," Charity remembered telling her, "that part of the man hasn't changed. The last time I saw him, just a few months ago, he was recovering something that had been stolen from a woman he didn't even know."

Savannah had gone on to tell her that she'd run into Jesse again, very recently. She explained that she had returned to Marathon for the first time in nine years, to claim her sister's body. She had been honest and forthright with Charity about how her sister had been killed. It was obvious that the circumstances of her sister's death had compounded the pain of losing her. Savannah said that she'd heard later that most of the people responsible had been killed in a gun battle near Fort Myers.

At the time, Charity thought that Jesse being involved in the gunfight seemed out of character. But now, in the cold light of a gray dawn, she realized that was just what a man like him would do — only he'd take steps to ensure he wouldn't be seen or caught. Much like the men at the blue hole, Charity surmised that the men in Fort Myers undoubtedly deserved everything they got and then some.

Going to the coffee maker, she set it up and switched it on. Then she reached up and slid the main hatch open and climbed the steps to the cockpit. *Sea Biscuit* was gone.

The wind whipped at Charity's clothes and hair as she stood on the deck and looked all around the anchorage. The catamaran was still there, but there wasn't another boat in sight.

Conditions were good for sailing. The wind was a steady twenty knots and seas hadn't built to anything appreciable yet. Charity and Savannah had both known the weather was coming and they both knew that this morning would be the worst of it. Most trawler skippers would stay put during the slightest blow. But the deeper keel of a sailboat and the way it worked with the wind and waves, meant that even though it was threatening a light rain, it would be a good day for *Wind Dancer*.

Why would she leave? Charity thought. For a trawler, anything other than flat seas and calm winds were reason enough to stay put in a safe harbor. The Bimini over *Sea Biscuit's* fly bridge was a good fifteen feet above the water, and the boat presented an awful lot of surface area to the wind.

Going back down to the salon, Charity turned on the VHF radio and plucked the mic from its holder. She checked that she was on the hailing frequency and called for *Sea Biscuit*. When there was no answer, she hailed again.

"*S/V Cattitude* calling *Wind Dancer*," a man's voice replied. "Go to seventy-two."

Charity switched frequencies and hailed what she assumed was the catamaran, judging by the name.

"*Wind Dancer*, the trawler you arrived with yesterday left before dawn. It went west-southwest, toward Northwest Channel."

Northwest Channel was a natural, very deep channel to the Tongue of the Ocean, part of the Bahamas surrounded by shallows with a bottom depth of over six thousand feet in places.

"I thought it was too shallow that way."

"It is for you," the man replied. "I've crossed it under power with the centerboards up at high tide. That trawler probably draws the same."

"Thanks, *Cattitude*," Charity said into the mic. "*Wind Dancer* standing by on sixteen."

She changed the radio back to the hailing channel and sat at the navigation desk. The chart of the Berry Islands was spread before her. She studied the contour lines of the shallows to the west of her location and saw that the guy was right: there was a natural winding channel of sorts. Not in the true sense of the word; it looked more like wide shallows that got barely four feet deep in some places, a tidal plain twisting this way and that. But Savannah had told her that they'd been to these islands many times. Perhaps she knew the way.

There was nothing to be gained by trying to figure out why she left without saying goodbye. In two hours, Savannah could be ten to fifteen miles away and there were dozens of small coves.

Perhaps she was embarrassed after her revelation, Charity thought.

So rather than ponder it further, Charity began preparing to get underway herself. She had no cell phone signal here, and Victor would be leaving Nassau within the hour. With no way to let him know she'd moved to a new anchorage, her best bet was to intercept him out on the blue, by sailing a reverse course from Hoffman's Cay toward Nassau.

Getting her foul weather gear from a small hanging locker, she stuffed it into a waterproof bag, along with some fruit for later. She poured the coffee into a large thermos, then carried it up to the helm. Opening the hidden compartment at the helm, she carefully wrapped her Colt in its oilcloth and stored it away.

The current had changed with the rising tide, and *Dancer's* bow was pointed toward the open ocean, about forty-five degrees off the wind. Charity sat at the helm and opened the little cabinet beneath the wheel house to start the engine, then thought better of it. Conditions were perfect to do something she didn't get a chance to do very often: sail off the anchor. Instead of starting the engine, she turned on the batteries and checked that they were fully charged. The small wind turbine mounted high above the aft rail had charged the batteries all night.

Everything was in the green, so she toggled the switch to raise the mainsail. The halyard slowly hauled the sail out of the boom furler, as she eased the tension on the main sheet, letting the wind move the boom out to port. The mainsail snapped at the wind, as if *Wind Dancer* were anxious to test herself against it. When the main reached the top of the mast and with the sail luffing in the strong wind, Charity flipped the switch for the anchor windlass.

Timing the maneuver was critical. When the anchor broke free from the sand, it would still be dangling ten or fifteen feet below the boat and could get fouled on something. She'd have to haul in the main just enough to hold the boat in place against the current until the anchor was seated.

With a deft hand on the toggles, she waited, feeling her boat's movement against wind and water, as the windlass slowly pulled *Wind Dancer* forward. Charity felt the anchor give and eased the boom inboard just a little, diminishing the luff. The anchor snagged again, but she held the main, turning the wheel slightly into the wind.

Soon she felt the anchor come up off the bottom and, after a few seconds, heard the heavy ten-foot chain rattle across the roller on the pulpit, as the anchor seated itself.

She turned the wheel off the wind slightly, the main snapped, and the seventy-six-year-old vessel heeled a few degrees, gathering forward speed. Toggling the port staysail winch, she unfurled the smaller foresail at the bow, adding more power. Once set, she eased off on the sheet as the staysail pulled *Wind Dancer* forward.

Manipulating both the main and staysail winches from experience, Charity set each, then quickly set the autopilot to maintain course and went to the bow to secure the anchor. Back at the helm, she took a moment to pour a mug of coffee, then switched off the autopilot.

Beating to windward, *Dancer* gathered a little more speed. It was a fine line to dance; pointing upwind too much would cause the sails to lose lift and not be able to provide the power to overcome the water's drag on the hull. Pointing more to port, away from the wind, would give her more speed, but it would also take her dangerously close to the shallows. And the channel was far too narrow to tack back and forth.

"Bravo!" she heard the man on the catamaran say over the radio, as she passed between the northern tip of High Cay and the rocks just off the southern end of Little Harbor Cay. She picked up the old conch horn from the corner of the cockpit and blew her reply. The old shell had been with the boat when she got it, and she just left it laying loose on the deck, a throwback to an earlier time.

The sonar showed the bottom swiftly falling away below *Wind Dancer's* hull, as the old sloop moved out into the open ocean. Once clear of the islands, Charity eased the wheel to port slightly, turning just a few degrees more to the north, away from the wind. This slight maneuver provided more lift and power to the sails, increasing *Dancer's* forward speed.

She spun the wheel to starboard, using the boat's increased speed to tack across the wind. At the same time, she glanced up at the wind indicator at the masthead and adjusted the sheets for a beam reach on the wind point she planned to steer. The sails continued to luff for a moment as the bow came about, crossing through the wind. The mainsail and boom swung across the Bimini top, then snapped again as the wind filled the sails from the port side.

She adjusted the main slightly, as *Wind Dancer* began to pick up speed after the turn. Her waterline length was just over thirty-six feet. On most sailboats, or any displacement hull boat, it was this measurement that limited speed. Unlike a planing hull, which used engine power to climb up and over the wave created by the bow, a displacement hull couldn't outrun its bow wave.

She glanced down at the small chart plotter on the pedestal. With only the two sails deployed, *Dancer* was making just over six knots.

Reaching down to the console, Charity toggled the starboard genoa winch, unfurling the larger headsail. *Dancer* heeled slightly more, as she began to accelerate.

Built in the thirties from a design by famed naval architect John Alden, *Wind Dancer* had competed in many long-distance races in her early years, winning quite a few. Charity looked at the knot meter again and smiled; just a shade under eight knots, nearly maximum hull speed.

Continuing her southeast heading, she waited until the islands were barely visible on the horizon, two miles to the west. Confident that she was near a rhumb line between Nassau and Hoffman's Cay, she turned slightly more to the south and readjusted the sails. Now all she had to do was keep an eye out for the boat bringing Victor to her.

Her radar screen was empty, save for the islands to her west — and she was moving away from them. The range on the unit, figuring the boat bringing Victor was a typical speed boat with a six-foot profile, was about ten miles. Zooming the chart plotter out so she could see New Providence Island, she judged that she was indeed very close to a line drawn from there to Hoffman's Cay. There wasn't any reason for the boat Victor hired to stray more than ten miles from a straight course, so she felt confident that she'd be able to intercept them. They might not have a radio on, but Victor should easily recognize her dark blue hull and dark sails against the dull gray sky.

Victor had messaged her two days ago, when she passed near Chub Cay, that he'd be leaving at nine o'clock local time, and gave her the name of the boat. Charity looked at her watch. It was near that time now.

For her to sail to Nassau would take most of the day, but it was only an hour or so in a go-fast boat, and she was headed toward them. She knew she'd be in Victor's arms within an hour, so she enjoyed the time with her boat.

Seas were beginning to build, but the slow rollers were barely three feet and at regimented intervals. Coming out of the east, *Wind Dancer* took them on the port bow, sending a sheet of fine mist into the air, as she charged through, unperturbed.

An hour passed, and Charity began to worry. She tried hailing the boat but got no response. She stared at the chart plotter again. There was nothing between Nassau and the Berry Islands except forty miles of ocean. Even if the boat changed course due to weather and headed for Chub Cay or one of the other islands in the southern part of the Berry Islands, she'd see them on her radar screen. Those islands were within its range still.

She turned slightly more south, to keep them in range of her radar, and adjusted the sails for a broader reach. *Wind Dancer* slowed slightly, and the waves were more on the beam than bow, sometimes sending sheets of spray high into the air. Protected by the Bimini and dodger, Charity forged onward. Every fifteen or twenty minutes, she tried to hail the other boat to no avail.

Off Chub Cay, Charity's cell-phone picked up a signal, chirping an alert that she had a message. Snatching it up, she saw that it was from Victor, saying he'd be leaving this morning. It was dated Wednesday evening, New Year's Eve.

She quickly replied that she had to change anchorages, and was underway, eight miles east of Chub and headed toward Nassau. The cell signal held for nearly twenty minutes, but there was no reply.

Another hour passed as the southernmost of the Berry Islands began to fall off the radar screen behind her. It was unlike Victor not to respond right away. He always had his cell phone on him. If he had a signal, which he would just about anywhere in Nassau, he would always reply within minutes.

The closer she got to the midpoint of the forty-mile crossing, the more she worried. She saw other boat's echoes on her radar screen, but all were either heading in the wrong direction, or were moving too slowly to be anything other than a trawler or another sailboat.

Maybe leaving the Berry Islands wasn't such a good idea, Charity thought, as she looked astern once more. He might have left earlier, due to the weather, and headed to the lee side of the island chain. He could be at Hoffman's Cay now and not have a way to contact her, but he'd see the ugly boat there and maybe guess that she'd changed anchorages to be away from it.

Checking her watch, she estimated that if Victor had left on time, he'd already have been there, found her gone, and would somehow have convinced the boat's owner to do some island-hopping to find her. It wouldn't take them long to get within cell distance of Chub Cay. Then he'd get her message and head back to Nassau.

By noon, Charity was certain that something had gone wrong. Maybe the boat Victor had hired had engine trouble and turned back. New Providence Island was on the horizon, but she knew from the past that she wouldn't get a signal on her cell phone until she was within three miles.

She had a satellite phone she could use, but it was for dire emergencies. They'd gotten separated a few times in the past, but had always known where they were headed and often reunited there. They'd come up with a plan in case something like this happened. They'd each get close to civilization and wait until they were both in range of communication.

When she did pick up a cell signal, she waited anxiously for a reply as she sailed as fast as possible toward the harbor, but none came. She tried calling several times, but it kept going directly to voicemail.

Charity contacted Harbour Bay Marina, just across from the boatyard where Victor had his boat hauled out, and requested a day slip, possibly overnight. The woman told her that they had plenty of room for as long as she'd like.

It was just after one o'clock local time when Charity spotted a massive cruise ship exiting the harbor. She passed the buoys at the harbor's western inlet, giving the ship a wide berth and staying to its windward side so the ship didn't deflect her air as it passed. She sailed into the cruise terminal's huge turning basin in Nassau Harbor and only dropped her sails and started the engine when the harbor's physical restrictions forced her to turn the bow into the easterly wind. More cruise ships were preparing to leave.

She couldn't understand why people thought that was enjoyable. Crammed in like sardines, going to tourist trap ports, and bypassing the real beauty of the islands.

A smaller cruise ship was docked on the outside of the terminal. Like the others, the crew was bustling around, preparing to take their passengers to the next so-called paradise. A dozen or so people stood on the *Delta Star's* sun deck, gawking down at her as *Wind Dancer* sedately cruised past them.

When she arrived at the marina, there was a young dock hand waiting to help with the lines. Using the bow thruster, Charity maneuvered *Dancer* around, backing into the slip with practiced precision. She tossed the smiling young black man a line as she shut off the engine, then hurried along the starboard side deck to tie off the bow. She tipped the young man, and he told her where to find the office to pay for the slip. When he left, she went

below to grab her bag, having already slipped the Colt into a hidden side pocket.

Hurriedly, she went to the office and paid for one night. Leaving the office, she walked to the entrance, where she could see the masts of Victor's ketch across the street.

When she arrived at the gate, the guard said that Victor had left less than an hour earlier and hadn't come back. She dug her phone out of her bag and reread the text message Victor had sent two days earlier.

"Do you know where I can find a boat called *Dripping Wet*?"

The man frowned down at her through the window. "Why yuh wanna find dat no-gooder?"

"My boyfriend," she began, pointing to Victor's boat. "That's his boat, *Salty Dog*; he hired the owner to take him to where I was in the Berry Islands, but he never made it."

"Don't suhprise me none," the old man said. "Dat mon ain't di most dependable one around here."

"Can you tell me how to find it?"

He pointed to his left, toward the bridge. "On di uddah side of di road," he replied. "Just past a place called *Celebrity Status* on dis side."

"Thanks," Charity said, hurrying off.

When she arrived at the marina's office, she asked at the desk where to find *Dripping Wet*.

"End of the dock on the right," a young British woman said. "You can't miss the bloody thing."

The disdain in her voice, coupled with the words of the gate guard, didn't paint a favorable picture of the person Victor had hired.

The woman was right; Charity spotted the boat before even reaching the pier it was docked at. *Dripping Wet* was a gaudily painted Cigarette boat, about forty feet long. A man of about thirty was lying on the padded engine cover wearing nothing but a Speedo.

"Are you the owner?" Charity asked.

The man raised his head and looked in her direction. "Guilty as charged. Name's Beaux Chapman; that's with an X."

"Did you have a charter this morning?" Charity asked, raising her sunglasses to her forehead. "To take a man to Hoffman's Cay?"

Chapman sat up, reached for a pack of cigarettes, and lit one. "Guy never showed," he replied, a bit of a south Louisiana accent in his voice. "Waited around for two hours for the sumbitch. You know him?"

"You were supposed to bring him to me," Charity replied. "His boat's here getting repairs."

The man's eyes moved up and down Charity's body. "I can't think of a single reason that'd hold *me* back."

"So you have no idea where he is?"

"Sure don't," Chapman said, stepping up to the dock. "But me and this boat are right here."

"I'll keep that in mind," Charity said, putting her sunglasses back on and turning to leave.

The man grabbed her arm to stop her. "Just a minute, sweet thing."

Her reaction was completely reflexive, elevated by the stress that had been building all day. She grabbed the man's wrist and turned under his arm, breaking his hold, then continued her turn, bringing the man's arm up behind his back. Easily deflecting his other hand when he reached for her, Charity stepped in behind her adversary.

She wrenched his wrist up to his neck and shoved hard, planting a foot well behind her for leverage.

Beaux was off-balance, off-guard, and way out-classed. He tripped over his boat's combing and sprawled sideways on the engine cover, toppling a beer, then tumbling onto the cockpit deck, legs and arms akimbo.

"I'm a woman," she hissed down at the man, "not a thing! And most certainly not a *sweet* thing. You can take this ugly, forty-foot penis extension of yours and shove it up your ass."

Several people on boats around them erupted in laughter and applause at the scene, hooting and yelling. Charity strode confidently back toward the foot of the pier, one hand covertly resting inside her bag, a finger on the Velcro tab that would open the Colt's hiding spot.

Back on Bay Street, she looked up and down the block. A couple passed her, the man carrying a suitcase, and turned into the marina. Behind her sunglasses, Charity noticed the tall young man's eyes stray toward her for a moment too long. His Asian-looking girlfriend yanked his arm and they continued toward the docks. She overheard the very petite young woman tell the man that Chapman was waiting, and she couldn't help but think the young man had better be on his guard.

His boat's here, Charity thought, looking around. Victor hated being away from *Salty Dog*; something she completely understood. She'd believed the guy when he'd said that Victor hadn't arrived at the appointed time. So that meant that he was still somewhere on the island. An eighty-square mile island with nearly three hundred thousand people.

CHAPTER SEVEN:

Leilani woke to see light coming in through the three back windows. "Get up," she said urgently.

Brent didn't move, which gave her a certain amount of satisfaction, remembering their activities the previous night. They'd continued searching, but found little else, and then turned their minds and bodies to other pursuits.

She shoved his shoulder roughly. He mumbled something, but it was unintelligible.

"We have to go," she said, grabbing his shoulder and shaking him with both hands. "Come on, the sun's already up."

That seemed to get his attention. "Timezit?"

"Do I look like a cuckoo clock to you?" She rolled to the edge of the bed and looked down for the steps.

She quickly pulled the little blue dress over her head, and slipped on her sandals, as Brent dropped down beside her. "We don't have to go back, you know."

"What do you mean?" Leilani asked, smoothing out her dress.

"All that cash," Brent replied. "And those passports. I'm the same size and build. I can color my hair like his and nobody would know."

Leilani stopped at the bedroom door and turned around. "And what about me? I didn't see any passports in there for a four-eleven, ninety-five-pound island woman."

"There's ways around that," Brent said, moving toward her. "With that kind of money, we can get you one. I know a guy in Miami that does stuff like that."

"Go back to the States?" Leilani asked. "Nuh-uh. No way."

"Why not? Just me and you and all that money. We could be anyone we wanted. Buy a boat and drive it back. You're American, nobody is going to ask for a passport."

"You're forgetting one little thing," she said. "I have an outstanding warrant in the States. I killed two people in Boston."

"Oh, yeah," Brent said. "So we color your hair and make up a name. You'd look super-hot with blond hair. And it's only until we can get you a fake passport — then we head to Mexico or somewhere."

"You're serious?"

"Think about it," Brent said. "With that kind of money, we could live big time in Mexico, and never have to work another day for the rest our lives."

Leilani unashamedly looked down at the naked man's loins. He'd been everything she was hoping for last night, and then some. The truth was, she'd considered running off with the money herself, until they'd overslept. Brent had been the only thing in her way. She moved demurely into his arms, feeling his manhood stir.

And he was right, she thought, reaching down, and hefting the weight of him. It was easily the biggest haul any in the group had come up with. She and Brent hadn't even counted it all. The bundles on top were twenties, but below that were a lot more bundles of hundred-dollar bills. The rush of the excitement had taken a different turn several times. But she was pretty sure there was at least three hundred thousand dollars in that black box. The guy Brent killed had been loaded.

"We have to move quickly, if we're going to do this," she said, slowly stroking him.

"Then you better quit what you're doing," Brent replied.

Her knee came up, and again Brent wasn't ready. True to her word, she'd tortured the man's testicles most of the night. Brent went down to his knees. This time, she resisted the urge to plant herself on his face.

"Get dressed then," she said, turning for the door. "We have to get to Florida before dark."

Going back up to the kitchen, Leilani looked through the cabinets for something to put the money and passports in. She didn't find anything, then remembered the trap doors in the living room and went toward the front of the boat. Boaters usually kept dry goods in those sorts of places.

Opening the first one, she saw just what she was looking for: boxes of canned foods. She selected the biggest box and opened it, dumping the canned food out, which rolled all across the floor.

When she returned to the bedroom with the empty cardboard box, Brent was buttoning his shirt.

"We can put everything in this," she said. "Less conspicuous. You realize that we don't have any clothes or anything?"

"We'll buy what we need when we get there," Brent replied, taking the box and placing it between the two watertight boxes. He started to take the money out of the container to put in the cardboard box, but Leilani stopped him.

"Put the whole thing in," she said. "If the cardboard breaks open, we won't have a bunch of cash flying away in the wind."

Brent took one bundle of twenties out and set it aside. "Think we can hire a boat for two grand?"

Leilani removed another of the bundles and put it with the one he'd kept out. "Better make it four. There's a few marinas just across the street. One has a small clothing store; I was checking it out yesterday. You're all set, but this dress isn't exactly the right clothes for crossing an ocean. I'll need to buy a few things."

Brent put the big, shiny handgun in the box with the money, then started going through the passports. He selected two. "American and Canadian," he said. "Both have the same name; Rene Cook."

He added the passports to the plastic cash box; the lid barely closed. Then he put the whole thing in the cardboard box. It fit snugly, bulging the sides slightly. He closed the flaps and carried it to the hallway, placing it on the counter, then opened the engine room door.

"I bet there's some duct tape in here."

"Yeah," Leilani said, joining him in the small room. She was right; he had to duck slightly to keep from hitting his head on the ceiling.

She went to a tool chest and opened one of the lower drawers, removing a roll of gray tape.

"Perfect," Brent said, taking it from her and returning to the box. He pulled off a long strip and with Leilani holding the flaps of the box, he sealed it. Hefting the box, he put it under his arm. "Heavy, but I can carry it so it looks light."

"Don't forget your hat," Leilani said, grabbing it off the counter.

"You just make sure the guard doesn't spend too much time looking at me."

They left the boat, and several workers in the yard stopped what they were doing to watch Leilani climb down the ladder in her little blue dress. At the bottom, she stretched her arms up over her head, both because she needed it after the previous night and to keep the workers' eyes on her. Brent was the same build as the guy he'd killed but looked nothing like him, and he was struggling with the weight of the box.

They crossed the street to the first marina they saw. At the door, Leilani looked back and didn't see anyone paying attention to them. Inside, she spent twenty minutes picking out clothes, and bought a suitcase large enough for her new things and the box of cash.

Going behind the marina store, they quickly decided to move on to another marina. The only boats tied to the piers were sailboats and a handful of older and slower-looking boats. At the second marina, they found even fewer to choose from, and none looked fast.

"We're going to have to hurry this up," Leilani said, taking Brent's free arm as he carried the suitcase. "The ship will sail soon. And the others are going to miss us."

"What do you think they'll do if we're not back in time?"

"That's right," Leilani said. "You weren't part of the group last summer. We had a guy who usually worked with Rayna; he said he wanted to leave. The Pences made us kill him. I don't know what they'd do if we didn't get back in time. They could all just leave the ship and come looking for us. One thing's for sure — they catch us trying to ditch them with all this money, we're both dead meat."

Brent reached into his pocket and took a throwaway cell phone out. A light was flashing. He flipped it open and looked at the screen.

"It's a message from Pence," he said, looking at Leilani. "He says the ship's departure is delayed. Something to do with the electronics."

"Let me see that," she said, taking the phone and stopping in the shade of a withered tree. She quickly composed a reply and sent it.

"What did you say?" he asked, as they entered another marina.

"I told him that was good." She handed the phone back. "Because the boat had lots of hiding places and we'd only found a gun after looking for hours, and that we were about to give up."

His phone vibrated in his hand and he flipped it open again. "He says to keep looking, but be back to the ship no later than one. The captain said they'd be departing at two."

"By then, we'll be halfway to Florida, if we can find a fast boat."

There was a fast-looking boat at the third marina, but nobody was around. Leilani went to the office to ask the man at the desk where the boat owner was.

"No good," she told Brent when she returned. "That boat has a dead engine; not going anywhere."

Leaving the marina, they walked toward the bridge. "This is the last one," Leilani said, as they approached the next marina. When they reached the docks, Leilani saw just the boat they'd need. "Over there," she said, pointing across the docks.

They walked toward a brightly colored boat that looked very fast. A man was lounging in the back. He looked impatient.

"Are you for hire?" Leilani asked as they approached the man.

He rose and looked up at the two of them. "Waiting for a client right now," he replied, "but he's late and I can't reach him."

"How long do you plan to wait?" Brent asked.

"Not a whole helluva lot longer. Where do you want to go?"

"Can this boat get us to Miami?" Leilani asked.

"Miami?" The man stepped up to the dock beside them. "Yeah, I can get you to Miami, but I'll have to take on more gas and do a thorough check of the engines."

"How long will it take to get there?" Leilani asked. "And how much will you charge us?"

He eyed them suspiciously. "It's just the two of you and the one suitcase?"

"Yeah, and we're in a hurry," Brent said. "We missed our ship, and we're about fed up with cruising anyway."

"Yeah, right," the guy said, looking the two over. "Twenty-five hundred. Five hundred before you walk away, so I can pull her around and get gas, and the other two grand before we leave the dock. Cash."

"How soon can we leave?" Leilani asked, as Brent counted out the money.

"Go get some lunch," he said. "There's a nice restaurant just next door. Be back here by two o'clock and I'll have you in Miami by ten. We'll have to stop at Bimini for gas."

"And if the other guy shows up while we're gone?" Brent asked.

"I'll tell him to find someone else," the man said. "He was only chartering me to run him about forty miles north to see his girlfriend or something. Besides, he didn't give me a deposit like you folks." They agreed, and the man gave him a card with his name and number on it. "Call me if you change your plans — but if you do, the five hundred's not refundable."

"We'll be here at two," Brent said, taking Leilani's hand and turning back up the dock.

Once out of earshot, Brent said, "We'll be in Miami by ten, but that guy's not gonna live that long."

Leilani looked up at Brent and smiled back. *You're never going to make it to Florida either*, she thought. *That money will last me a lot longer than it will the two of us.*

Though she'd never intentionally hurt anyone since poisoning her captives, she felt certain that Brent would kill her and keep the money once he'd used her for whatever he needed.

Self-defense in advance, she thought.

They turned left upon reaching the street, still holding hands. Brent even held the restaurant door open for her. She knew it was mostly so he could look at her ass again.

After a leisurely lunch, Brent paid the tab, then he and Leilani left the restaurant. They'd be half an hour early but figured if all he had to do was gas up the boat, it shouldn't take more than an hour.

"Where's your hat?" Leilani asked, as they walked along the sidewalk.

"Left it at the restaurant," he replied. "I won't need it anymore."

A woman came through the marina's gate as they neared it. She had long blond hair in a ponytail, and tanned skin nearly as dark as Leilani's own. Even in simple boating clothes and dark sunglasses, she was quite beautiful.

Brent's eyes lingered on the woman a touch too long, and Leilani grabbed his arm and yanked him away.

"Chapman's waiting," she hissed, when they were out of earshot of the woman. "And I owe you a kick in the balls for that."

"A guy could get used to that, knowing what comes with it."

When they reached the boat, Beaux Chapman looked pissed. Which was difficult to pull off wearing only a Speedo.

"Ah, you're back early," he said. "Come aboard, I was just about to go down and change after checking the engines over."

He disappeared through a small door in the console and Brent stepped down into the boat, offering Leilani a hand.

"Got the money?" Chapman asked, when he returned from the cabin.

Brent reached into his pocket and took out the cash bundle they hadn't spent any money out of. "Two thousand," he said. "Where can I put our bag?"

The man took the money and reached for the bag, but Brent pulled it away.

"Take it below," Chapman said, a bit indignantly, as he turned the key to start the first engine.

CHAPTER EIGHT:

Walking back toward the marina where her boat was located, Charity stopped at the entrance. She hadn't intended to hurt the guy, but when he'd grabbed her arm, her instincts took over.

Behind her, she heard two powerful engines start and rev several times. It was probably Chapman revving the boat's engines to reestablish his manhood among the other boaters that had seen what happened — or maybe to impress the young couple with the suitcase.

Charity looked across Bay Street at the boatyard where Victor's boat sat on the hard. Crossing the street again, she approached the gate shack once more. Through the fence, she could see Victor's boat, but didn't see anyone on it. If he wasn't here and he hadn't taken the boat he'd planned to, Charity was worried that something bad had happened.

"I see yuh found him," the old man at the window said.

"What? No, I found the boat he was supposed to leave on, but the man said he never showed up. Why do you say that?"

He pointed down the road. "Dat was him, yuh jest walk past."

Charity spun around, searching the street. There were several people walking this way or that, but none was Victor.

"I'm not following you," she said, turning back to the man. "I didn't pass Rene on the street."

"Yes, miss, yuh did. He was carryin' a suitcase and was wit di tiny Asian princess."

She heard the roar of two powerful engines, as a boat left the marina where she'd just met Beaux Chapman.

"That wasn't Rene!" she said urgently, as she stepped closer to the window. "The man with the Asian woman was a lot younger and had dark hair. Rene's hair is lighter. I think the man you saw with the suitcase has robbed Rene's boat."

"I don't know 'bout dat," the guard said. "Mistuh Cook left jest 'bout di time I went home. Di night guard say di Asian woman came with di key, and Mistuh Cook was jest a minute behind her. Dey left together a few hours ago. I saw dem enter di marina yuh jest came from."

"I'm telling you, that wasn't Rene," Charity said, leaning closer to the window, and removing her sunglasses. "Do you let anyone come and go here without asking for iden- tification? I'd like to speak with your boss. Would you get him please?"

Whether it was the look in Charity's eyes or the sudden realization that he might have let a stranger in, the old man became much more cooperative. He picked up the receiver of an old rotary phone and dialed a number, explaining to whoever answered that he had a problem.

A few minutes passed, then another man appeared. He was younger, early thirties maybe, dressed in work clothes with a bright red bandana tied around his forehead. He opened the gate from the inside and invited Charity in.

"Hello, miss. I am John, di owner. What seems to be di problem?"

"My boyfriend is missing," Charity replied, pointing to Victor's boat. "His name is Rene Cook, and he owns that ketch. I think that your guard let someone else aboard who was pretending to be Rene."

"Is dat possible, Caleb?" the man asked, turning to the guard.

The old man explained the events as he knew them; seeing Rene leave just after sunset and how the night guard told him that he returned with a young Asian woman a few hours later.

"And you're sure it was him?" John asked.

The guard shifted his weight back and forth uneasily. "No, suh. Di truth is, I was looking more at her dan at him."

"How do I know you're a friend of Mistuh Cook?" John asked her.

Charity opened her bag and removed a small wallet. From it she pulled out a neatly folded document. "We each carry one of these," she said, handing the man the paper. "We have separate boats. Mine is across the street. That's a power of attorney, allowing me to take care of Rene's assets if anything happens to him, and vice versa."

John studied the document carefully. "All I can do is allow yuh to go aboard di boat," he said. "But I will have to go wit yuh, and yuh cannot sell it until di police tell me."

"I don't want to sell it," she said, taking the document back and returning it to her wallet. "I just want to find him."

Together, they walked toward the *Salty Dog*. Charity immediately sensed something wrong. There were far too many lights on inside.

"Allow me to go up first," John said, starting up the ladder.

Charity followed right behind him. When they reached the cockpit, she knew something was wrong; the companionway hatch was open.

"Rene never leaves his boat unsecured," she said.

"Perhaps I should call di police," John said, looking down into the cabin. "I don't like to go in someone's boat without permission."

"His boat's here for repair," Charity said. "You'll be going aboard sooner or later, right?"

"Yes, miss," he replied, looking down into the cabin again. "But dis is a bit different."

"Then step aside," Charity said, forcing her way past the man. She descended the steps quickly.

The lights in the galley-up pilothouse were on and several drawers and cabinets were open. She crossed quickly to the navigation desk and looked back toward the hatch. The man was holding back. She depressed the underside of a bookshelf and a false panel opened just below it. Inside were neatly stacked bundles of hundred-dollar bills, part of the stash of cash they both carried. The cash had come to them from a land developer turned money launderer named Brad Whitaker. He'd no longer had a need for it when his yacht burned and sank.

She closed the panel and started to go toward the aft stateroom, but something out of place caught her eye in the lower salon. A can of green beans. Going down the forward companionway, she saw more, scattered across the deck. The dry goods storage hatch was open.

Retracing her steps and crossing the pilothouse, she went down the aft companionway. The stateroom hatch was wide open, and she could see that the bunk hadn't been made and was completely disheveled. Victor was fastidious about neatness.

When she stepped through the hatch, she knew instantly that whoever had been aboard had found the watertight cash box under the engine. The matching one, which Victor kept his false identities in, lay open on the bunk. A small stack of passports was in the box and several more were scattered on the bunk. She quickly counted them; three were missing along with Victor's Kimber .45 caliber handgun.

She put them all together, and carried them to the engine room, leaving the empty box on the bunk.

It was a long reach under the engine, Charity had to lay on her side by the engine to get her arm and shoulder under it, but she managed to get the passports inside the hiding spot and put the false panel back in place. The police would arrive soon, and she didn't want them to find Victor's fake papers.

Returning to the hatch, she climbed up. "Call the police," she told John. "Rene's boat has been ransacked, and his money is gone."

The police arrived within minutes. They immediately went aboard Victor's boat to make sure it was secure. Then one of the policemen, a short, squat man of about forty wearing sergeant's chevrons, motioned for Charity to climb up. When she reached the cockpit, two other officers went down the ladder and waited.

"Mistuh Brown say dat you know di owner of dis boat?" the sergeant asked.

"Yes, Sergeant," Charity replied with a slight Cuban accent, as she handed the man her own fake passport. It had been created by the best — the American government — so she knew it wouldn't be a problem in any way.

"My name is Gabriella Ortiz Fleming," she said, perching her sunglasses on her head. "I am a Cuban-American citizen, and this is my boyfriend's boat."

"I'm told dis boat belongs to, uh," the sergeant flipped a page in a small notebook, "Mistuh Rene Cook. Is dat right."

"Yes," she replied, taking back her passport, and handing him the power of attorney. "Rene and I have been sailing together for some time. We each carry one of these, in case something happens to the other."

The sergeant studied the paper. "We are not at dat point yet," he said, handing it back. "How do you know dis boat has been robbed?"

"I offered it only as evidence of our relationship," Charity replied, folding the document, and putting it away. "Rene had a charter arranged so he could meet me at Hoffman's Cay. When he didn't arrive, I started this way, looking for him. The man who owns the charter boat said that Rene never arrived for the charter. As I said, we've been together for some time; I know the man. Things down below are in disarray, and his hatch was left open. Rene is fastidious about maintenance and keeping his boat neat and orderly."

"Do you know what was stolen?"

"I haven't looked thoroughly, but I know cash is missing. Did you see the watertight box on the aft bunk?"

"Yes. It is a cash box?"

"It held over one quarter million dollars, Sergeant."

The cop's eyes came up. "How much?"

"We're both semi-retired professionals," Charity said. They both maintained and developed their cover stories, sometimes just out of fun. "Rene is a shipwright. He owns a very successful business in the States that does quite well without him there. He always carries cash in case he comes across a boat he thinks might be worth salvaging."

"And you?"

"Owner of a not-so-successful travel magazine," she lied. "One that gets smaller and smaller the longer I'm away from it."

"Are you comfortable doing a quick inventory on dis boat?"

"No need," Charity replied. "The guard pointed out to me that I'd passed the man who was posing as Rene. He was carrying a suitcase just big enough for Victor's cash."

"I see," the sergeant said. "My men checked di marina where Caleb said di man and woman went to. A boat dere recently left, and witnesses say dat di man and woman hired di boat to go somewhere."

"A man named Beaux Chapman and his boat *Dripping Wet*?"

The sergeant removed his sunglasses and looked Charity in the eye. "Di same witnesses say dat just minutes before dat, a blond woman in sailing clothes roughed up dis Mistuh Beaux Chapman. Would you know anything 'bout dat?"

"That was me," Charity admitted, unfazed. "The man made a lewd advance and grabbed me. I have every right to defend myself."

He put his sunglasses back on, producing a business card from his shirt pocket. "I am Sergeant Bingham. Dis Chapman character is known to us. Do not worry 'bout it. My men are checking our logs and di hospital. Dat is my cellphone numbuh on di card. Call me if yuh remember anything else. How can I reach yuh?"

Charity gave him her own card, embossed with the logo of her phony business, *Tropical Luxury Magazine*. "That's my cell number. Call me as soon as you hear anything?"

He agreed and held the ladder as she climbed down. John Brown was waiting at the bottom. "I'll make sure di boat is secure when di police are finished, Miss. I am very sorry dis has happened and hope dey find Cap'n Cook very soon."

With nothing else for her to do, Charity started across the yard. She wanted to get aboard her boat. Maybe she could use her laptop to learn something. One of the policemen got out of his car as she approached. He tipped his hat as he walked past her toward the sergeant. A moment later Sergeant Bingham called out to her.

The sergeant's face was grave, as Charity approached. "Dere is a man at Doctor's Hospital, just a few blocks from here. He was brought dere with no identification, late in the evening, two nights ago. He was mugged and beaten. Dis man matches di description dat Mistuh Brown gave us. I can take yuh dere and find out if it is Mistuh Cook."

"He's not conscious to say who he is?"

Bingham took her arm, guiding Charity toward his police car. "He is hurt bad. Di doctors are keeping him mostly sedated. He was hit in di head with something very hard and has lost his vision and his ability to speak."

"Blind?" Charity asked, as she got in the car.

They arrived at the hospital ten minutes later, and Charity was rushed to the room of the unknown man. A doctor was just coming out as they approached.

"How is he, Doctor?" Bingham asked. "Dis young lady may know who your patient is."

The doctor looked solemnly at Charity. "He is badly hurt and may not survive. He has a broken jaw from a dreadful beating. There are multiple fractures of the cranium, along with swelling of the brain. The swelling is most intense around the occipital and left temporal lobes, where he was struck at least twice by something round and very hard. This is the part of the brain where vision and speech reside. He's heavily sedated, but awake. I think he can hear, though he isn't responding to questions."

"How long will di swelling affect his ability to see and talk?" the sergeant asked.

"If we can get the swelling under control, his vision and speech may return. We just don't know the extent of the damage yet."

"Anything on di tox screen?" Bingham asked.

"When he was first brought in, his blood panel showed mild intoxication. The only other thing the screen shows

is a high level of methylenedioxy-methamphetamine, a drug commonly called *ecstasy*."

"Then that can't be Rene in there," Charity said. "He doesn't do drugs, not even weed."

"This wouldn't be di first time something like dis has happened," Bingham said. "Dere is a high level of gang activity here in Nassau, and on other islands in di Caribbean. Dere has been a rash of tourist men robbed and killed, two women, as well. Dese gangs use women to lure di men into a trap. Sometimes, dey use ecstasy to make dem easier to control."

The doctor nodded to the sergeant and walked away. Bingham opened the door and motioned Charity inside.

At first, Charity wasn't sure if it was Victor or not. The man lying in the bed had a bandage around most of his head and face. The parts that she could see were purpled and swollen. He'd obviously been the victim of a terrible beating before the final blows to the side and back of his head. A nurse stood next to the bed, checking a chart.

"Can you pull the sheet down a little?" Charity said.

The man's head jerked almost imperceptibly, as the nurse looked at the sergeant. Bingham nodded, and she folded back the sheet that covered the man up to his neck. On his chest was a tiny tattoo of a leaping dolphin.

Charity had one just like it. They'd had them done together on Tortola, a symbol of their freedom after Charity had returned from Florida, having learned she wasn't being sought after.

Charity went quickly to Victor's side and took his hand in hers. His grip was weak, but it was there. He was also lightly tapping her wrist with his finger; three quick taps, then three longer ones, followed by three more fast ones. An SOS.

The nurse moved a chair over next to Victor's bed. "I be right outside," she said, herding Bingham toward the door.

Charity sat down in the chair. Still holding Victor's hand, she whispered, "Vic, can you hear me?"

His index finger pressed against her wrist for a moment, then once more quickly, and twice more long. Charity recognized it as Morse code for the letter Y.

"They said you were mugged by a gang," Charity said.

For the next several minutes, Victor slowly tapped out a message in code, first asking if they were alone. When she replied that they were, he continued, recounting what happened, using the antiquated language of dots and dashes to tell her that it wasn't a gang but cruise ship people who'd drugged him, and that he was sorry.

"You don't have anything to be sorry about," she said, a tear streaking down her cheek. Though he'd been beaten nearly to death, he was more concerned that he might have let her down.

She held him for a moment, then his hand found hers and he continued his tapping. He seemed agitated and hurried. After a moment the tapping stopped, and his hand gripped hers tightly.

The machine that had been quietly beeping, showing a weak pulse on its screen, suddenly went flat and emitted a continuous, monotone sound, a light flashing on the screen.

The nurse suddenly rushed into the room. She moved Charity out of the way. A stream of tears was already flowing from Charity's eyes. The doctor came in, followed by several other technicians with a crash cart. Sergeant

Bingham came in and pulled Charity to the side so the medical team could work.

For several minutes, the technicians tried in vain, using the defibrillator several times, trying to restart Victor's heart. Finally, the doctor stopped and looked up at the clock on the wall.

"Time of death, sixteen-oh-four," the doctor said, laying the paddles aside and pulling the sheet up over Victor's ruined face.

When Sergeant Bingham turned around, Charity was gone.

CHAPTER NINE:

Clive and Yvette Pence relaxed on the ship's sundeck, a bright colored sunbrella blocking the early afternoon rays. Yvette couldn't spend more than a few minutes in direct sunlight; her skin would become a bright pink. Being British, Clive wasn't much of a sun seeker, either.

"That's a pretty one," Yvette said.

The dark blue sailboat the woman he called his wife was pointing at was one of those older ones with a long pole at the front holding the front of the boat's brown sails. As it went past, he could see the name on the back; *Wind Dancer*.

"Clever name," Clive said. "And yes, my dear, it is quite a lovely vessel. But it won't be fast enough to suit my tastes."

"I'd expect that from one of *my* countrymen," Yvette said. "But I always thought you Europeans were far too sophisticated."

"British, my dear. There *is* a difference. I just like fast things."

"Is that why you like me?" Yvette looked at him over her red-rimmed sunglasses.

Clive chuckled. "You did set quite a pace that first time."

"Do you mean in picking your pocket?" she said, looking seductively at the man she called her husband. "Or how fast I got you into my bed when you caught me?"

"Oh, absolutely the latter."

The two continued to watch the boats coming and going in the bay as they waited for the crew to fix whatever the problem was that delayed their departure.

They'd only known one another for a few years, and though they called one another husband and wife, they weren't married. Nor did they even know each other's real names.

Clive looked over at Yvette and smiled lecherously. She was a stunningly beautiful woman with skin like porcelain. Her thick auburn hair captured and refracted the sun's light like a flaming halo. He knew that she only wore the bikini so others would admire her body. And why wouldn't they? The woman had been a model and, later, an aerobics and fitness instructor. Not one of those anorexic-looking women one would usually associate with those occupations, but a curvy, full-figured woman with a narrow waist and washboard abs.

One of their protégés approached.

"What is it, Doug?" Clive asked.

"Excuse me for interrupting, Mister Pence," Doug Bullard said. "But Brent and Leilani haven't returned yet."

Clive picked up his cell phone and touched a few buttons on the screen. "I told him to be back by one," he said absently.

"Yeah," Doug muttered. "It's after that."

Clive eyed the younger man. Doug wasn't quite as bright as the others, and he lacked the guile to keep unspoken words from his voice. Clive ignored him and studied the tracking app on his phone. All the phones his people carried were tracked by GPS. The display showed that Brent's cell phone was moving toward them at a fairly high rate of speed.

"That one should be fast enough for your liking," Yvette said, pointing to a brightly colored racing boat moving past the cruise ship. The boat's engine nearly drowned out her voice.

Clive looked at the boat, then looked at his phone. "Bloody hell!"

Rising quickly from his lounge chair, Clive strode to the rail and looked down at the passing boat. He recognized Brent, sitting in the back of the boat with his head back on the rear cushion. A woman who looked a lot like Leilani was kneeling in front of him, her face buried in his lap.

Brent looked toward the ship, right at Clive. He raised an arm high, extending his middle finger. Suddenly, Leilani sat back on the deck and punched Brent in the groin. The man fell out of his seat, gripping himself in obvious pain.

"Bloody hell," Clive muttered again as Yvette joined him.

"I wonder what they found that they'd risk their lives for," Yvette said, her voice cold and flat.

Clive strode back toward Doug. "Get everyone together in Rayna's room, Doug. Yvette and I will be there shortly."

The young man hurried off.

"I bet it was that slut Leilani's idea," Yvette said, lifting her glass and draining it.

"We'll soon find out."

They left the sundeck and returned to their luxury suite to get a few things before going down to the lower cabins.

Clive had gone to a lot of trouble finding the people for his group — not to mention the considerable time he and Yvette spent teaching them the subtleties of their new roles. Each of them had been hand selected.

The first criteria he and Yvette had in selecting possible apprentices was their family situation. Early on, they'd found that men and women who'd been orphaned as adolescents were the most suitable candidates. They had no family. Any with strong ties to step- or foster families were immediately dismissed. They soon found that the best candidates were those who'd been abused in foster care.

Even then, they didn't always fit the mold. It came down to whether they had any empathy toward their victims and little or no conscience about what they were doing.

Clive tapped lightly on the door. When it opened, Jeff Maple stood there for a moment, then stepped aside to allow entry. Jeff was nearly as tall as Clive's six-one, but being addicted to weight rooms, he outweighed Clive by an easy fifteen pounds, most of it in his chest and bulging biceps.

Clive waited for Jeff to close the door and take a seat. "Brent and Leilani have decided to abandon our group."

"Any idea what they found on that guy's boat?" Fiona asked.

Yvette stepped closer to her protégé and looked down at her. "You met the man. What do you suppose they might have found?"

The dark-haired woman furrowed her brow for a moment. When Yvette had found her five years earlier, she'd been living on the streets of San Diego, getting by as a street hustler. That was before Yvette had met Clive and started their new enterprise. At the time, Yvette ran a small but very successful stable of some of LA's finest call girls. Yvette had taken the seventeen-year-old girl in, groomed her, taught her to look and act like a lady, and then tricked her out for a thousand bucks an hour, mostly to the Hollywood elite.

"He was clean shaven," Fiona said. "Smelled nice and had recently showered. He wore clean clothes. He didn't strike me as a typical boat bum, although he was wearing boat shoes. My first guess would have been that he was some sort of professional, maybe a lawyer or doctor." She looked over at Rayna. "But remember his hands? They were rough and calloused." She shrugged. "Could have got that way from boating, but I got the feeling that he worked with his hands and had been very successful. Too young to retire, but probably wealthy enough to do it anyway. My bet would be they found a big pile of cash."

"Would that be your assessment, Rayna?" Clive asked.

Rayna Haywood had only been with the group since last summer. Clive had found her in a bar, where she'd propositioned him. He'd gone along, just to see where it led. When they got to his room, she'd slipped something in his drink. He'd deftly switched their drinks, turning the huntress into the prey.

"Yeah," Rayna replied. "I'd guess cash, too. He didn't seem like the drug dealer type."

"The boat turned west out of the harbor," Clive said to Jeff. He knew that Brent and Jeff were friends, constantly picking on Doug. "Where would Brent be going?"

Jeff looked blankly at the man. "He's from Florida, she's from up north somewhere. In a boat? They'd head to Miami."

"Why there?" Clive asked, moving closer to the younger man.

Jeff shrugged. "He's got friends there, and it's close. Besides, it's Miami, man."

Retrieving his phone from his pocket, Clive scrolled through his contact list, then stabbed the screen and put the phone to his ear.

"It's me," he said into the phone. "I need some work done." He paused for a moment, listening. "Yes, later this afternoon. My apologies for the short notice. A very fast boat just left Nassau for Miami. One of those flamboyant racing boats, all gaudily painted. The name on the back is *Dripping Wet*. There will be three people on board, two men and a woman. They will have something that belongs to me."

After listening for a few seconds, Clive said, "No, what they have is valuable, it can't be lost. You'll have to stop them some other way." He paused, listening again. "It matters little to me what you do with the occupants. But you're right; the woman will bring an excellent price. You'll see what I mean when you stop them. The usual fee for taking care of the other two? We can split what you get for the girl, and I'll add ten percent of what you recover, to compensate for the short notice. Do whatever you want with the boat."

Clive listened a moment longer, then ended the call without saying anything more. He put his phone back in his pocket and turned to the others. "Brent will be feeding the sharks before the day is over, and Leilani will belong to some rich Arab by Monday."

"Sucks for them," Jeff said, shrugging again.

"Until we find replacements," Yvette said, "Clive and I will be going with you. It's too dangerous with just two men."

"I met someone last night," Rayna said. "Another passenger here on the ship. You should check him out."

Clive watched as Yvette turned toward Rayna. The blonde had once been as hard as the Oklahoma dirt she came from, but now she visibly drew back from Yvette's gaze.

"What kind of person?" Yvette asked.

Rayna subconsciously tugged at the hem of her skirt. Clive was delighted at the juxtaposition of the two women. Physically, they were nearly identical: same height, weight, and very nearly the same build. Rayna was younger by a dozen years and might normally have a slight edge in stamina, if it weren't for the fact that Yvette had once taught aerobics. In a physical contest, they would be almost a dead heat. However, Yvette had a ten-mile lead in mental toughness and had made short work of the younger woman's aggressive behavior and superior attitude the night she'd tried to drug him. When Rayna had awakened from her drug-induced nap, she'd found herself tied to the bed. Naked and gagged, at the hands of a merciless mistress holding a pair of jumper cables. The other end of the cables already had one of the clamps connected to a car battery.

"Like us," Rayna replied. "No family."

CHAPTER TEN:

Moving aimlessly, Charity found her way out of the hospital, rage slowly overtaking the pain of loss. The late afternoon sun on her face felt out of place. Victor was gone, and there was no bringing him back. He'd never feel the sun on his face again, nor could he point out the stars to her and talk to them like they were old friends.

A car's horn blared, but Charity ignored it as she walked across the street. She continued walking, the sun on her left cheek, until she reached Bay Street. Crossing it, she turned right toward the marina where *Wind Dancer* was patiently waiting. Stopping, she looked back, then turned and wandered through the parking lot of a group of warehouses until she found herself at the waterfront. She could see the cruise terminal. No ships were docked there.

Charity left the warehouses and continued toward the marina, a little over a mile away. She walked in a fog, paying little attention to what was going on around her.

When she reached the marina, she paused and looked across the street. The masts of Victor's boat were visible. The sight of his boat sitting on the hard drove home the finality of his death. She would now have to use that document in her wallet. Victor would hate it if his boat were left there, abandoned. She turned and went to the dock where *Wind Dancer* was tied up.

Stopping at *Dancer's* bow, she stared blankly, almost reverently, at the old boat's lines. There was a light chop in the bay, and *Dancer* lunged against her dock lines like she knew exactly what Charity needed: speed, wind, and the taste of the sea. With Victor gone, *Wind Dancer* was her whole world and meant more to her than anything else.

Victor had felt the same about his boat. That was why they hadn't sold one and moved in together. Charity knew what she'd have to do. She would need to find someone that would take care of *Salty Dog* the way Victor had.

She stepped aboard, unlocked the hatch, and went down into the salon. The air inside felt hot and heavy. She collapsed at the nav-desk, staring blankly at the chart spread out in front of her.

Victor had told her that the people who'd attacked him had let it slip that they arrived in Nassau aboard the cruise ship *Delta Star*, and that there were five of them, three men and two women. Her mind on autopilot, she opened her laptop and searched for the cruise ship.

Delta Star wasn't one of the bigger ocean liners that visit the islands carrying thousands of Midwesterners to what they were told would be a tropical paradise. The *Star* was only six hundred feet, and carried eight hundred passengers. In her mind, Charity imagined them stacked like so much cord wood.

The ship's next port of call was Half Moon Cay and would be there for "a full day of fun and sun", including a beach blowout dinner party. But the schedule said it should have left Nassau this morning. Charity remembered seeing it at the docks when she arrived in the early afternoon.

Finding Half Moon on the chart, she guessed it was more than eighty nautical miles away, a full day's sail for her. Scrolling further down the web page, she found the ship's statistics and read that the *Delta Star* had a top speed of eighteen knots. A departure delay would mean they'd be doing every bit of that to make up time. The small ship could easily cover the eighty miles in less than five hours, arriving just after dark.

There was no way she'd catch the cruise ship, and chasing Chapman's Cigarette with the man and woman who'd robbed Victor was out of the question. He'd said there were five, and she had no idea if the young couple were even part of the murder.

Two targets, she though. *Neither of which I can catch.*

At least not with *Wind Dancer.*

After Charity's trip to Florida, and learning that her boat and helicopter were hers and hers alone, she'd reunited with Victor on Tortola. They'd decided to cruise the Bahamas for a while, so they'd sailed the short distance to Puerto Rico and retrieved her helicopter. Victor waited there until she moved it to a more central location where they planned to cruise. It was now in a hangar at the San Andros Airport, just thirty-five miles from Nassau. The mechanic there was a young helicopter pilot, and she'd paid him to maintain it and run the turbine once a week.

She calculated that if the couple on Chapman's boat were heading back to the States — and that was the direction she heard the go-fast boat going when it left the harbor — they'd arrive there in about three hours. If she could get to Andros Island in less than an hour, she could catch them before they made it to the mainland.

Get there how? she thought. *And do what?* Her head fell to the desk in utter despair.

Just getting a cab to the airport would take half an hour and there was no way she could immediately board a departing flight to Andros that would get her there in time. Dejected, Charity sobbed quietly.

"Ahoy, *Wind Dancer*," a voice called from outside.

Recognizing the voice, Charity raised her head and, in a flash, she was up the companionway to the cockpit. There on the dock stood none other than Jesse McDermitt.

"How did you find me?" Charity asked, stepping over to the dock and into the man's arms.

It was unlike her to be so emotional, and Jesse must have sensed it. He held her for a moment, then took her shoulders and pushed her away. Charity's eyes were red and puffy.

"What's wrong?"

Charity fell against him again. Then the choking spasms she'd been holding back came. She shuddered in his embrace, sobbing. Finally, she stepped back and wiped the tears from her eyes.

"Victor's dead," she said, driving in the final nail by uttering the words aloud for the first time.

Jesse wrapped her in his arms once more, holding her head against his shoulder. "I'm so sorry, Charity."

She cried again. Not convulsively this time, just a slow stream of tears and the occasional barely audible yelp of pain. When she stepped back again, she looked up at the man's face. She'd always looked to him as a sort of father figure. Not fatherly, but a trusted man who she could talk to.

"I can make some coffee," she offered, remembering Jesse's penchant for strong brew.

Jesse's eyes scanned the immediate area, wary as always. Then they softened as he looked back at her. "My boat's just down the dock," he said. "I already have some brewing."

They walked together toward the other end of the dock. Charity saw his boat, *Gaspar's Revenge*, and realized she'd walked right past it without noticing.

"How did it happen?" he asked as they reached the stern of his boat and he swung a leg over the low gunwale.

Charity stepped over and joined him as he unlocked the main hatch. "He was murdered," she said.

Jesse paused and looked deeply into her eyes before pushing open the hatch. He was instantly met by his dog, a big goofy-looking yellow lab named Finn. He told the dog to go back inside, and they followed.

"When did it happen?" he asked, going forward to the little galley.

"I was up at Hoffman's Cay," Charity replied. "Victor had to come here for repairs and was supposed to charter a boat to meet me there this morning. I had to change anchorages yesterday, so I sailed out to meet him. There's no cell signal there."

"A lot of the Bahamas are like that," Jesse said, passing her a cup of coffee. "I take it that Victor never arrived?"

She took a tentative sip, and it reminded her of Savannah. "No," she replied. "The reason we had to move was because we were attacked. We had to kill four men, Jesse."

"We?" he said, looking over the rim of his cup. "He did get there? And why did four men have to die?"

"No," Charity said, watching Jesse carefully. "On my second day at Hoffman's, a woman arrived. Someone I'd met briefly a couple of years ago. Savannah Richmond." Charity could tell everything she needed to know by his reaction. He was looking for her. And he was in love with her. "You'll never find her in busy ports like this."

Jesse sat down hard on a stool. "Wait, you were with Savannah? Where was Victor?"

"Four men attacked us at Hoffman's," she said. "Savannah's dog took one of them out, she got a second one, and I dropped two more."

"Savannah killed someone?" he asked, surprised.

Looking into his wide eyes a moment, she saw fear. It was strange seeing this reaction from a man she'd always considered fearless. She knew he was afraid for Savannah, but it was still disconcerting.

"No," Charity replied. "She knocked one of them out with a heck of a spinning back kick, though. The dog sent one over the cliff into the blue hole, where it looked like he landed head first on the rocks." She paused again. "After I sent her and her daughter back to their boat, I went back up there and cleaned everything up."

Jesse studied her face while he mulled it over. "A man dead, three unconscious, no cops around for hours, and no way to get help."

"These were bad people, Jesse," Charity said. "Very bad. I did the world a favor."

"Not judging," he said. "You were there, and you did what had to be done."

"Savannah and I moved south a few miles to another anchorage. She tried to act as if nothing had happened, but I could tell it weighed on her. The next morning, she was gone. That's when I set sail to intercept Victor. I ended up sailing all the way back here, only to find him in a hospital."

For the next few minutes, she explained how Victor had told her what had happened using Morse code, the drugging and the beating by the three men from a cruise ship called *Delta Star*, and then she told him about the young couple that had apparently robbed Victor's boat.

To his credit, Jesse stayed on track, asking pointed questions about when and where things happened, although finding Savannah must have been a high priority. Savannah had mentioned seeing him just a few weeks ago, and Jesse meeting her daughter for the first time. Had he been searching for her since?

"You never said how you found me," Charity said.

Jesse gave her that lopsided grin of his. "I didn't. I'd just locked up the salon and turned around. You walked right past me."

She smiled back, though it felt foreign somehow. "You came here looking for Savannah?"

The man fidgeted on the stool. "Well, we sort of knew each other a long—"

"She told me," Charity interrupted. "It didn't take long before we realized we knew people in common."

"What did she tell you?"

"About your affair, the kidnappings, the hurricane." She paused. "Then she told me about when she learned she was pregnant. She'd already filed for divorce."

"Did she—?"

"Tell me that Flo was your daughter? No. She doesn't know. Her husband might be the father. She just doesn't know and doesn't want to know. At least that's what she said."

"What do you mean?"

"I think she doesn't want the ex to be the father ... and as long as she doesn't know, she can pretend that you are."

Jesse sat there on the stool a moment, then went around the counter and rinsed his mug. "Want more?" he asked.

"No." She slid her empty mug toward him.

"So the possible murderers are on a cruise ship," he said, washing her mug. "They're headed southeast, and the thieves, who may or may not have been in on the murder, are on a go-fast boat headed northwest."

"And my boat can't catch either," she said.

"Well, the *Revenge* can easily outrun a cruise ship. How long ago did it leave?"

"Less than an hour ago. And the thieves left just before that."

She could see in his eyes that he was calculating speed and distance. "So this cruise ship has, what? A fifteen-mile head start? The *Revenge* can catch up to it in less than an hour."

"You want to help me?"

"It'll take a Cigarette at least three or four hours at cruising speed to reach the mainland," Jesse said, ignoring the question. "Those guys are all show and will only

run wide-open if there's an audience around. Once out in open water, he'll cruise at thirty or forty knots to save gas. We can probably catch them, too. But not both."

"My Huey's at San Andros Airport," Charity said.

"Really?"

"If I could get there fast, I could catch the Cigarette boat."

"Andros is only forty miles west," he said, his mind again working out the logistics in his head. "I can get you there in an hour and have someone waiting to take you straight to the airport. You still have that sat-phone I gave you."

"Yeah," Charity replied.

"Call the airport and have them wheel your bird out and warm it up. I can drop you off and still beat the cruise ship to Half Moon Cay, but we're losing daylight fast. Go get your gear."

"You're serious? What about Savannah?"

"Do you want to leave this in the hands of the Bahamian police?"

Charity scanned the man's eyes, seeing nothing but resolve. "No," she replied. "I want to catch them myself."

"Get going then. Savannah can wait. I'll make some calls and possibly get you some backup on the water. Don't forget the sat-phone."

Leaving Jesse's boat, Charity sprinted down the dock. When she arrived at the *Dancer*, she realized she'd left the hatch unsecured, and mentally slapped herself for losing focus.

Inside, she stuffed her flight bag with some extra clothes and ammunition, then grabbed her bugout bag from its hiding place. She blocked the hurt she was feeling out of her mind, pushed it down into a little box to be opened later, in private. Right now, she had purpose. She had a mission.

And, with Jesse's help, maybe vengeance.

When she returned to his boat, Jesse had the engines running and was loosing the bow line. Charity remembered how fast the big luxury fishing yacht was, and it gave her a sense of moving in the right direction. Knowing the arsenal that the man kept on his boat gave her a better sense of preparedness.

She checked her watch as she stepped aboard. An hour to Andros, then ninety minutes to Miami. If the thieves were making a beeline for the city, she'd catch them in international waters. What she'd do then, she had no idea.

"Get the stern line," Jesse said, as he climbed up to the fly bridge.

A minute later, she was on the bridge with him, as the boat idled away from the slip. Jesse turned toward the high bridge carrying traffic over to Paradise Island and pushed the twin throttles forward. The big boat effortlessly climbed over the bow wave, sending a jolt of adrenaline through Charity's system as she was pushed back in her seat.

"Are you sure you want to get involved in this?" Charity shouted over the engines.

At twenty-five knots, Jesse pulled back on the throttles to maintain speed. "I talked to Deuce," he said, steering through the wide bay toward the western entrance. "Andrew Bourke and Tony Jacobs were there in the office. Andrew has a boat and they're heading out now. They'll be off the Miami coast within two hours, max. What do you want to do when you catch these people?"

Charity considered the question. "I don't know for certain that they had anything to do with the attack on Victor," she replied. "But I'm certain they're the ones who ransacked Victor's boat and took most of his money."

Jesse was a careful man, she knew that. He rarely spoke without giving thought to each word. "So, you want to talk to them first?" he finally asked as he turned toward open water and accelerated. "Find out if they were involved in the attack on Victor? And then get back what they stole?"

Charity thought about his question for a moment. "It's just a little too coincidental," she finally admitted, practically shouting over the engines. "The attack was Wednesday night, New Year's Eve, just before midnight. The guard at the boatyard said the man who was impersonating Victor, and the woman he was with, arrived a few hours later. They had the keys to his boat."

Making a wide turn out of the bay and into open water, Jesse turned toward the setting sun, pushing the throttles all the way forward. A rising high-pitched whine joined the roar of the big diesels.

"You're right," Jesse said, "too coincidental. If they weren't involved in the actual attack, they were with those who did."

"I don't care about the money," Charity said. "I just want the three men who beat Vic to death."

They rode on in silence for several minutes, chasing the sun. Charity looked around the immaculate fly bridge. Everything had a place, on Jesse's boat and in his life. He'd allowed her into his life, due to circumstances, and he'd allowed her more when they'd been together chasing Smith. He was habitually neat, just like Victor.

"I think you should have his boat."

"Have whose boat?" Jesse asked.

"*Salty Dog*. Victor's boat."

He looked over at her and pushed his sunglasses up onto his forehead. The diffused light from the setting sun made the lines around his eyes more pronounced. "What the hell would I do with a sailboat? And it's not really yours to give, is it?"

"Look," Charity said, turning in her seat to face him, now certain of her sudden decision. "Victor and I loved each other. And we both had a love affair with our boats. When we met up again in Tortola last summer, after I'd sailed his boat up to see you, we very nearly ran past each other to get to our own boats."

"Yeah," Jesse said wistfully. "I can understand that. But it doesn't answer either of my questions."

"I know you're the same way about your boat as Victor is—was about his. And I've seen you at *Salty Dog's* helm, she suits you. That first night back together, we couldn't decide which boat to sleep on. We'd been apart for over a month, yet that first night, we both slept on our own boats. The next morning, we went into San Juan and met with an American ex-pat attorney. He drew up powers of attorney for each of us, just to cover the sale of our boats and everything in them, in case something happened to one of us."

Charity paused a moment, then let out a sigh. "At the time, I thought it was very romantic, like we were married or something, and our boats were our children. Does that make any sense?"

CHAPTER
ELEVEN:

Jesse had to slow to pick a spot to get through the barrier reef, but they'd soon arrived at a desolate dock jutting out into the Atlantic. It was dark and the only lights at the dock were the headlights of a pickup parked at the foot of the short pier.

It seemed like McDermitt had friends everywhere. A man who looked to be in his eighties was waiting for them at the dock. Jesse had only told her that the man was a friend of the family and his name was Henry. Which family, he didn't say.

Before leaving the boat, Charity gave Jesse a quick hug and whispered another thanks. He knew her better than most and knew exactly what she needed to get her mind past losing Victor.

When she stepped up beside Henry, Jesse reached over the gunwale and shook the old man's hand. That was it, no words were exchanged.

Pushing his sunglasses back down, Jesse looked out over the broad foredeck at the calm water ahead. The sun was barely ten degrees above the horizon, painting the low clouds a little off to the north a burnt red. "Yeah, it does," he said, barely loud enough for her to hear. "It makes a lot of sense. Don't forget to call the airport and have your bird ready."

"So, where do you know Jesse from?" Charity asked as the truck rattled and bounced through the streets of a small town.

"Don't really know the boy all that much," Henry said. "I served with his grandpa during the war in the Pacific. Jesse's daddy was my godson. How is it you know him?"

There was a lot about her and Jesse's relationship that wasn't for public knowledge. In fact, there was more to it than anyone knew. The weeks together on his boat, criss-crossing the Caribbean. To this day, the circumstances of Jason Smith's death were known only to the two of them. Their co-workers suspected, but never asked.

"We worked together once," she said. "What's the name of this town?"

Henry glanced over as he turned onto what looked like a main road, though it was devoid of anything but man-groves on either side for as far as the headlight beams reached.

"Ain't really a town," Henry replied. "It's called Mastic Point Settlement. So you and him worked together in the Corps? Or after that, doing that government work?"

The last question told her that this old man was someone she could trust. If he knew what Jesse's job was with Homeland Security, Jesse must trust him complete-ly, and that was good enough for Charity.

"I was a helicopter pilot for the same agency," she replied.

He seemed satisfied with that answer. The ride to the airport took only a few minutes and they only passed one car on the way. Henry didn't ask anything more or offer any further explanation of his relationship to McDermitt.

The fixed base operator at San Andros was very small, and the airport didn't have lights, so there were no arrivals after dark. When she called, she'd had to promise the guy an extra twenty to stick around another hour. They were about to close and go home.

"I don't know what you're involved in," Henry said, when he pulled up at the FBO and Charity started to get out. "But best of luck to you."

"Thanks, Henry." She stepped out of the truck. "And thanks again for the lift."

"Any friend of any McDermitt," the old man said. "No questions asked." Then he ground the old truck into gear and drove away.

Shouldering her flight bag, Charity picked up her other bag and turned toward the building. Henry's last statement left her wondering. He'd said it almost reverently, like there was some sort of debt there that could never be repaid.

When Charity pulled on the door, it was locked. She could hear a helicopter's turbine, which she assumed was hers, out back. She rapped on the glass with her knuckles.

After a second, more insistent knock, a woman came out of a side office, unlocked the door, and pushed it open for her. "You be Miss Fleming?"

"Yes, ma'am," Charity replied. "I spoke with Derrick about an hour or so ago."

"He out back, going over your aircraft," the short, round, black woman said. "Di moon be up soon; nice night for flying. Yuh want me to put di fuel and extras on di same card?"

Charity had opened an account at the FBO when she'd brought the Huey there, paying for hangar space for four months. The FBO — or, more precisely, Derrick — per-formed some light maintenance and spooled the turbine up once a week.

"Yes, thanks," Charity replied, extending her hand to the woman, a twenty-dollar bill in it. "This is for waiting for me."

It was her helicopter that was running, all the naviga-tion and landing lights turned on. The young man she knew only as Derrick was at the controls, going over a checklist. When she'd first met him, she'd been impressed by his knowledge of older Bell helicopters.

The powerful landing light winked off, making the area look much darker. Leaving Derrick to finish, she walked around the helicopter checking things out. The black paint job gleamed with the reflected light from inside the build-ing. They must have washed it recently.

"Thanks for staying, Derrick," Charity shouted when she reached the open door on the pilot's side.

"No trouble, miss," he replied with the typical broad smile of the Bahamian people. "I like to sit in dis bird when I bring her out and start her up," he said, stepping out. "She has many stories to tell."

"Hopefully, she'll have more stories in the future," Charity said, getting in and placing her bags on the co-pi-lot's seat.

"I'm sure dat she will, Miss."

"Here," she said, handing the young man another bill. "I really appreciate everything."

Derrick took the twenty as Charity pulled the seatbelt harness through the bags' straps, clicking it into place.

"Yuh didn't need to do dat, Miss. Me and Momma 'bout live here anyway. But we thank yuh just di same. Your aircraft is all set."

When Derrick closed the door and latched it, the sound of the turbine diminished slightly. Charity donned her headset and the noise was reduced to a hum. She adjusted the mic so that it was directly in front of her mouth and then looked over her instrument panel. Derrick must have taken the time to wipe things down each week, as there was no dust on the gauges. Everything was reading normal.

After a quick pre-flight check, Charity was satisfied that the bird was just as she'd left it, full of fuel and in top shape. She reached down beside her seat to her left and twisted the throttle slightly, bringing the turbine up to flight speed. It whined louder as the rotors picked up speed.

Turning the mic switch to voice-activated, she called out her intention on the airport's frequency, checked all around her, and pulled up on the collective slightly, just enough to take some of the weight off the skids.

The main rotor began beating the air heavily. Derrick was standing by the door of the FBO and gave her a thumbs-up. She returned the signal, then raised the collective slightly more. The Huey responded, lifting a few feet off the ground.

Using the foot pedals, Charity turned the chopper until she was facing the taxiway, then raised the collective a little more, while nudging the cyclic stick forward.

Five feet off the ground, Charity taxied her helicopter toward the long, unlit runway. The lights from the FBO barely illuminated the tarmac in front of the hangar,

but the powerful spotlight under the belly of the Huey pierced the blackness easily, illuminating the length of the short runway.

Twisting the throttle to takeoff speed, Charity raised the collective and pushed the cyclic forward, the chopper responding by dipping the nose and accelerating quickly to seventy knots. The black Huey slowly rose higher into the dark, moonless sky. At a hundred knots and a hundred feet above the runway, she added more collective, and pitched the nose up and to the left.

The heavy whump-whump of the blades resonated through the whole aircraft as she pulled it into a climbing turn to the northwest.

Leveling off at twenty-five hundred feet, she set a course that would take her toward a spot further north on the Florida coast. The Cigarette would probably run between the Cat Cays and the Biminis, which were straight ahead. It would be somewhere between those islands and the Florida coast that she'd catch the thieves.

She had the sky all to herself. Ahead and below, the ocean was inky black, with just two tiny points of light in the distance ahead.

She still had no idea what she would do if and when she found them. She couldn't set down on the water. Even if Andrew and Tony were able to help, would their boat be fast enough to overtake a Cigarette? The boats were noted for their high speed. She couldn't put her former work associates and friends in harm's way, nor could she ask them to do something illegal. Maybe they could just follow the boat, while she went ahead.

Slowly, the ocean surface began to lighten from inky black emptiness to varying shades of dark gray. It took a moment for Charity to realize that the moon was rising. She pushed on the left foot pedal, crabbing the bird slightly sideways, as she eased the stick a little to the right to compensate. Looking out the side window, she could see the moon directly behind her; a bright moon, more than half full.

Thinking about Victor, Charity's eyes clouded with tears again. The last few months they'd spent together had been wonderful. No pressure, no expectations, just two people enjoying life together. She wiped the tears with her shirt sleeve and tried to concentrate.

Before arriving on Andros, Jesse had given her Tony's and Andrew's contact information. She reached over to get her sat-phone out of the go-bag and turned it on. She knew she wouldn't hear anything from Jesse until he'd located the cruise ship, which wouldn't be difficult. Commercial vessels have transponders, so they can be located by anyone. All he planned to do was get to Half Moon Cay ahead of the ship and watch the people getting off, looking for a group of two or three men together with one or two women, all in their twenties.

As she flew on, the two lights in the distance began to break apart, and she could see the sparsely populated islands of North and South Bimini, and the Cat Cays more clearly. Farther east, a lighter patch of sky glowed on the horizon: the twenty-four-hour city of Miami. She checked her watch. It was still early, barely an hour after sunset, but enough time had passed that the Cigarette would probably be beyond Bimini, unless they made an extended stop for fuel.

Flying over North Cat Cay, with Gun Cay and its lighthouse just ahead, Charity started her turn to the east.

Chapman's boat, with the two thieves aboard, was somewhere ahead. The moon illuminated the white sand beaches of the uninhabited Gun Cay as she passed over. Two boats lay at anchor just off the northern tip, where the lighthouse and the ruins of the light keeper's home were located.

Straightening out on a course that would take her to Miami, Charity heard her sat-phone beep twice, signaling an incoming text message. When she looked over to grab it, a red light caught her eye down on the surface.

Picking up the phone, she banked right slightly for a better view. A boat was just coming out of the channel between North and South Bimini. It was the boat's red navigation light that had caught her eye, telling her it too was headed east. From the altitude and distance, she couldn't be sure in the gray darkness of a half-moon if it was the boat she was looking for, but it did appear to have the same lines.

Continuing her turn to the left, she circled around, crossed over the lighthouse at Gun Cay, and descended to fifteen hundred feet, as she finished a wide circle to approach the boat from the stern. When she came out of the turn, she lined up on the boat ahead of her and slowed, to just a little faster than the boat was going.

The sound of the boat's engines, probably at half throttle, would make it difficult to hear themselves talk, let alone hear her helicopter. When she was a mile behind the boat, she reached into her flight bag and pulled out her clip-on night vision monocular. She attached it to her headset and turned it on, adjusting it in front of her right eye.

It took a second to find the boat through the two-power optics, but when she did, even in the gray-green display of the night vision, she saw immediately that it wasn't the boat she was after. Pitching the nose down, she applied full power and pulled up slightly on the collective.

She passed over the speeding boat at double their speed, while scanning the water ahead. Seeing nothing, she flipped the monocular up and looked at her phone. She didn't recognize the number the text message had come from, but the area code was southeast Florida and the Keys. She opened the message, which read, *On loc, 4 mls off M.*

It had to be from Tony or Andrew, letting her know they were off the coast of Miami. She quickly typed a short reply telling them that she was one hundred miles away and no sign. Digging out her phone's cord, she patched it into her headset. When she found the boat, she didn't want to be texting. She alternated with the monocular, scanning the water ahead for a few minutes, then flipping it up to look all around with both eyes. *Dripping Wet* was out there somewhere.

After another twenty minutes of searching, she saw another boat in the distance. Angling toward it, she could see quickly that it wasn't the Cigarette, but a charter fishing boat.

As she resumed course, her phone beeped again. Another text message from Tony, she assumed. *Now 8 nm off M. Inbnd bogey, 13 nm, closing at 40 knts.*

Checking her position, she estimated the Florida coast lay just fifty miles ahead, meaning the boat they had on radar was twenty-six miles in front of her.

Charity cursed softly and pushed the Huey to its maximum speed of one hundred and thirty-five miles per hour. She'd reach Tony's and Andrew's position in eighteen minutes. About one minute ahead of the Cigarette, if that was even what they were tracking.

A ringing in her headset told her she had an incoming call on her sat-phone. The display indicated that it was the same number that was texting. She answered it.

"Déjà vu," she heard Tony say. "Didn't we do something like this a couple years ago?"

He was talking about the time she'd flown Andrew and two other men out to where Tony was piloting Jesse's own Cigarette boat, and the three men had jumped into it at sixty knots. It was the same night that Charity had disappeared.

"Thanks for doing this, Tony. I really don't have a plan, though."

"How soon are you going to get here?" he asked. "That boat's coming straight toward us."

"I'm at full speed," Charity said. "I'll reach your position ahead of the boat, but not by more than a minute or so."

"Take her right down on the deck," Tony said. "Does that thing still have the spotlight and PA?" He meant the public-address loudspeaker mounted next to the spotlight on the helicopter's belly.

"Yeah," she replied, wondering how he knew it was the same bird.

"Get right up behind the boat. You should be able to ID it before it reaches us. Tell them to heave to and prepare to be—wait one. It's slowing down."

Putting the nose down, Charity dove the helicopter to just two hundred feet. The dive increased her forward speed for a few precious seconds.

"The boat's stopped," Tony whispered. "About five miles east of us. You should be able to see it in a few seconds. We're heading that way."

Flipping the night vision scope back over her eye, Charity studied the water ahead. "I'm going to come in hot and flare right behind them."

"Roger that," Tony said. "That should hold their attention long enough for us to get close."

Spotting the boat, Charity adjusted course and put the Huey into a shallow dive. She wanted to be no more than fifty feet off the wavetops when she got to the vessel. Through the low-power scope, she could now see that it was Chapman's boat, *Dripping Wet*.

Almost on top of the boat, Charity saw a long, sleek center-console in the distance, and guessed that it was Tony and Andrew. She pulled the cyclic to her lap and hauled the collective up fully. Being nearly empty, the chopper was light and agile. She knew from experience the sound such a maneuver created. The heavy whumping of the main rotor, beating the air hard to bring the big chopper to a stop from a hundred and thirty-five miles per hour, could certainly rattle a person's cage.

Just as she started the maneuver, she saw one of the people on the boat swing a high right fist at another person, who fell to the deck instantly.

CHAPTER TWELVE:

Bringing his brand-new Yellowfin down off plane in the calm Atlantic water, Andrew Bourke studied the radar. The screen was empty, and they were a good four miles from shore.

"Think this is far enough?" he asked his partner, Tony Jacobs.

Tony came around the console and looked at the screen. "I'll text her our position," he said, "but maybe we should keep heading out."

"Any guess what this is all about?" the burly former Coast Guard senior chief asked.

"No idea," Tony said, tapping away at his satellite phone, "but she's one of us and needs our help. That's good enough for me."

Putting the boat in gear, Andrew brought it up on plane again, heading east. Somewhere ahead, on the ocean's dark, glassy surface, a flashy Cigarette boat was heading toward them, with a helicopter trying to catch it.

Andrew wasn't concerned about the production racing boat outrunning his new offshore tournament boat. A new company would be starting production next year of the world's most powerful outboards, and Andrew was close friends with one of the design engineers. He had a pair of five hundred and seventy-seven horsepower prototypes hanging on the transom that could push the boat to an easy seventy knots.

"I don't know, man," Tony said glancing back. "They just don't sound like outboards."

"You're just a purist," Andrew replied, his deep baritone sounding like a rumbling freight train. "My buddy on the design team says that once they introduce these babies at the Miami boat show in a year or two, they're gonna fly off the shelves."

They continued east, barely on plane, while they both watched the radar screen. With the range of the Furuno unit, any boat coming toward Miami from Bimini would show up on the radar screen.

"There," Tony said, pointing at an echo that had just appeared on the unit's peripheral. "Twelve miles and coming pretty fast."

Tony quickly sent another message to Charity, as Andrew brought the boat down to idle speed. They watched the other boat's echo on the screen, as it approached the mainland. It was going fast, but not full throttle, and was still a good fifteen minutes away.

"You better call her," Andrew said. "Screw all that texting."

Tony nodded and made the call. As he updated Charity on the approaching boat's direction and speed, Andrew noticed that the target boat was decelerating.

"They're slowing," Andrew said.

Tony relayed the news to Charity, then turned to his partner. "What the heck are they doing?"

"I'm gonna head towards them," Andrew said, pushing the throttles forward.

The twin supercharged vee-eight outboards whined like banshees as the boat accelerated. Tony was somewhat correct: the engineers would have to do something about the high-pitched whine of the superchargers. More sound-proofing or something. And the truth was, the shape of the engine's covers was odd, kind of futuristic-looking, to enclose the closed-loop cooling system.

Tony looked at the screen and said into the phone, "Roger that. That should hold their attention long enough for us to get close."

He ended the call and put the phone on the console. "She said she's gonna create a diversion by coming in fast and loud, flaring at the last second."

"Get up on the bow," Andrew said. "Have your Tavor at the ready."

When they were within a quarter mile, Andrew began to slow his boat. Snatching up a pair of binoculars, he studied the other vessel carefully. The moon was bright enough that he could see the people on board. It didn't look like they'd heard or seen them yet, and he didn't see any weapons.

Three people were aboard. Two of them, standing in the front of the cockpit, were obviously a man and a woman. The woman seemed to be talking to the man standing at the helm.

A second man stood in back, behind the couple.

Suddenly, the man in the back swung something white at the other man. The helmsman went down instantly. Andrew watched for a moment longer, as the woman bounced up and down, shouting at the man who'd just cold-cocked the helmsman.

"That's not good," rumbled Andrew.

"What's going on?" the former SEAL on the bow asked.

"One of the people on that boat just clobbered one of the others."

Andrew watched as the attacker, with help from the woman, heaved the other man overboard, just as the beating sound of Charity's rotor reached Andrew's ears.

He put down the binos and mashed the throttles. In seconds they were alongside the Cigarette, Tony shouting orders at the confused man and woman still in the boat. Shifting to neutral, Andrew quickly moved to the port gunwale, as the two boats began to drift closer together.

The helicopter hovered about fifty feet above the water and slightly astern the racing boat. A bright spotlight came on, aimed at the couple in the boat.

"Hands on the back of your head!" an amplified voice boomed from above. "Prepare to be boarded!"

The man dropped something white on the deck, as he pulled up his shirt front with his left hand.

"Gun!" Andrew shouted, as he aimed at the man and squeezed off two quick shots.

At the same instant, Andrew heard two more popping sounds from Tony's suppressed bullpup. The two men had trained together for more than three years in Homeland Security's Caribbean Counterterrorism Command. One of their group was a former Marine sniper who always chided the CCC's field operatives about superior firepower.

"Anytime you have to shoot at someone, shoot twice," Jesse McDermitt often said. "And when in doubt, empty the magazine."

Andrew had no doubt about his or Tony's marksmanship, but a double tap was less expensive than their lives.

The woman, no bigger than a twelve-year-old girl, screamed as the man in the back of the boat went down.

"Don't move!" Tony shouted at her. "Keep your hands where I can see them."

The woman put her hands behind her head, her face blank, as she stared at Tony in the bow.

"Stand between the seats," Tony ordered, "hands on your head, and face forward!"

As she complied, the boats drifted close enough together that Andrew could reach out and grab a cleat on the other boat's port side. He trained his own Israeli-made machine pistol at the woman, who was now staring at him. Something about the woman's expression bothered him. It wasn't fear, and her scream had been more one of surprise than anything.

"Go," Andrew shouted over the noise from Charity's helicopter.

Instantly, Tony vaulted the gunwale, landing lightly in the cockpit of the other boat. He moved forward, pushing the woman against the boat's dashboard and windshield to control her.

Andrew slung his weapon over his shoulder, then swiftly lashed the two boats together. He turned and waved both hands over his head at the helicopter.

Charity backed off a hundred yards, keeping the bright spotlight on the Cigarette's stern.

Taking the woman's right hand, Tony pulled it down behind her. He had two interlocked flex cuffs looped on his arm, and slid the first one over her hand as he held it firmly. Then he did the same with her other hand, cinching the interlocking loops tight and depositing her in the passenger seat.

"What the hell?" Tony asked, reaching down to the deck, and picking up what the man had dropped. "It's a sock." Grabbing the toe of the sock, he dumped a yellow ball into his palm. "With a pool ball in it."

Moving forward, Andrew stepped over to the other boat. He picked up the gun lying on the deck next to the dead man.

"It's a Kimber 1911," Andrew said, securing the weapon and thrusting it into his pocket.

Tony took his phone out and stabbed the screen. After a moment he said, "Couldn't be helped. He started to draw a gun on us." Pausing to listen, he added, "A Kimber 1911. What do you want to do with the woman?"

CHAPTER THIRTEEN:

Watching the activity on the two boats below her, Charity gasped as the man in the back moved suddenly. She saw Andrew and Tony fire at the same time, and the man went down.

Tony stepped over to the boat to restrain the woman. The second man was nowhere to be seen. When Andrew waved Charity off, she moved the helo fifty yards away, adjusting the powerful spotlight to keep the two boats in its circle of illumination.

A moment later, Tony took something from his pocket and held it to the side of his head. Her sat-phone rang through her headset, startling her. This wasn't the outcome she'd envisioned.

She touched the *Accept* button. "Why did you shoot him?"

"Couldn't be helped," Tony replied urgently, shouting to be heard over the buffeting wind the chopper was making. "He started to draw a gun on us."

"What kind of gun? One of Victor's was missing."

"A Kimber 1911. What do you want to do with the woman?"

"They stole it from Victor," Charity replied. *What do we do with her?* she thought.

"Another boat is approaching, Charity," Tony said. "Coming out of Biscayne Bay and headed this way very fast."

Charity looked to the west but could only see the glow of lights from the city. She shook off what had just happened. "Feel like going for a ride, Tony?"

"Bring her down," he replied. "I'll move the woman to the casting deck of Andrew's boat."

She ended the call and moved the bird into position just in front of the sleek-looking center-console. The Huey's rotors were more than fourteen feet above its skids, so there was no real danger in the maneuver; the trick was in the weight transfer. When someone steps off the boat onto the skids, the boat will rise slightly and the helo will drop, due to the extra weight. It was something she'd done many times before, though.

Standing on the raised foredeck, Tony waited, letting his knees absorb the up-and-down movement of the boat while his torso remained motionless. Andrew stood on the lower part of the deck, guiding Charity closer with hand signals. When she was in position, Tony timed the rise and fall of the boat then stepped up onto the skid and slid the big cargo door open.

Charity adjusted for the additional weight and kept her bird in position, as Andrew lifted the small woman bodily and held her up for Tony to drag inside. Then she moved the chopper away from the two boats.

Andrew spent less than a minute looking through the Cigarette's cabin. When he returned to the foredeck, he had the suitcase Charity had seen the man carrying when he and the woman went to Chapman's dock.

Charity eased the helo back into position and Andrew handed the luggage up to Tony. She could barely hear the exchange of shouted words between the two, then the cargo door closed.

A moment later, Tony stepped into the cockpit and removed her bags from the right seat, taking their place. He quickly donned the headphones hanging on the dash, adjusting the mic boom.

"She's strapped in," he said in a low voice. "No headphones."

Charity understood. If they talked low over the intercom, the woman in back wouldn't overhear anything, due to the noise from the turbine.

"What happened to the boat's owner?" she asked.

"Andrew said the guy they threw overboard is nowhere to be seen. He must have gone under."

"I didn't see him go overboard," she said. "But I saw the other guy punch him."

Below, Andrew had the boats untied and was at the helm. In just a few seconds he had his boat up on the step and was headed south at a very high rate of speed.

Tony held up a yellow sphere in his gloved hand. "It wasn't a punch," he said, turning it to show her a small white circle with the number one on it. "The dude used a homemade sap — a sock with a billiard ball in the toe."

Pulling the collective up, Charity turned back toward the islands, though she had no idea where to go. "Did the woman say anything?"

"Not a word," Tony replied. "Maybe she's in shock. She was just staring blankly at us the whole time. Where are we going?"

"I don't know," she replied. "Jesse is following the cruise ship that this woman's partners are on. It's headed for Half Moon Cay, between the northern tip of Cat Island and the southern tip of Eleuthera."

"Head that way," Tony said. "There's a little rock of an island about two miles off the eastern end of Little San Salvador. It's smaller than Jesse's island, not much bigger than a football field and completely barren."

Charity glanced at her fuel gauge, which was down to nearly half a tank. The standard tanks on a Huey gave it a range of just over three hundred miles. Her former boss had added auxiliary fuel cells giving her bird a range of almost five hundred miles.

"I'll be on reserves when we get there," Charity said, the dissipating adrenaline apparent in her voice.

Tony took his phone out and pulled up a map, typing on the little keyboard and moving the map around on the screen.

"Arthur's Town Airport is fourteen miles from the rock. When's the ship supposed to dock at Half Moon?"

"They left Nassau late," she replied, putting the information into the GPS. "At full speed, they could be there now."

"Cruise ships never run full speed." Tony said, closing the app on his phone and opening another one. "All they have to do is get there before the tourist shops open in the morning What's the ship's name?"

"*Delta Star*," she replied.

Working with his phone for a moment, Tony finally looked over at her. "Got it. Departed Nassau just after fourteen-hundred. Currently about halfway to Half Moon Cay, and cruising at a sedate seven knots. Scheduled to arrive at oh-seven-hundred."

Scrolling through his contact list, Tony stopped and stabbed the screen with the stump of his index finger. Pulling the headphone from his left ear, he wedged the phone under it. "It's me," he shouted. "I'm with Charity. Remember that little rock about a mile east of the island you're heading to? Meet us there in about" — he paused and looked at the GPS and air speed indicator — "two and a half hours."

He listened for a moment. "We're all okay. One of the guys on the boat killed the other guy before we arrived. We watched it go down. When Andrew and I got there, the killer drew a gun. We had no choice but to shoot him."

Listening for a bit longer, he finally said. "No, no bodies retrieved. One sank, and the other's still on the boat. Guns are untraceable, and we wore gloves."

Charity glanced back at the woman. She was small enough to pass for a child, but she was obviously an adult. Charity guessed her to be early- to mid-twenties. Her expression was one of passive acceptance, as if being plucked from a boat after seeing two men killed was an everyday occurrence.

Charity looked over at the black man seated next to her. Tony's eyes were on his phone as he typed something. Like Jesse, he and Andrew had come to her aide, no questions asked.

Finally, Tony put his phone away. "Had to let Tasha know I wouldn't be home tonight."

"Tasha?"

"My wife," Tony explained. "We got married last July."

"Congratulations," Charity paused for a moment. "Why did you come out here, Tony?"

"Jesse called Deuce and said you needed some help. Andrew and I weren't sure what kind of help, so we came prepared for anything. What'd those people do?"

"Jesse didn't tell you?"

Tony looked at her questioningly. "All Deuce said was you were in trouble and needed our help."

Charity turned and looked through the windshield again. The moon was well above the horizon, creating sparkling reflections on the water below. The sky was devoid of clouds, and stars competed collectively with the moon for brightness.

"The woman and one of those men might have been involved in Victor's murder," she said.

"Victor Pitt?" Tony asked, staring at Charity's profile.

She nodded, fighting back the tears.

"I'm really sorry, Charity," Tony said. The timbre of his voice was one of genuine concern. "You said one of the men was involved. Who was the other guy?"

"His name was Beaux Chapman," she replied. "That's Beaux with an X." She jerked her head toward the back. "That woman and the other man chartered his boat to take them to Miami."

"But you're not sure if he and the woman were involved?"

"I'd bet my life on it," she replied, "especially after seeing that pool ball. Victor was hit by something similar. His cash box is in that suitcase, and they stole his gun. Did you get it?"

Tony dug into his pocket. "Andrew gave it to me, after I told him that it might be Victor's." He quickly dropped the

magazine out of the grip, turned the weapon sideways and ejected a cartridge into his lap, before handing it to her.

Charity took the Kimber and looked at it in the dim red light. It was definitely Victor's. "Before he died, Vic told me there were five attackers; three men and two women. If these two didn't actually take part in the murder, they were with those who did."

Reaching back, Tony pulled the suitcase forward and examined it. The case was a cheap piece of crap one would use for an overnight bag. He undid the clasps and lifted the lid. Inside, he found a Pelican watertight storage box, which he pulled out and opened.

Letting out a low whistle, Tony kept his voice low. "That's a shit-ton of cash." He lifted a leather folio from the box and opened it. "Yeah, this is pretty damning. An American passport with Victor's picture, issued to Rene Cook. That's the name Victor used when I met him last year."

"You met him before?"

"Last July, just before Tasha and I were married. He was living on Andros, working for an old friend of Jesse's grandfather; a man named Henry Patterson. We accepted a last-minute mission to rescue a woman and her grand-daughter from a Jamaican gang on the south end of Cat Island. There were some unusual developments and we brought Chyrel in, when we went to Andros for fuel. She recognized Victor."

They flew in silence for quite a while. The northern tip of Andros Island passed beneath them. Charity was flying as straight a course as possible to the spot where they would meet Jesse, but was also giving Nassau and any inquisitive air traffic controllers a wide berth.

The flight lasted a little over two hours. Charity descended to fifteen hundred feet, as they approached Little San Salvador, where the private resort of Half Moon Cay was located. There were no cruise ships anchored off the crescent-shaped bay on the west end, but Tony had said it would still be hours before it arrived. She continued her descent as they flew the length of the island's desolate north shore.

Ahead in the distance, Charity saw a light. A moment later, she could easily make out the sleek lines of McDermitt's sport fisherman *Gaspar's Revenge*. Flipping the night vision scope back in front of her eye, she studied the little island.

"It's not barren, Tony."

"Well, it was last year," he replied, craning his neck to look down.

Jesse's boat lay at anchor on the southwest side of the island, shielded from the easterly rollers by a natural breakwater. It was this rocky promontory that probably created the island behind it, as waves broke on the rocks and wrapped around the ends, forming a sandbar.

"It's called Tee Cay," Tony said. "Not like a Tiki hut, though. It's spelled T E E, I guess because it's shaped like a T."

Charity studied the island as they got closer. "The beach on the far side looks large enough."

Tony consulted his phone again. "Tide's high. A few hours from now that beach will be bigger than the island. The water's less than a foot deep."

Without a word, Charity turned and made her approach from the water. She turned on the powerful spotlight, which revealed nothing on the beach that could cause a problem, and set the Huey down gently on a beautiful white sand beach, about twenty yards beyond the tiny waves lapping at the shoreline.

Shutting down the turbine, she went through her post-flight and opened the door. The blades were still spinning as she and Tony stepped down onto the sand. The moon was bright and high in the night sky, lending a tranquil glow to the little island.

Charity wasn't very concerned that air traffic control on Nassau might take notice of their descent. These waters were home to some of the best sport fishing in the Caribbean, and anglers were ferried out to the good spots by helicopter all the time.

Jesse appeared at the top of the dune — if you could call it that. No part of the little island looked to be more than two feet above the high tide mark. He strode down to where Tony and Charity stood in front of the helicopter.

"She say anything?" Jesse asked, as he approached.

CHAPTER FOURTEEN:

The three former special operators stepped away from the helicopter and spoke quietly. They didn't want the woman, still trussed up in the back of the helo, to hear them.

"Are you a hundred percent sure?" Jesse asked. "She's definitely the woman who broke into Victor's boat?"

Charity nodded. "The guard at the gate where his boat is being worked on pointed them out. They had his keys, and the man had been wearing his hat."

"They also had a suitcase onboard," Tony added. "Andrew found it. Inside was a Pelican box full of cash and two passports; one Canadian and one American. Both were Victor's."

"And this," Charity said, extending Victor's Kimber, butt first. "It's Victor's, too."

Jesse took the handgun, racked the slide slightly to look in the chamber, then turned it over in his hands. "She's a thief," he said quietly, handing the gun back, "but is she a killer?"

Extending the pool ball, Tony said, "The man she was with killed the boat owner with this, while she distracted him. It was in the toe of a sock, and Charity said that Victor had injuries that could be consistent with being hit like that."

"But it wasn't her that did it."

Charity didn't take exception at his doubtful questions. McDermitt was a professional and had a deep-seated need to see a situation from as many angles as possible before acting.

If he had the time.

"Andrew was watching through binoculars," Tony said, "when the one guy hit the other, probably caving in his skull Andrew said the woman might have been clapping."

Always wary, Jesse's eyes moved out over the water, scanning all around for approaching danger. Charity knew that his mind was in tactical mode. She'd now made three friends accomplices to murder and kidnapping. At least that was the way the courts would see it.

"We'll take her aboard the *Revenge*," he told Charity. "Then you fly to the airfield on Cat Island; you gotta be low on fuel."

"Where will you be?" she asked.

"The airport is just half a mile from shore," Jesse replied. "There's a public pier where I can pick you up; just follow the road west from the little terminal building. The facilities won't be open until morning, so we'll have the rest of the night to get some answers, sleep, and figure out what to do with her. The cruise ship won't get here until early morning, and the launches won't start ferrying people ashore until zero-eight-hundred."

"We need to find out who her friends are," Charity said. "For all we know, they could already have their sights on another victim. A policeman in Nassau told me there had been a rash of murders of tourists and cruisers throughout the Caribbean, all with similar MOs and injuries. They were chalking it up to gang activity."

"We'll find out," Jesse whispered. He pointed a thick finger at Tony. "She needs to become a little worried first. You're the bad guy, and I'm the good guy. You think it was Rene Cook who you shot. You were after him and his Cuban girlfriend. Got it?"

Tony nodded his understanding, then said through a grin, "Why am I always the bad guy?"

Jesse smiled back at him. "Because you're good at it." Then he raised his voice. "That's not a lot of proof, Malcolm. She and Cook might have just found it."

Tony's rebuttal sounded adamant. "Not enough for the courts, no. But damned sure enough for Mister Livingston. Besides, the guard at the boathouse IDed them."

"Eyewitnesses make mistakes," Jesse said. "We should at least question her first."

"No," Tony replied quite forcefully. "My orders were clear. Kill them both."

As Tony turned to walk toward the back of the helicopter, Jesse pushed him, knocking him to the ground.

"Not on my watch!" Jesse growled. "Not until I know for certain. I don't care what Livingston says."

Charity stood off to the side, watching the exchange. She'd seen the two of them work like this before. In fact,

all the members of her former team had learned to improvise from a stage actress who was also the team's armorer, making things up as they went along. In this case, Charity was playing the role of the indifferent transporter.

Tony stood and brushed the sand off. "Okay, Stretch," he growled, with just a touch of a southeastern accent. "We'll do it your way. *This* time. But if things go south, it's your ass in the sling."

"Good," Jesse said, opening the side door to the cargo area. The woman stared at him blankly. Jesse turned to Charity. "Take the bird and get refueled. We'll meet you there in an hour."

Reaching inside, Jesse unbuckled the harness holding the woman in place, then roughly took her arm and dragged her from the helicopter. Standing next to the tall man, the woman looked even smaller, though her figure was that of a grown woman and her eyes showed some age.

He started marching the woman toward the dune, half-dragging and half-pushing at times. "Bring the suitcase," he said over his shoulder.

Tony stuffed the Pelican box back into the case and closed it, hurrying after Jesse.

Producing a bright flashlight, Charity did a quick walk around, then climbed into the cockpit and went through her check list as she watched the two men cross the narrow spit of land.

After a moment, the rotor slowly spun up. She watched Jesse lift the woman to his shoulder like she was no more than a laundry bag. He sloshed into the water, with Tony alongside him. She knew that they'd still be in character, arguing over the merits of questioning her or doing as the mysterious Mister Livingston had ordered.

The turbine fired, and Charity closed the door. The fuel gauge was way lower than she was comfortable with, especially flying over water. But the warning light wasn't on, so she knew there was at least thirty minutes of reserve left in the tanks. It wouldn't take her half that time to reach nearby Cat Island.

As she lifted off the beach and turned, she saw Tony climbing onto the swim platform of Jesse's boat. Jesse himself was standing in water up to his chest and the woman was squirming to keep her face out of the water.

Turning toward the east-northeast, Charity climbed to just a thousand feet. Within minutes, she could see Cat Island in the moonlight. She circled to the north of the airfield and, even though she knew that there wouldn't be anyone around to hear her, used the little airstrip's Unicom frequency to declare her intention to land.

As she crossed the nearly desolate beach north of Arthur's Town, she banked right and reduced power to line up with the runway. That was when the low fuel warning light came on. Ignoring it, she brought the chopper in low over the apron, bleeding off speed as she neared the small terminal building.

The airport had only the one building — small, squat, and concrete, like most buildings in the Bahamas. Next to the tarmac sat a decrepit-looking DC-3, pushed way back onto the grass, its tail section practically obscured by the trees that had grown up around it. Parked on the tarmac next to the hangar was a fairly new Citation. She felt relieved. The jet used the same fuel her Huey did.

Picking a spot opposite the derelict transport plane, she brought the Huey in low and turned it, so she was facing

toward town. With the warning light flashing, she set the bird on the ground and shut down the turbine.

After going through her post flight, she went to the cargo area and opened the secret hiding spot in the belly. There she stashed her guns and ammo. She never liked being unarmed in an unfamiliar place, but she didn't want to be stopped by some airport security guy who lived nearby as she walked toward town.

Writing a quick note saying she'd return in the morning for fuel, Charity taped it to the inside of the window, then locked up the Huey. She shouldered her two bags and looked around the area.

Aside from the ticking noise the turbine made as it cooled, there wasn't a sound. She didn't see any lights — or anything moving, either — so she started toward the road that led west.

Arthur's Town was small, even as small towns went. Charity moved quietly down the dark road. Occasionally she heard a bird, or maybe an iguana moving through the brush next to the road. The road's shoulder was almost nonexistent. Fragments of ancient coral and limestone, used as the road base, extended a foot beyond the pavement, then dropped down into tangled underbrush. Here and there, pools of standing, brackish water with new growth mangrove came right up to the edge of the road.

After ten minutes, she sensed that she was nearing the shore. There was light ahead, at a crossroads, where she passed the shells of a couple of houses. In typical island fashion, they looked like they'd been under construction for quite a few years.

In the distance, she could hear the rumble of powerful engines slowing down. Staying close to the last of the vacant block structures, she looked carefully up and down the two-lane cross-street. The light was coming from a lamp post a couple hundred yards to the south. Directly across the road was a walkway to a pier, illuminated only by the silvery moon. Beyond the pier, she could see the hulking apparition of Jesse's boat's dark hull slowly slicing through the water toward the dock.

Staying low, Charity sprinted across the street, then continued down the walkway, toward the beach. The pier extended fifty or more yards beyond the water's edge. She reached the end only a moment before the big boat stopped, twenty feet from the end of the pier.

CHAPTER FIFTEEN:

All the way out to the boat, Tony continued to harass Jesse. "I'm telling ya, Stretch," he said, as they neared the large vessel, "quick and simple. That's what Mister Livingston said. Remember?"

The woman Jesse was carrying was in danger of drowning if she wasn't careful. She'd been compliant when he'd reached over and scooped her up onto his shoulder, but as soon as they'd started walking out into the water, she began to struggle.

The water was up to Tony's chest when they reached the swim platform. He climbed the short boarding ladder and stepped up into the cockpit.

"Here," Jesse said, "grab her."

"The hell with that," Tony said, water dripping from his clothes onto the deck. "Just drop her and hold her under for a minute. The sooner we get done with this, the sooner we can part company."

Jesse heaved the woman sideways onto the platform, then climbed the ladder. "I told you, man. We're not killing anyone until I'm sure."

"Sure?" Tony said, flailing his arms. "How much more proof do you need? She was with Cook. They *had* the money on them. Good enough for me, man. So we shot Cook, and now she's gotta die, too."

"His name wasn't Cook," the woman spat out.

"Ah, she does speak," Jesse said, grabbing the woman, and lifting her to her feet. Her shirt was wet and clung to her tiny frame, accentuating the curves of a grown woman. He squared her shoulders in front of him, nearly lifting her off the platform as he lowered his face to hers. "But do me a favor. Shut up for now."

Spinning her around, Jesse shoved the woman roughly, nearly causing her to trip on the step up to the cockpit.

"Get up on the bow and secure the anchor," Jesse ordered, forcing the woman into the fighting chair and strapping her in,

Tony stepped up onto the side deck, muttering, "Do this, do that. Yeah, you're a real tough guy."

"Just get the anchor!" Jesse shouted, as he started up the ladder to the fly bridge.

On the bow, Tony waited as Jesse started the engines, and activated the windlass. It only took a few minutes for it to haul the rode aboard. The rattling of the chain as it dropped into the anchor locker seemed out of place. When the anchor seated in the pulpit, Tony secured it with the safety chain, then started toward the stern as the boat began to idle slowly toward the south.

The woman turned her head toward him as Tony jumped down to the cockpit. "You killed the wrong person."

"Just shut up," Tony said, as he leaned in close. "Did you enjoy the sunrise this morning? I hope so. It was the last one you're gonna see."

She started to say something, but Tony raised his hand, as if to backhand her. She cringed toward the far side of the seat. Tony laughed, then went up the steps to the bridge.

Sitting in the second seat, Tony leaned over. "It's working," he said softly, as Jesse nudged the throttles forward. "I made like I was gonna hit her and she cringed."

"Good," was Jesse's only reply.

Though he'd never struck a woman, and believed the same to be true of the man sitting next to him, Jesse's simple reply still left an unsettling feeling. Tony had known Jesse for a few years now and knew him to be steadfast in his belief of what was right and wrong. To him, the woman down below was a common criminal, nothing more. Scaring her with physical violence didn't bother him in the least. But Tony knew he'd never follow through with it.

Once the boat cleared the breakwater, the bottom dropped away quickly. Jesse pushed the throttles about halfway forward and the big twin diesels rumbled as the bow lifted.

The crossing over to Cat Island only took thirty minutes. Jesse slowed as they neared the shoreline, then reached up and turned on the infrared camera mounted on the roof.

"See if you can spot the pier," he said, bringing the boat down to idle speed. "Should be just at the north end of town."

Tony used the camera controls to pan the beach, as he watched the monitor. "There it is. Just a few degrees north of this heading."

Leaning over, Jesse whispered, "I have an idea. Take her down to my cabin, make sure she can't move or get up. There's a couple of belts in the top drawer; tie her legs. Before you come back up, call me on the intercom and ask if I need anything. Then leave the intercom open."

Grinning broadly, Tony rose from his seat. "You're devious, man."

The woman was still strapped to the chair. For really large gamefish, a fisherman wore a harness which attached to the reel for added leverage. Jesse had simply looped the harness through the chair's back slats and buckled it around her. With her hands behind her back, she couldn't release the simple catch.

Unbuckling the harness, Tony took the woman by her arm and pulled her to the salon hatch.

"I was wondering when you'd want me," she said as Tony opened the hatch and pushed her inside. Upon seeing Finn, lying on the deck by the settee, she jumped back, apparently afraid of the big yellow dog.

"Shut up," Tony growled. "I don't *want* you. I want you *dead*. Luckily for you, Stretch won't let me do that yet. Otherwise, I'd just put two in your brain and feed you to the fish."

Taking both her shoulders, he pushed her forward and down the companionway to Jesse's forward stateroom. Inside, he easily lifted her onto the big centerline bed. He went to the chest of drawers and opened the top one. There he found a web belt with an adjustable clasp. He looped it around the woman's ankles several times and drew it tight, cinching the buckle.

"What's your name?" Tony asked.

"Does it matter?" she replied, staring at him with a vacant look in her eyes.

"Not to me," he said, pointing upward. "He wants to know. I can put a bullet in your brain whether I know your name or not."

"The man you shot wasn't Rene Cook."

Tony grinned as he looked down at the woman. "I never said his first name. Gotcha."

"My boyfriend stole his money and passport," she said. "That's all. That's how I know the guy's name"

"Yeah, I heard that one before. What's your name?"

"Leilani," she replied. "And the man you killed was Brent, my boyfriend."

"Boyfriend, huh? Yeah, you seem real broke up about that."

Without waiting for a response, Tony stabbed the intercom button, opening the channel to the whole boat. "Hey, Stretch. She's secure. You need anything up there?"

"Yeah," a scratchy voice replied from the speaker. "Bring me a bottle of water."

"I'm telling you," Leilani said, "we're not who you think we are."

Tony used the distraction to his advantage, whirling to face the woman and leaving the intercom on. "Too bad for you," he said menacingly. "I was told that Cook would be in the company of an Hispanic woman, and here you are. With the money that Cook stole and the gun that he used to kill my boss's partner."

"You're an idiot," Leilani said. "I'm not Hispanic. I was born on the island of Tahiti and kidnapped when I was ten. I was held captive by a couple of pedophiles in Boston until I killed them."

Tony was moved by her declaration, if it was true. He was also somewhat impressed that a woman so small could kill anything, but he didn't let it show. "Whatever," he said. "You all look alike to me."

With that, he turned and went out the door, closing it behind him. Before returning to the bridge, he took three bottles of water from the reefer.

"Here ya go," Tony called up to the bridge from the cockpit.

Jesse rose from the helm and reached down to take the bottles. "The pilot's coming down the dock," he said, more for the benefit of the prisoner. "Go to the starboard side and fend us off that post beyond the end of the pier, while I turn the boat around."

"Her name's Gabby," Tony said, giving Jesse a thumbs-up. "Gabby Fleming. And the girl laying on your bunk is Leilani. She didn't give a last name."

Nodding, Jesse turned back to the helm, as the big boat idled toward the pier in the darkness. When Tony reached the starboard rail, just forward of the salon, he heard the pitch of the engines change, as Jesse shifted them to reverse and brought the boat to a stop.

Through the darkness, Tony saw a figure approaching on the dock. He could tell by the long, confident stride that it was Charity. Thinking back to the first time he'd met the woman, he remembered being quite enamored. She'd been all business back then, and pretty much gave him the cold shoulder, along with most of the other guys on the team.

Pivoting the boat so the stern was toward shore, Jesse slowly backed toward a spot ten feet off the pier but right alongside the post, which was meant to tie off a much nar-

rower boat between it and the dock. When the *Revenge* was in position, he bumped the transmissions to forward, bringing it to a stop.

Tony had a fender ready to drop between the widest part of the hull and the post, as Jesse maneuvered the stern sideways toward the pier. The fender wasn't necessary. With the boat at an angle to the pier, Charity stepped over the gap and dropped down to the cockpit deck. Putting the fender in its keeper, Tony hurried aft to bring Charity up to speed on things.

Stepping down beside her, Tony held a finger to his lips, and motioned Charity over to the stern. "The com's open in the cabin," he whispered. "Disinformation."

Charity nodded, opened the hatch, and placed her bags just inside the salon. Then the two of them climbed the ladder to the fly bridge.

"Where do you wanna dump the body?" Tony asked, taking the second seat, while Charity moved toward the port bench.

"You already killed her?" Charity asked, following Tony's lead.

They'd used disinformation many times working for Homeland Security. It was especially effective if the person believed they were getting the information covertly.

"Not yet," Jesse said. "I'm not satisfied that she was in on the murder."

"I'm just transportation," Charity said. "But if it were me, I don't think I'd let someone I'd just kidnapped go free, whether she was part of it or not. Definitely not after killing the man she was with."

Jesse slowly advanced the throttles. "We'll go offshore a little way, anchor up, and find out."

CHAPTER
SIXTEEN:

Sitting at a corner table with Yvette and Rayna, Clive watched the young man at the bar. He had his back to them, talking to another man.

"How much were you able to find out?" he asked his wife, glancing at his watch. It was past midnight and there were few patrons in the bar.

Yvette tapped on her tablet's screen. "Quite a bit," she replied, opening a dossier she'd compiled after Rayna got the man's name and where he was from. "His name is Bruce Wheeler. Twenty-four, born in Jacksonville, Florida. His parents were both killed in a car wreck in ninety-five; he was nine at the time. No family, no adoption possibilities, so he went into the foster care system, where he lived with four families. He started getting in trouble with the law at age thirteen and was convicted of armed robbery when he was sixteen. That landed him in juvenile detention until he was an adult. Then he promptly went back

to his old ways and wound up doing a year in prison in Raiford, Florida."

"He might be worthy," Clive said. "Depends on whether he can fit in or not." He looked at Rayna. "Did he come on to you, or the other way around?"

"He's not gay, if that's what you mean."

Clive smiled. "Exactly the answer I was hoping for."

He nodded to Yvette and she put her tablet in a bag, tucking it next to Clive. "Don't wait up, lover."

"Oh, you know I'm going to," he said with a lecherous grin.

Yvette reached into the plunging neckline of her blouse, alternately adjusting her bra cups to show more cleavage. Then she stood and tugged her skirt up slightly higher. She smiled at Clive, then turned and walked slowly and seductively toward the bar, three-inch heels clicking on the hardwood floor. Clive knew the show was for his benefit, since her prey had his back to her.

"Watch carefully, Rayna," Clive said. "Yvette is mistress of many things, as you well know, not the least of which is making a man feel as if he's the aggressor, when in fact, she is the lioness on the hunt."

"Can I ask you something?" Rayna said, somewhat sheepishly.

"How can a man allow his wife to be with other men?" he asked.

"Yeah," the younger woman said. "I mean, I know she's working. But it doesn't bother you? Not even a little?"

"Why would it?" Clive replied. "Neither of us has any feelings for the other, aside from physical. Always remember that. A sociopath is incapable of love, though they can play the part quite convincingly. You are a true sociopath, Rayna. Embrace it. Throw off the rules society has tried to force on you since the day you were born."

"So she's going to make him think that she's fallen for him?"

"Before this night is over, your young Mister Wheeler will totally believe that he has found his soul mate in an older woman. And by this time tomorrow, he will be broken and putty in her hands. I give him until Tuesday, before he will either come willingly into the fold, or be dead."

Clive glanced at his watch again. He'd been expecting a call from his Miami associate. As if on cue, his phone's screen came to life on the table in front of him, displaying an incoming call.

Clive snatched up the phone and stabbed the *Accept* button. "I was expecting your call an hour ago."

"Sorry," the voice on the other end said. "There was a problem."

"What kind of problem?" Clive asked, thinking the man was going to try shaking him down for more money.

"Someone beat us to it."

"Someone—" he nearly shouted, then lowered his voice. "What do you mean by that?"

"Another boat intercepted your package," the man said. "You didn't double-book the contract, did you?"

"Double— Now wait just a moment. Tell me exactly what happened."

"Just what I said. Another boat got to your package first. And there was a helicopter helping them. Both civilian, as far as I could tell. When we got to the boat, they'd already bugged out, the boat going south, and the chopper headed east."

"And the people on the boat?"

"There was only one man aboard, but he wasn't in any condition to say what happened, if you get my drift."

"What did he look like?"

"Young guy," the man said. "Dark hair, tall, tan and fit, like he worked out at a gym all the time, all the good it did him."

"Brent..." Clive muttered. "What about the girl?"

"Nobody else on board. And nothing worth hanging onto anywhere on the boat."

"Bloody hell," Clive cursed. "What did you do with the boat?"

"Strapped the guy in and ventilated the bottom. It's under two hundred feet of water now. And I'm out time and fuel with nothing to show for it."

How could this have happened? Clive thought.

"I'll take care of you, Joe," Clive said. "I always do, don't I?"

The man mumbled something, but Clive ended the call.

"What happened?" Rayna asked, watching Yvette casually flirting with the two men at the bar.

Clive stared at a spot on the far wall, trying to understand what he'd been told. "Brent's dead," he finally said, "but not by my direction."

"And the little whore?"

Clive looked at her sternly and saw her cringe under his gaze. "Be careful of your words, Rayna. You are all my little whores. And I'll do with any of you as I please."

The younger woman looked down, picking at her nails. It was a nervous habit Clive had noticed before, whenever she tried to organize her thoughts before speaking.

"Say what's on your mind," he ordered.

"Leilani was your favorite," Rayne blurted out, then looked down at her nails again. "We all knew it. She bragged about being with you."

"And you'd like to take her place?" Clive asked.

When she looked up at him, Clive could see it in her eyes. She'd been by far the hardest one to break and still had a stubborn side. Breaking the recruits was Yvette's job, and she did it well. Clive knew that they all feared him and what he was capable of, but feared her even more. Still, over the years, each of the new female recruits had come to him of their own accord. Now Rayna, with her curvy, wasp-waisted, hard body, was practically begging to get into his bed.

"You'll have to say it," Clive said. "But make no mistake, once you cross this line, you will cater willingly to my every whim. And I do like to play rough."

She stared straight into his eyes. "I want it rough. I want you to make me pay for all the things I've done."

A lewd grin came to his features, as a waiter approached the table.

"We'll be closing this bar soon, Mister Pence," the young Hispanic man said. "There is another on the port side, directly opposite, that opened just a few minutes ago."

Clive's eyes went quickly to the waiter's name tag. "Thank you, Eduardo. Please close us out and add twenty percent for yourself."

"Thank you, sir," he replied and turned back to the bar.

"They will be leaving soon," Clive said, nodding toward Yvette with the two men. "Watch how she separates the two. Our young man will be beaming with pride, and the other will be dismissed in such a manner that he will never want to see my dear Yvette again."

The second man had changed seats, so that Yvette was between the two men. Under the bar, her hands worked skillfully in both men's laps. Rayna slid closer and put her own hand on Clive, kneading him through his pants.

"It looks to me like she might take them both," Rayna whispered in his ear, as Yvette leaned toward the other man. "What's she telling him?"

Clive stretched his legs, enjoying Rayna's ministrations. "Quite simply that he's not man enough to satisfy her," he replied.

The second man rose suddenly. Even from across the room, Clive could see the color rise in his face. Yvette turned and smiled at Wheeler, then leaned close and whispered something to him as well. Wheeler smiled back, oblivious to the fact that the other man had left.

"Pretty obvious what she said to Bruce," Rayna said.

Yvette rose and took Wheeler by his hand, leading him toward the table where Clive and Rayna sat. Clive glanced over at Rayna as she continued to rub him through his pants. Her eyes were locked on Yvette's.

"Young Mister Wheeler has no idea what he's in for," Clive said as the couple approached.

Yvette was pulling him, almost like an errant child, save for the lascivious expression on the younger man's face. She had such a succulent stride, there was no way the young man could resist. As they passed, Yvette smiled and winked at Rayna, then pursed her lips at Clive.

"Is she taking him back to your suite?" Rayna asked.

"We have two," Clive said, standing and taking her hand. "Just in case something like this happens."

Rayna rose and took his arm as they followed Yvette and Bruce out the door into the night air. "So we're going to the other one?"

"They are adjoining suites."

CHAPTER
SEVENTEEN:

With the anchor set firmly and two hundred feet of chain rode out, Jesse shut down the engines. "Once you secure that, get up here," he yelled to Tony on the bow. "We need to talk."

Charity watched Tony in the moonlight as he made his way back to the cockpit and ladder.

"There really isn't anything more to talk about," Tony said, climbing the ladder to the bridge. He spoke just loud enough to be heard on the intercom, though it seemed as if he was keeping his voice low.

"Sure there is," Jesse said. "For instance, you said that she called herself Leilani. Hardly a Cuban name. And the woman Cook was seen with was a tall Cuban."

"She said she was from the island of Tahiti," Tony said, feigning ignorance. "Maybe that's off the coast of Cuba somewhere. I don't know, and I really don't give a crap. The boss gave me a job to do, and I'm only half finished."

"Look, Malcolm," Jesse said. "There's a chance that what she says might be true. Tahiti is in the South Pacific, not the Caribbean. And she looks more Polynesian islander than Cuban. And damned near a foot shorter in height. Maybe you did kill the wrong guy."

Tony stood and stomped around the bridge deck, really getting into his part, but mostly to make noise. "If that's the case, it's all the more reason we should just get rid of her right here and now, so we can get back on the hunt for Cook."

Charity listened, partially detached. She'd managed to suppress her emotions throughout the ordeal of the day before, except for crying on Jesse's shoulder. Numb to the pain, with adrenaline waning, now all she felt was tired.

"You need to just cool your jets, man," Jesse said.

"Why? If that wasn't Cook I shot, he was someone who stole the money that Cook stole from Mister Livingston. She was with him, which makes her a thief, too."

"And that means she might be useful," Jesse said. "Maybe she knows where the real Cook is hiding out. Maybe she can be useful in other ways. Kill her and we might never know."

"She's not gonna roll over," Tony said, "so her only use to me is for target practice."

"I'll go down and see if I can get something more out of her."

Before he climbed down, Tony stood and leaned in close. "She's afraid of dogs."

Jesse nodded and went down the ladder. Tony motioned Charity forward and they sat on the small bench in front of the helm, away from the intercom.

"How do you think he'll get her to talk?" Tony whispered.

Charity thought back to the time she'd spent on his boat. "By not asking her anything," she whispered. "He's good at this."

A moment later, there was a clicking sound over the intercom. "What was that?" Tony whispered.

"No idea," Charity replied.

They heard the sound of the stateroom hatch opening and Jesse speaking. "You want some water or something?"

Tony and Charity both turned in their seats and leaned toward the speaker on the console.

"I'm hungry," the woman replied.

There was a rustling sound over the speaker, then Jesse said, "We're anchored miles from land. I'm gonna free you now. But don't try to swim for it, cuz Malcolm will just shoot you in the water."

A minute passed, then Charity heard galley sounds, as Jesse opened the refrigerator and a couple of cabinets or drawers.

"He patched the galley comm in," Charity whispered.

"Thanks," the woman said, followed by a barely audible grunt.

There were more galley sounds, which Charity recognized. He was setting the coffee maker up to brew another pot. In the two weeks she and Jesse had spent on his boat, his coffee ritual was employed constantly; she often thought that he measured time by the mug. It was his easygoing manner while brewing and drinking what he called *lifer juice* that had finally gotten Charity to reveal her emotions and secrets. The machine seemed to take a long time, and the man had just stood watching it, waiting patiently. In her mind's eye, she could see him doing that now, leaning against the counter, waiting for the brew to finish but really waiting for the island woman to speak.

There was silence for several minutes, then Charity heard a cabinet open and close and the sound of two porcelain mugs being placed on the counter. The woman's voice came over the speaker. "The man your friend killed wasn't Rene Cook."

"Coffee?" Jesse asked.

Charity couldn't help but smile. He'd used the same tactic on her nearly three years ago. The near silence drew on. Over the speaker came other sounds, as Jesse moved around the salon and galley, straightening things that probably didn't need it.

"I'm serious, mister," the woman said. "And to be honest, he wasn't really my boyfriend."

"Oh?"

"We were sleeping together, but he was just a guy I met."

The rattle of the coffee pot came over the speaker. Charity had heard that sound so many times that it was easily recognized and somehow comforting.

"More coffee?" Jesse asked.

"His name was Brent," she said. "I don't even know what his last name was. We...worked together."

"You can see how it might be viewed differently," Jesse said, his voice measured and reassuring. "Is Leilani your real name?"

The woman hesitated a moment. "Well, yeah," she said. "It was a completely understandable mistake. And yes, Leilani is my name."

There was silence for a moment, then Jesse said, "French Polynesia? The Society Islands?"

Charity could picture the scene just below them. His innocent questions about her would get Leilani talking, and he'd get answers without asking questions.

"I was born there, on Tahiti, but don't remember much about it."

"Too bad," Jesse said. "It's a beautiful place."

A few more seconds of silence followed, then the sound of running water. Suddenly, the woman couldn't shut up. With just a little bit of prodding or steering from Jesse, she wove a story about how her and the man she'd been with had gotten aboard Victor's boat and stolen his cash box. She made it clear that they'd actually stolen it from the group she worked with, her rationale being that if she and the man she called Brent didn't take it back to the group, they would have sent someone else for it. The way she described it, she almost made it seem like it was okay.

"So you don't have to worry about Cook, mister," she said. "Brent and the others killed him. I was late and wasn't even there when it happened, but I did crawl through the little places of his boat, after Brent stole his keys and wallet."

"The others?" Jesse asked.

She hesitated for a moment, as if unsure. Charity knew from experience that the retired Marine was probably going about some other chore, as if he weren't very interested and just making small talk. Over the intercom, they'd fed the woman enough misinformation for her to be certain that Jesse was her only hope.

"Brent, Doug, and Jeff," she finally admitted. "I don't know their last names. They were the ones who killed Cook. Rayna and Fiona lured him out to them. I was supposed to help but was late getting there."

"So Brent was the leader?" Jesse asked.

It took a while, but Jesse managed to get names and descriptions of everyone involved, as well as the locations of several other attacks on tourists the group had perpetrated.

Finally, Jesse said, "Okay, I need to go up and talk to Malcolm. You've been real helpful, Leilani. I'm not going to tie you up again, but I would like you to sit over there on the corner of the couch.

"Why?" Leilani asked.

"Because I still don't completely trust you, and this boat cost me a whole lot of money. I just don't want you moving around. As long as you sit on the couch, my dog won't bother you."

A moment later, Charity heard him tell Finn to lie down and stay. Charity knew the woman was in no danger from Jesse's dog; he was obedient and would stay right where his master ordered him, even if the girl got up. But he was also a naturally curious animal and his attention would be on her constantly. To a person with a fear of dogs, having one that weighed more than you stare very intently at your every movement could be unnerving.

The hatch below opened and closed. Then Jesse climbed up to the bridge. He first turned off the intercom, then sat down at the helm.

"Some crazy shit," Tony said, quietly. "She just confessed to being in on half a dozen murders."

"We need to get all of them," Jesse said, his brow furrowed.

"You have a plan?" Charity asked.

"I'm working on it. For now, we all need some rest. Tomorrow—er, today might be a long one."

"You're not going to tie her up?"

"No," Jesse replied. "I think she trusts me a little now. We can use that to our advantage. I'll put her in my cabin with Finn. He'll stay on the deck and she'll stay put on the bed. You were right, Tony; she's scared to death of dogs."

"I'll take the first watch," Tony said.

"Okay, wake me in three hours. Charity, you take the guest cabin; you're not in the rotation since we may need you in the air. I'll get some shut-eye on the couch."

Charity started to object, but Jesse shut her down, with a hand on her forearm. "You've been through a lot, and we need you at your best. Tony and I can function on three hours' sleep for a few days."

She was tired, and she knew it. The practical side of her brain told her that he was right. This whole ordeal had drained her. And flying in this condition was unsafe. The emotional side, the part that she strove constantly to keep buried, had a great fear of being alone. Twice since Afghanistan, she'd opened up and allowed a man to get close. Both times they'd died.

Before going below, Jesse turned to Tony. "Send Chyrel an email. Ask her to cross-reference the names she gave us against the passenger manifests of ships that were in port in the places and times Leilani said the murders took place. From that, she should be able to get better intel on

who the players are. They seem to be living aboard cruise ships, and we need to know how long they'll be on *Delta Star* and which ship they'll be on next."

Tony nodded, and Jesse led the way down the ladder. Once inside, Charity went forward, while Jesse explained to their *guest* what her sleeping arrangement was going to be. She didn't like it but went forward with him anyway.

Charity entered the small cabin and closed the door. With the lights off, only a narrow shaft of moonlight on the outboard bunk lit the cabin. She kicked off her shoes and unbuttoned her work shirt. Removing it, she folded it on the bunk, then stepped out of her shorts and did the same, folding them neatly on the inboard bunk. She fell onto the outboard bunk, wearing just a tank top and panties. Through the boat's bulkheads she could hear Jesse explaining to Leilani that Finn wouldn't bother her if she stayed on the bed. A moment later, she heard the stateroom hatch close and Jesse's bare feet on the companionway steps outside her cabin.

Lying on her back, Charity stared blankly at the ceiling. There were a few sounds from the stern, then everything was quiet, but for the lapping of water against the hull. She'd been alone many times. In fact, for the better part of the last two years, she'd been in self-exile, living off the grid and out of touch with everyone.

That had all changed several months ago in the Virgin Islands, when she'd run into Victor again. Since then, they'd been together most every night, and she'd come to rely on his physical presence. Not that she needed a man to protect her — she and Victor both knew that wasn't necessary. It was the physical contact that had become so important. Being completely cut off in the cabin made her feel lonelier than she'd ever felt before. Emotional pain, isolation, and vulnerability were all things she'd not felt in many years. The feelings that were foreign to her. The one constant had been the warmth of Victor lying next to her at the end of the day.

Just a few feet away was a woman who had taken part in Victor's murder, or at least she was working in conjunction with the three men who had beaten him to death. It hadn't been easy, listening to the woman recount the details to Jesse. One of the three men was already dead. From what the doctor had told her, the ball in the sock was most likely the injury that had eventually killed him. The fact that the man who'd swung it was already dead seemed to take all the wind from Charity's sails.

After an hour of staring at the ceiling in the dim moonlight through the porthole, sleep still eluded her. Quietly, she rose from the bunk and reached for her shorts, then decided against it and sat back down. Tears flowed freely as she quietly sobbed.

Finally, she stood and went to the hatch, opening it quietly. In bare feet, she went up the steps to the salon. It was much lighter, with all the large windows letting the moonlight in. Jesse had pulled the convertible couch out into a bed and was sleeping under a lightweight camouflage blanket, which she recognized as a military poncho liner. He was against the outboard side.

Quietly, she lifted the cover and slid down alongside him, with her back to his chest. He didn't stir. In fact, for several seconds he didn't even breathe. Then he gently rested a hand on her waist.

Charity knew the contact was meant as a comforting gesture, much like the night she'd gone to his bed after killing Jason Smith. Finally, her tears subsided, and she drifted off to sleep.

Some time later, she had no way of knowing how long, Charity awoke alone on the tiny bed. She listened for a moment, then rose to a sitting position. Her shorts and over-shirt were neatly folded on the chair at the foot of the couch and her shoes were on the deck below them. She took her watch from the pocket and saw that it was nearly morning.

Dressing quietly, Charity went to the galley and opened the cabinet below the sink, where she knew Jesse kept a collection of insulated bottles. She filled one from a fresh pot of coffee that either Jesse or Tony had set up while she was asleep.

Probably Jesse, she thought.

She hoped that he'd risen on his own before Tony came down to wake him and found them together. That seemed likely, as he'd moved her clothes from the guest cabin, to make it look to Tony as if she'd slept on the sofa bed and Jesse had taken the guest cabin.

Carrying the thermos and a clean mug, she stepped out into the cool pre-dawn air and climbed the ladder to the bridge. Jesse was sitting at the helm, reading something on his phone.

"Good morning," he said, laying the phone on the console and looking up at her.

"I brought a peace offering," she said, holding up the thermos. "I'm sorry about last night."

He took the thermos and mug, filling it and another one he had in a drink holder. "Thanks, but you have nothing to apologize for."

Charity accepted the offered cup and sat down on the port bench seat. "Well, I don't usually crawl into bed with a man like that."

His lopsided grin looked endearing in the moonlight. "Okay, I'll bite. How do you usually crawl into bed with men?"

That made her laugh. "You know what I mean."

He turned the chair to face her, stretching out his long legs. "Before my divorce, my oldest used to have these nightmares. Sometimes two or three times a week. She said the only place she ever felt safe was lying beside me. I don't think it was a safety thing, but more just a need for physical closeness. Humans are a social animal."

"Yeah, but I'm a long way from being a little girl."

He took a sip from his mug. "You have a valid point there."

Charity looked down at her own mug. "You could have had me."

"No, I couldn't have. Your heart's with Victor. What you needed was physical presence."

She looked up at his face and saw the eyes of her father. "How old are you, Jesse?"

Looking out over the bow, he seemed to have to think about it for a moment. "I'll be forty-seven in a few months."

"I'll be thirty, next weekend," she said. "Seventeen years is hardly a May-September thing. May-July, maybe."

"I've never taken advantage of a person's vulnerability," he said softly. Then his eyes danced, and he grinned. "No matter how high the temptation."

She smiled back at him. "Thanks."

His expression changed; his eyes took on his usual seriousness. "Chyrel was still up, when Tony emailed her."

Sitting forward on the bench, Charity's mind switched gears instantly. She knew that Chyrel Koshinski's abilities were second to none once she started snooping around on the internet. Victor had told her that Chyrel's skills at the Agency were legendary. She remembered him telling her of a time that the woman had hacked into the FBI's main frame. Probably the second most difficult computer hack on the planet, he'd told her, second only to backing out without leaving a trace. All traffic on their super-secure computer system was embedded with a tracker that was supposed to be foolproof. Yet, she'd penetrated all their firewalls and safeguards, avoided the tracker, retrieved the information the Agency needed, and made it look like it never happened.

"What'd she find out?"

CHAPTER EIGHTEEN:

The foggy veil slowly lifted. Through the loud buzzing in his head, Bruce Wheeler could hear people talking. The voices came and went, and he couldn't quite understand what they were saying. The buzzing seemed to be coming from inside his own head, as if he had stereo headphones on and someone kept changing the dial.

"We need a woman," he heard a man's voice say. He had some sort of accent, like the guys in the old black and white movies.

As he became more aware of his surroundings, Bruce realized he was lying down, his arms and legs spread wide. He tried to move his right hand but couldn't. He hurt everywhere, especially his mouth.

"I think he's waking up," a woman's voice said.

Bruce struggled to open his eyes, trying in vain to say something. His mouth was open very wide, and something hard was pressed firmly against his teeth and tongue. Suddenly aware, his eyes flew open and he thrashed his head from side to side but saw only darkness.

The memory came flooding back. He'd left the bar with the hot, redheaded cougar and went with her to her suite. By the time they got through the door, she'd nearly been carrying him.

She'd helped him to get onto the bed, where he'd seemed to lose control of his muscles completely. He remembered lying there helpless, fully aware of everything going on, but unable to move any part of his body. The woman slowly removed his clothes, wrestling them off him. Then she'd climbed on top of him, straddling his hips. Though he hadn't been able to move a muscle, he'd felt every contact she made, as if she set fire to whatever part of his body she touched.

Raising his arms above his head, she'd snapped leather cuffs onto his wrists, stretching to attach them to the bed frame. The softness of her breasts, crushing against his face as she stretched to manacle each wrist, had felt wonderfully suffocating.

When she'd climbed off, she'd even turned his head for him, so he could watch as she fettered his ankles with the same leather straps. He also remembered thinking that she'd drugged him unnecessarily. He would have willingly allowed her to subdue and dominate him. In fact, he enjoyed it.

She'd gagged him then, even though he couldn't move his mouth to form words, then propped several pillows under his head so he could watch. What happened next was beyond anything he'd ever imagined. His mind had been fully functioning, and he could feel every sensation of her touch. He just couldn't do anything about it.

Looking down he remembered seeing electrical wires leading to a box of some kind. The box had switches and lights on the face and one large knob. But it was the contraptions on top of the box that filled him with horror. One wire led from the box to a cylindrical metal cage that would fit only one part of a man's body. Next to it was a small device, like a miniature microphone stand, with a flat base plate. It also had a wire going into the box. But it was the cage that had frightened him most.

Standing beside the bed, the woman had put her hands on her hips and smiled at him, as if admiring her handiwork. Then she took the microphone stand and wedged the flat base under his thighs and butt, positioning the mic over his groin. She'd picked up the small cylindrical cage, and the smile on her face could only be described as evil.

It was at that moment that Bruce realized it wasn't a microphone at all, just a flat piece of metal suspended horizontally just above his groin. He also noticed that it was insulated from the metal stand, and the wire from the box was connected to the flat piece of metal with a wingnut, not an audio jack.

The cage and the metal plate made up a simple electrical switch.

A hand grabbed his chin, stopping his thrashing movement, and bringing him back to the reality of the present. The effects of whatever drug she'd given him had worn off, and Bruce could move.

It was the redhead. "Do I have your attention?" she asked. "Nod your head if I do, Bruce."

He nodded quickly.

"Good," she said. "You've been chosen to join our little group. Your options are none."

She released his jaw, pushing his head away and slapping him hard across his cheek. "First, you'll be tested. I'm going to give you a shot now. Basically, the same drug as before, but without the sensory stimulation added. Do you know what that means?"

Two hands gripped his left arm, one above the elbow and one below. It was the green-eyed blond woman he'd met the night before. His arm was forced hard against the bed he was lying on. He felt a sharp sting on the inside of his elbow, then something cold moving up his arm.

"I asked you a question, Bruce," the redhead said. "Do you understand what I just said?"

Eyes focusing, Bruce saw a third person in the room; an older man. He remembered seeing the blonde with him when he'd left the bar with the redheaded hard-body. The redhead was looking at him expectantly. He shook his head side to side.

"What it means is," the redhead began, moving up alongside his head, "that in a moment you're not going to be able to move again. Like before, you'll still be aware and can see, hear, and feel, but this time there's no X, so you won't be as easily aroused."

She again propped pillows under his head, and to his revulsion, he saw that he was still inside the cage, connected to the electrical torture contraption.

"Rayna," the man said to the blonde, "it's nearly dawn. Go wake the others. They're to keep a wary eye out for a possible female recruit. We never know when our next enemy will show up and we need six. Also tell them to watch for anyone suspicious. Remember, someone got to Leilani and Brent before me. Then you come back here. It's time you take part in the training."

As the blonde left, the man walked around the bed and joined the redhead. Bruce tried to turn his head to follow him, but he couldn't. The drug was already in his system.

"What was that about Leilani and Brent?" the redhead asked, absently checking the bindings on his wrists. Bruce remembered her telling him her name at the bar, but it escaped him now.

"Someone else got to their boat before Joe. Whatever they took from the last mark is gone. Brent's dead, and the boat captain and Leilani have disappeared. My guess is she double-crossed Brent and had an accomplice on the outside."

"Did you enjoy yourself with Rayna?" the woman asked, stroking Bruce's inner thigh.

Her touch didn't feel quite as provocative as before, though Bruce couldn't help but get excited a little. He squeezed his eyes closed, trying desperately to ignore the feeling.

"No comparison to your antics, my dear Yvette," the older man said. "Not even as good as Leilani, but she will learn. Can I help with anything here?"

"No, you run along and get rested. You'll need your energy when I come to you in a few hours. I've thought up a new *antic* that you might enjoy. Young Mister Wheeler will be going to sleep again soon. But I want to wait until Rayna returns, so she can help with the milking."

Bruce clenched his eyes tighter, as he heard the door open and close.

"Closing your eyes will do no good," Yvette said. He was certain that wasn't the name she'd given him last night. She walked to the foot of the bed, letting her fingernails trace lines down his thigh. "True, visual stimulation is important in what we do. That's why you were chosen. You're quite attractive, you know."

A knock on the door startled Bruce. He opened his eyes, hoping it was someone that would help him. Yvette looked through the peep hole, then opened the door. The green-eyed blonde came in.

"You're just in time," Yvette said. "He thinks if he doesn't watch, he won't get excited."

"What would you like me to do?" Rayna asked.

"Just follow my lead."

Bruce clenched his eyes tightly, concentrating on the image of the ugliest woman he'd ever seen. The room fell silent for a long minute. Nobody touched him, and he started to think that the ordeal might be over. He slowly opened one eye. The women were on either side of the bed, facing one another. They were both slowly unbuttoning their blouses while staring down at his manhood.

"Oh, he's peeking," Yvette said.

They both began to seductively caress his thighs and belly, getting closer and closer to the cage.

Bruce closed his eyes, apparently the only motor function at his disposal.

Suddenly, he heard the spark of the closing circuit, even smelled the ozone it created, then pain shot through him. It wasn't as powerful as before, though. The electrical charge was lower and actually stimulated him even more.

He chanced another look. Just as he opened his eyes, Yvette turned to the box and twisted the knob next to the glowing switch. In less than a second, the pain increased ten-fold, and Bruce blacked out again.

CHAPTER NINETEEN:

The *Revenge* slowed as Jesse brought her around the tip of the island in the darkness. On the radar screen, the cruise ship was hard to miss, three miles out and closing. They'd left the previous anchorage before the sun was up and made the short fifteen-mile run to Half Moon Cay in less than half an hour.

Arriving under cover of darkness, they could see the lights of the big cruise ship as it approached. Jesse had hugged the shoreline of the western tip of the island, idling slowly as he followed the ten-foot line on the chart plotter, keeping a cautious eye on the forward scanning sonar. The idea was to use the island itself to create enough backscatter on the ship's radar that an inattentive operator working late at night might miss the *Revenge* slipping in.

The effort, they soon realized, was for nothing. There were two other yachts at anchor off Half Moon Beach, a small pocket schooner and an Albin trawler. The cruise line owned the resort, and while one of their ships was at anchor, other boats weren't allowed to disembark. They could anchor, during those times, but could only go ashore if there weren't any cruise ships there. The island was strictly off-limits when a ship of the line was anchored.

Like many police stakeouts Charity had been on when she was with Miami-Dade, sitting and watching from a distance was monotonous. The three of them talked about common friends and what was going on in everyone's life, but Jesse didn't bring up his search. He'd seemed to just put his life on pause for now.

"Looks like they're getting ready to start ferrying people ashore," Tony said. "It's getting light, and service people ashore are starting to move around."

Tony had been at the controls of the rooftop camera, watching the activities ashore and on the *Delta Star* for over an hour. The powerful zoom function of the high-resolution system allowed clear images from a distance if the platform it was on was steady enough. There was little wave activity on the lee side of the island, so the boat barely moved.

"They're scheduled to be here until late tonight," Tony said. "With a beach dinner party just after sunset. Next stop is Little Stirrup Cay."

"The last shuttle from shore will be about midnight," Jesse said. "That would be the best time."

"You really think this will work?" Charity asked.

"Cruise ship employees work long hours. And it being a private island, owned by the cruise line, they'll barely be checking."

"You don't have a dinghy."

"Tide's rising and the wind should hold out of the east. At sunset, I can move around to the windward side, drop

anchor, and let out enough rode to put the stern in four feet of water."

"I don't think a bathing suit is going to be acceptable dinner attire," Charity said.

Jesse glanced at her with that half-cocked grin and winked. "It should be." Then his more somber expression took over. "Under the inboard bunk in the guest cabin, there's some clothes that Devon left behind. You're about the same size — a little taller, maybe. I think there's a couple of cocktail dresses in there."

"Cocktail dresses on the *Revenge*?"

"We enjoyed the night life sometimes," he grumbled. "Docked for a whole weekend in South Beach once."

"What happened with her?" Charity asked, genuinely concerned. She'd only met the woman Jesse had been dating a couple of times, under what Devon might have thought suspicious circumstances.

"Just didn't work out," he said. "She took a job in rural Georgia."

His tone said more than his words. It was a touchy subject, as was Savannah.

Changing the topic, Charity asked about the old man on Andros, who had given her a ride to the airport and was apparently part of a hostage rescue with Tony and the others.

"He and Pap served together, during the Second World War," Jesse said. "On Guadalcanal and Peleliu."

"I got the impression that he held your grandfather in very high regard."

"Pap never mentioned it," Jesse said. "Henry told me at his funeral. They were in a fighting hole — Pap, Henry, two other grunts, and a lieutenant. It was the second night after the landing on Peleliu. A Japanese soldier got close and threw a grenade in with them. Henry told me that Pap didn't even hesitate, he just threw himself on the grenade."

"Oh my God," Charity said, her voice heavy. "What happened?"

Jesse grinned mischievously. "It happened a year before my dad was born."

"The grenade didn't go off," Charity surmised.

"Nope," Jesse replied, off-handedly. "Japanese grenades were notoriously faulty."

That one little thing, Charity thought. A single grenade that failed sixty-five years earlier was the reason she was here right now. Had that grenade gone off, there would never have been a Jesse McDermitt for her to turn to.

"Better get her up here," Jesse said, moving toward the ladder.

"You really think she'll rat out her friends? Tony asked.

"Yeah," Jesse replied. "I think she will."

He went down the ladder and was inside only a minute or so. When the hatch opened again, Jesse's dog was first out. He went to the transom door and waited patiently.

"Go up there and sit at the wheel," Jesse told the woman, opening the transom door for the dog to do his business. He waited, a water hose in one hand to wash down the swim platform, as Leilani moved cautiously toward the ladder.

Charity watched Leilani closely, as she climbed up to the bridge. She looked suspiciously at both her and Tony, before sitting down at the helm.

"We'll wait until they start boarding the ferry," Jesse said, climbing up the ladder. "Then try to ID the group as they go ashore. Leilani has promised to help. And I want to see them in real life."

"I never really fit in with them," the tiny island woman said, trying but failing miserably to act contrite. "I'll do anything I can to make things right."

"First ferry is heading out," Tony said.

"Leilani, keep your eyes peeled," Jesse said. "I want you to watch the screen carefully and point out the Pences if they get off."

Jesse moved around behind the helm, and Charity joined him. Together they looked over Tony's and Leilani's shoulders at the screen. Tony zoomed in on the cruise ship, panning the camera along its length. A hatch was open amidships, about four feet above the waterline and a uniformed man stood in the opening behind a yellow rope.

"The ferry's probably gonna block the view," Tony said. "If we can't spot them through the ferry's windows, we'll have to wait until they disembark at the pier."

"The Pences probably won't be on the first excursion," Leilani said. "They hardly ever get up before noon. Jeff and Doug might be, though."

All four of them watched carefully. The camera's powerful lens was able to look through the ferry's window at each person as they stepped aboard. The image was a little fuzzy, but each person was facing the camera as they stepped down into the ferry.

Barely half full, the ferry pulled away, heading toward the dock. They watched again, as the small boat disgorged its passengers there.

"None of them," Leilani said.

While they waited for the ferry to make its next run, Jesse went down to the galley and brought up a package of cinnamon rolls. "Sorry, I hadn't had a chance to reprovision. I have enough fruit and junk food to last a few days, though."

Leilani wasted no time, snatching one up like some sort of starving street urchin.

Tony had told her and Jesse what the woman had said about being kidnapped as a child. Whether it was true or not, Charity didn't know. The woman was exotically beautiful, but lacked any sort of refinement or manners, licking the glaze from her fingers with a smacking sound.

The ferry started out toward the cruise ship again and Charity moved back to her seat on the port bench. She watched the young woman, who sat forward on the helm seat, leaning on the wheel for a better look. It did appear as if she had a genuine desire to help them, but a person like her might consent to anything to save her own life. Considering her possible background, that would make sense.

When the ferry was in position, more passengers began to file aboard from the open hatch. Leilani watched intently, as if to justify her own existence. Suddenly, she pointed at the screen. "That's Jeff!"

Tony picked up his phone and scrolled through some documents.

"And that's Doug right behind him!" Leilani said. "They'll be on the hunt for anything that squats to pee."

"Jeff Maple," Tony said, reading from his phone. "Twenty-five years old, from the Bronx. Five-ten and one-ninety, dark blond hair, blue eyes. Says here that he was orphaned at seven, and lived in foster homes most of his life, then juvenile detention. A couple of arrests as an adult, nothing serious."

"The other guy?" Charity asked.

"Doug Bullard, twenty-three, five-nine, one-sixty-five, brown hair and eyes, from LA." He paused a moment. "Huh," he said, obviously puzzled. "This guy was orphaned too. At age fourteen, and he also spent time in foster homes and juvenile detention. Minor arrests as an adult."

"We're all orphans," Leilani said, as if it were the most obvious thing in the world.

"The whole group?" Tony asked.

Leilani nodded. "The Pences, too." She pointed at the screen again, practically bouncing in her seat. "And there's Fiona!"

Charity moved around behind the helm seats with Jesse. Leilani had said that Fiona and another woman named Rayna had lured Victor out of the bar, after drugging him with ecstasy.

The image on the screen wasn't sharp. The cruise ship was anchored almost half a mile away and the *Revenge* was moving slightly. The camera's automatic image stabilization kept the subject centered but did so by sacrificing definition.

The woman had Mediterranean features, probably Italian, with long wavy brown hair and a light olive complexion. Attractive, but she'd never have been able to entice Victor without the help of the libido-altering drug.

Tony flipped through images on his phone again. "Fiona Russo," he said. "Age twenty-two, five-seven, one-twenty-five, born San Diego. Orphaned when she was four, raised in foster care. Had some trouble with the law as an adolescent. Ran away at fourteen, arrested for prostitution at sixteen, and put in juvenile detention. A year later, she escaped custody and disappeared."

"Why orphans?" Charity asked.

"We don't have families," Leilani said. "It's a rule with the Pences. No ties and no families."

"How long have you been with them?" Charity asked, sensing the reason even if the girl didn't see it.

"From the start," she replied. "I worked for Mister Pence before Missus Pence came along. Rayna, too, but not as long. When Missus Pence came along, she brought in Fiona. Then the Pences started adding the guys."

"So you and Rayna," Charity said. "What kind of work did you do for Mister Pence?"

The diminutive woman glanced over at Charity, then up to Jesse, who nodded.

"Escorts," Leilani said. "Usually rich old guys."

"Prostitutes."

Leilani glared at her. "No. *Escorts*. The men paid for our time, that's all. Sometimes it was just dinner, or maybe a show or something. If there was sex involved, it was only because we liked the guy we were with. Call it whatever you want, but at least I wasn't locked up, beaten, and gang-banged by my captors and their friends."

The last part was said with such venomous hate that Charity found herself believing it to be true. "What happened to the people who kidnapped you?"

"They *died*, okay? Dead and buried nine years ago."

"And that's when you went to work for Pence?"

"About a year later," Leilani said watching the screen again. "I was sixteen when Mister Pence found me and gave me a home."

Sixteen? Charity thought. *A year younger than me when Dad died.*

Looking up at Jesse, Charity saw sadness and revulsion equally present in his eyes.

"How old were you when you were kidnapped?" Tony asked.

"Ten," she replied. "Do we have to talk about this?"

Jesse put a hand on her shoulder. "No, not unless you want to. You're being a big help to us."

Leilani looked around at the three of them. "You guys aren't what you led me to think, are you?" She jerked a thumb at Tony. "This guy knows things about the Gang of Six that I don't even know."

"No, we're not," Charity said, taking the lead. "We used to work together. For the federal government."

"You work for—wait, so why did you kill Brent?"

"He started to draw a gun," Tony said. "He gave us no choice."

"And you don't work for the government now?"

"Not since last summer," Jesse said. "The man Brent killed in Nassau two nights ago was a former CIA operative." He nodded toward Charity. "He was her boyfriend. They were in love. And I'd like to think that he and I parted as friends, the one time I met him."

"CIA?" Leilani breathed out slowly. She glanced at Tony beside her, then at Jesse, and finally Charity. "That's why he had more than one passport? He's a spy? That's who you guys used to work for?"

"A different branch," Charity said. "We were part of the fight against terrorism. Malcolm there is an explosives expert, and Stretch was a sniper." Jesse's eyes cut sharply to hers. She smiled and added, "But now we're just boat bums."

"What was your job?" Leilani asked.

Charity's smile disappeared. "Among other things," she said, her laser-like blue eyes becoming cold and calculating as they fixed on the island woman's, "I was an assassin."

CHAPTER TWENTY

Throughout the morning, two ferries moved leisurely back and forth, taking passengers to the island, and returning others to the ship. Each time one of them loaded, the group on the bridge of *Gaspar's Revenge* watched the monitor. The Pences and Rayna never left the ship. Or at least none that looked like the pictures Chyrel had sent them.

Watching Leilani watch the monitor, Charity thought it possible that she'd changed her mind and was possibly reluctant to ID them. There were two men who looked somewhat like the picture of Clive Pence, if that was his real name.

The only thing Chyrel had found out about him and his wife were a string of passport stamps and cruise tickets. Usually on smaller, less expensive ships. Chyrel had relayed that the passports were definitely fake, but pretty good ones in her opinion.

The two men who resembled the pictures of Clive Pence were with wives and kids, and none of the women leaving the ship looked anything like Yvette Pence's passport photo. Leilani had made no mention of kids, nor did the Pence couple buy tickets for anyone but themselves.

No, Charity decided. *They're still on the ship.*

Just before noon, Tony went down to the cockpit with a small fishing rod and managed to catch a couple of snappers. He broiled them on the outdoor grill in the cockpit and made sandwiches. The sun reached its azimuth and began its descent into the western sky. The group ate on the bridge, and the two men talked about a variety of subjects to pass the tedious hours away. Charity mostly listened, lost in her own thoughts.

When the ferry wasn't actively loading or unloading, they used the camera to scan the beach, keeping an eye on the woman and two men from Leilani's group.

In the afternoon, Tony and Jesse went down to the engine room to do some maintenance work Jesse had admitted neglecting, leaving Charity alone on the bridge with Leilani.

While watching the beach, Charity noticed that the two men from Leilani's group had been staying relatively close together, just meandering around on the sand, stopping in little Tiki huts for a drink, and talking to young women. The Russo woman spent most of her time lounging in the sun, alternately moving a sunbrella around to cool off.

"Do they not like each other?" Charity asked Leilani.

"Who?"

"Jeff and Doug seem to be ignoring Fiona on the beach. They're hitting on every woman they meet, just like you said they would, but neither has said a word to Fiona."

Leilani's eyes lost focus, staring off into space. "What are you going to do with us?"

Charity sat forward on the bench. "That would depend on your level of involvement and cooperation," she said, trying to keep the woman placated. "I'm not a psychologist, but I know people. I don't think anyone is beyond redemption. I'm living proof."

"What do you mean?"

Charity considered not answering the question. Finally, she said, "I'm also an orphan. My birth mother abandoned me and Dad when I was little, and he died when I was seventeen. Stretch is an orphan, too."

"Him?" Leilani asked. "He seems too level-headed."

"His dad was killed in Vietnam and his mother took her own life. He was eight and went to live with his grandparents."

Leilani looked at the monitor again. Charity could see that she was trying to process this information. "The Pences don't let us fraternize. The girls and guys, I mean. We had adjoining rooms, but the boys' rooms were on another deck. They're real strict about that."

"Why?" Charity asked.

Leilani glanced over at Charity, then back at the screen. "It's just some rule. We're not allowed to screw each other. But screwing them is okay." She shrugged her tiny shoulders. "I don't know why."

"Screwing them?"

Leilani went on to tell her how the Pences liked to have more than just each other for sex. Both she and Brent were often allowed into their bed, as well as occasional strangers on the ships.

"Not in groups or anything," Leilani said. "I guess they just like variety. You know, like swingers."

"I've been watching them," Charity said, nodding toward the monitor. "Jeff and Doug have probably talked to every woman on shore, but Fiona is ignoring everyone."

Leilani looked at the monitor for a moment. "The Gang of Six is missing two," she said. "It's happened before. Brent and I will be replaced. They've probably already found a guy and are now looking for a suitable girl."

"Suitable? You mean someone with no family ties?"

"Not just that," Leilani said, her voice dropping to a mournful whisper. "They look for people like me, someone who's had a rough life and has been broken before."

Charity could see that the woman was changing, becoming less of a hot head. In just the few hours since morning, it seemed as if the realization of the things she'd done to survive were becoming heavy for her. It was obvious that she was easily influenced and had a need to feel wanted. At first, she'd been flippant about what Jesse and Tony would do to her. Now Charity sensed that she was really trying to do what was right.

"Why does there have to be six?" Charity asked, already surmising the answer.

Leilani looked out over the side of the boat at the sun sparkling on the water and didn't answer. Then she bowed her head, looking down at her hands.

"Two to hold the victim?" Charity asked, softly. "One to kill him?"

Leilani nodded somberly, her head still bowed.

"Would you like to get away from that life, Leilani?"

The woman scoffed. "I thought I had when we took off—" She seemed to realize she was about to say something wrong and choked back her words.

"When you robbed Rene's boat and tried to escape?"

"He was already dead," she said, swallowing hard. "The group was going to have it, anyway. And the Pences are big spenders. That money would have lasted me and Brent for years. But in their hands, maybe a few weeks."

"What if I said I could help you get out, legit?" Charity asked, staring into the younger woman's almond-shaped eyes until Leilani blinked and looked away.

"Why would you do that?" Leilani said. "Why do you even care? We killed your boyfriend."

Charity studied the side of the girl's face. "You're not a killer," she said. "You might be a lot of things, but that's off the table."

"Oh, yeah?" Leilani shouted back, suddenly vehement. "How do you think the pervs in Boston died, lady?"

Charity could see the tears the woman was fighting back. She was doing a good job of it, but the hurt was visible. She tried one of Jesse's tricks and just calmly looked into the woman's eyes, waiting.

"I killed them," Leilani said. "Me! By myself. And I'd do it again."

"Defending yourself when there's nobody around to help isn't the mark of a killer, Leilani. Trust me, I know this. You weren't late when Fiona and Rayna lured Rene out of that bar. Were you?"

Leilani turned back to the screen. "There ain't nothing you or anyone else can do. Fate is what it is."

"Don't confuse fate and karma," Charity said. "If you exude negative energy, karma will come up and slap the back of your head, knocking you down. Some people think that's their fate, because it happens over and over. But fate walks hand-in-hand with free will."

"You can't change fate."

"No, you can't. But what if this isn't your fate? What if karma is trying to get your attention to change something? And when you do, some new life will be revealed as your true fate?"

Glancing over at Charity, Leilani held her gaze, thinking. "Why would you even want to?" She finally asked. She pointed at the screen. "Jeff and Doug held your boyfriend while Brent beat him. I'm part of that group."

Charity was also having a hard time choking back the tears. "But you tried to change it. You'd been a part of it for a long time and saw your chance at a new, better life. Maybe your methods were suspect, but you wanted out. That's free will stepping in and guiding you toward your true fate. I can see it in you. You're not a lost cause, Leilani."

Suddenly, Charity's mission became clear. The woman sitting in front of her was barely ten or twelve years old mentally. She'd been dealt a terrible hand by a pair of degenerates and bent to their will. She'd escaped that hell for a slightly better version. She needed help, and not the kind of help a prison or asylum would provide.

A better plan began to formulate in Charity's mind. First, they needed to separate and isolate the two men. Then Charity had to get Leilani someplace safe. Someplace close.

"Stay here," Charity said, rising, and moving toward the ladder.

When Charity dropped down into the engine room, Jesse and Tony were sitting on a pair of upturned washdown buckets. Both men were grinning. Tony reached over and punched the intercom button with the thick stump of his index finger.

"You were listening?" Charity asked.

Jesse reached behind the port engine and handed her a third bucket.

"I saw it right off," Tony said. "When I told Jesse, he said he was thinking the same thing. Whatever that girl has done in the past has been because of what's been done to her."

"She needs guidance," Jesse said. "Someone to show her how to survive and thrive in a positive way. How can we help?"

"Your friend on Andros?" Charity said, placing the bucket on the deck, and sitting on it. "Can he keep an eye on her for a while?"

The former Marine sniper slowly nodded his head. "What about getting aboard and infiltrating the group like we talked about?"

Charity smiled. "I was thinking more along the lines of what Chyrel did out at Stiltsville."

"Stilts—" Tony started to say. Then he, too, grinned. "Yeah, I see what you mean. I'm not Chyrel, but I think I can put together enough information. Get me one of their phones and I'll put it on there. Leave a note pinned to one of their shirts."

"I can get you the phone," Charity said. "And the breathing body of the person carrying it. You heard what she said about looking for a female recruit?"

"You want to sneak ashore and get them to notice you?" Tony asked. "That could be danger—" He paused and grinned. "Never mind."

"I can lure them away from the others one by one, then bring them out to the boat."

"What about the woman?" Jesse asked.

"I don't know yet. I get the feeling the Pences use these *kids* as pawns. All of them come from terrible backgrounds — Leilani's perhaps the worst. They're broken emotionally. These people use them up and throw them away. It's a wonder she's survived as long as she has."

"We need to move the timetable up," Jesse said. "If those two guys are actively looking for another victim, we need to get to them before they find one."

"And she said they may already have one," Tony added.

Charity looked from one man to the other. "I want to help her."

"Then we're here to help you do that," Tony said, extending a closed fist.

Charity bumped his fist with her own, and Tony pulled his up and away, waggling his fingers and making an exploding sound.

Jesse stood up as far as the cramped engine room would allow. At his height, he was hunched over with his back against a beam. He put his bucket back in its place. "I'll call Henry."

As he started to move past her, Charity stopped him. "I know none of this will bring Victor back."

"No, it won't," the old war-horse said. "Ya just gotta endure the pain, and live a life he'd have been proud to be a part of."

"Is it right to seek revenge, Jesse?"

Looking up at him, his head and shoulders against the overhead, she again saw her father's wisdom in his eyes, something she guessed just came with age.

"Revenge?" he asked. "No, revenge just leaves an empty hole in your heart. Besides, the man who killed Victor is already dead. And he brought that on himself."

"And the others?"

"There's nothing wrong with seeking justice," Jesse replied. "I think we should all be armed with loud whistles, and when we see someone stepping out of the lines of societal norm, blow it and point them out for everyone to see. Whether it's instant justice, or a long, drawn-out court battle, is up to the wrongdoer. If someone backs you in a corner where you have no choice, what happens is on them not you. We'll just put these people and their activities under the spotlight and let the authorities do the rest."

Charity understood Jesse's hidden message. He wasn't just talking about Leilani. The four men on Hoffman's Cay had backed her and Savannah into a corner.

"Let's move to the far side of the island," Jesse said, slipping past her, and mounting the steps up to the cockpit. Charity and Tony followed.

"Nothing's changed," Leilani said, as Charity climbed to the bridge, Jesse right behind her.

Sitting down at the helm, Jesse started the engines. He flipped a switch on the console and the windlass on the bow, where Tony was standing, began to drag the big boat forward.

"We're leaving?" Leilani asked, suddenly frightened.

"Just moving the boat to a better spot," Jesse said.

While Jesse and Tony prepared to get under way, Charity pulled Leilani over to the port bench and explained to her what their new plan was.

After securing the anchor, Tony joined them on the bridge and Jesse turned away from shore, slowly idling toward deeper water. Tony sat forward studying the sonar screen. "Ten feet under the keel. No obstructions."

Jesse advanced the throttles slowly, bringing the big boat up to cruising speed, then backed off as he made a wide turn around the tip of the island.

"You're gonna have to hike a ways," Jesse said. "This end of the island is mostly cleared. We'll have to go a little farther east, to where the resort people won't see us."

A few minutes later, he slowed the boat, and Tony went back down to release the anchor. Jesse turned the boat away from shore in fifteen feet of water and flipped the switch to release the anchor. He then backed the boat toward shore, paying out more anchor rode. When the sonar showed they were in only six feet of water, he set the windlass brake and backed down hard, setting the anchor deep in the sandy bottom.

"We'll let the wind push us a little closer," he said, releasing the brake. "At best we'll be in four feet of water, fifty feet from shore."

"That's fine," Charity said, "I think all I'll need is a swimsuit. And a plastic zipper bag."

"For the phone?" Jesse asked. Charity nodded. "Bottom drawer in the galley."

Charity went down to the guest cabin, where she'd stored her bag, and changed into her red one-piece. She'd bought it on Saint Thomas after Victor commented how good it would look on her. He'd been right; the suit was

cut high at the hips, with a deep neckline and no back. She stuffed the plastic bag in next to her belly, smoothing it as best she could.

"Wow!" Leilani said, as Charity came out of the cabin to join the others in the cockpit. "You look like a model."

"One of us can slip ashore and help," Tony offered.

"We'd only slow her down and be in the way," Jesse said, opening a gear locker and taking out a pair of powerful binoculars. He scanned the beach slowly, stopping now and then. Finally, he set them on the fighting chair and opened the transom door. "The beach looks deserted, but go in as covert as possible."

"Roger that," Charity said, stepping down onto the swim platform, and pulling her tinted goggles down over her eyes.

She began hyperventilating, taking quick deep breaths to oxygenate her lungs. She pressed the small goggles against her eyes with the heel of her palms.

"Be careful," Tony said.

Charity nodded, then dove off the starboard side of the platform. Underwater, she turned toward shore and started a dolphin kick, arms extended ahead of her. She knew she could cover a lot more distance below the surface than above. Her goal was to get far enough away that anyone who might have seen her dive off the side wouldn't be looking for her halfway to shore when she surfaced. Behind her, a small stream of bubbles rose as she slowly exhaled.

Her air nearly gone, Charity slowed and rose to the surface. Her head breached for only a second, as she gulped another lungful of air. Then she was underwater again, kicking toward shore.

She finally rose to her feet in hip-deep water and moved quickly up onto the beach, removing her goggles. Jogging across the loose sand, she made it to the dune and hung her goggles on a dead tree branch.

When she looked back, Jesse was standing on the swim platform, scanning the beach in the direction of the resort. When he lowered them, she waved, and he waved back. Then she disappeared into the tropical foliage at the top of the dune.

CHAPTER
TWENTY-ONE

Spotting Doug making his way back toward the little Tiki bar, Jeff angled toward him, and jogged to catch up.

"This is fucking boring, man," Jeff said, as he came up beside the smaller man.

"Why don't they ever book us on bigger ships?" Doug asked. "These little ones are always full of old farts trying to save a buck. I'm pretty sure I've met everyone on board by now."

"Rayna said that the guy they found last night looks like he might be a good fit," Jeff said, as the two men sat down on wooden stools at the open-air bar.

"I want a real drink," Doug complained. "We got lucky finding the one. We don't need a third girl."

"Speak for yourself," Jeff said, puffing his chest out in a macho display. "I can handle three easy enough."

"Yeah, right," Doug said as the bartender approached them. "We can't screw 'em, and if two can't get a guy to leave the bar, then a third ain't gonna be much help. Our real need is three guys. A third girl is just another ticket to buy and mouth to feed."

"Another mango smoothie, gentlemen?" the bartender asked, his teeth smiling brightly in his dark black face.

"Add some vodka to mine," Doug said.

The bartender frowned. "That's not really going to taste very good at all, sir."

"What would you suggest then?"

"The only spirit to drink with tropical fruit is a tropical spirit," the bartender said, smiling broadly. "Rum."

"Surprise us," Jeff said. After the bartender walked away, he pointed with his chin toward Fiona, reclined on a lounge chair, absorbing the sun. "Why ain't she helping look?"

"Guess she figures hitting on girls is man work. She don't like to get her hands dirty."

"I'd hit it," Jeff said, as the bartender placed two orange-colored drinks in front of them.

"Dude, you'd hit a knothole in a fence post."

"Tell me you wouldn't."

"No, I wouldn't," Doug replied. "And if you're smart, you won't try. She's tight with Red. Besides, she used to work the streets, man. No telling what you'd get from her."

Out of the corner of his eye, Jeff saw color and movement through the palm trees. He took a long sip of whatever the bartender had made for them and looked across the island. A long-legged blonde in a red swimsuit was slowly strolling along the far shore, at the edge of the resort property.

"There's only a couple dozen people on the whole ship who are the right age," Jeff said, licking the remnants of his drink from his lips, as he continued to watch the blonde.

Jeff was certain that he'd seen everyone on board at one point or another. The woman had either stayed holed up in her cabin in Nassau or lived here on the island. Even from more than a football field away, he could tell she was hot.

"There's probably still a few people that haven't come ashore," Doug said. He nodded out toward where the *Delta Star* lay at anchor, one of the ferries just pulling away from the side. "Another ferry coming this way. I think I'll head over to the dock and see if anyone looks like a prospect."

Jeff grinned, tearing his eyes away from the blonde over Doug's shoulder. "You do that," he said. "I'm gonna take a walk down the beach, see if we missed anyone."

"Remember, we need to get back to the ship by sunset," Doug said, standing, and dropping a ten on the bar. "Red wants us cleaned up for dinner."

"You shouldn't call her that," Jeff warned.

"What? You gonna tell? That's low, man."

"Nah," Jeff said, then lowered his voice. "But Fiona has other things in common with rabbits. She can hear a mile away."

After Doug left, Jeff tilted his drink and drained it. When he looked across the island again, the woman was gone. He stood and scanned the far shore through the trees. Finally, he saw her, walking away from him, close to the water's edge.

"Hey," he said to the bartender. When the man approached, Jeff nodded at the ten Doug had left. "That cover the drinks?"

"Six dollars each," the man said. "American or Bahamian."

Jeff reached into his pocket and took a five from a small roll of bills, laying it on top of the ten. "What do you call that, anyway?"

"Make Me Disappear," the bartender replied with a smile. "White rum, orange cognac, demerara, and orgeat. I make my own orgeat."

"No mango?"

"You said surprise you," the bartender replied, gathering up the bills and quickly replacing them with three ones. "Like it?"

"Yeah, thanks," Jeff said. "Keep the change." He then hurried away from the bar toward the other side of the island.

Jeff had no idea what the last two ingredients the guy had mentioned were, but he liked the drink and would order it again, and maybe find out what those ingredients were.

Once he was away from the beach, the loose dry sand of the island's interior made it difficult to hurry. Unbeknownst to Jeff, the three ounces of liquor he'd just consumed was masked by the very ingredients he was unaware of, and that was making his feet move a little slower as well. But the blonde was just a few hundred yards down the shoreline and walking slow.

Angling through the tropical greenery, he half-trotted to catch up with her. But she suddenly turned and started walking the other way. Adjusting his course, Jeff walked out onto the beach less than a hundred yards ahead of her.

He straightened his shirt, brushing it off as he strode toward the woman. His shadow stretched more than twice

his height toward the leggy blonde, with the late afternoon sun over his shoulder. The closer he got, the better she looked. Tall and athletically built, she moved with a slow, methodical grace, like a lioness on the hunt. The sun cast a golden glow on her dark bronze skin. She had her head down, as if looking for something.

The woman started when Jeff's shadow passed in front of her. When she looked up, Jeff saw the bluest of eyes looking back at him.

"Did you lose something?" he asked.

She gazed at him for the briefest of moments, then smiled. "No," she said. "I am looking for a shell. Usually, the northeastern shores of these islands are more dynamic."

Jeff looked down at his feet. The whole beach was littered with shells of all sizes and shapes. "Not sure what that means," Jeff said, smiling. "But there's lots of shells here. My name's Jeff."

"Pleased to meet you, Jeff" she said, extending her hand. "I am Gabriella."

Taking her hand in his, her grip was firm and confident. "Pleased to meet you, too."

"Sorry for the lab speak," she said. "A lot of shells is just what I meant. The northeast side of most of these islands get heavier surf, so more shells wash up."

"But you don't have a bag or anything to carry them in. Be glad to offer my pockets."

She smiled again, then reached a hand under the side of her swimsuit and pulled out a plastic bag. "I would be lucky if I find one murex shell; that's what I am looking for. They are very rare."

"What's it look like?"

"They are white," she replied, walking again. Jeff fell in beside her. "Some have streaks of light brown and pink on the bottom. They have long spurs that grow out all around the bottom and across the newer portion of the whorl."

"Like a conch shell?"

"Similar, but the spines are much longer and thinner compared to the size of the shell. They are very small, only an inch or two in length."

"Are you on the cruise ship?" Jeff asked. "Because I'm sure I'd remember having seen you before."

"No," she said, pointing up the beach. "I arrived on a private yacht. I had the captain come around to this side, so I could come ashore. The cruise line doesn't allow anyone but passengers ashore when the cruise ships are here. You won't tell, will you?"

Farther down the beach and just a hundred yards off-shore was a big, dark blue power boat. "Nah, your secret's safe with me. You own that?"

"It used to belong to my adoptive father," she said. "He passed away last year."

"You were adopted?" Jeff asked, incredulous. "I was too. It's a small world."

Jeff couldn't believe how easy that information was gained. It's not something a person usually asks when meeting someone new. Being new to the Gang of Six, he wasn't real sure on all the rules still, but first and foremost everyone had to be an orphan. The fact that this woman seemed to have money should be a plus.

"My biological parents died when I was a baby," she said. "I have no memory of them at all. Neither had any relatives, so I was put up for adoption. My adoptive parents were unable to have children and raised me as their own."

"You were lucky," Jeff said. "I was seven when my folks died. Nobody wants to adopt a boy that age. Where are you from?"

"Florida," she replied, "but my parents were Cuban, so I picked up some of their accent. You?"

"The mean streets of New York," Jeff replied. "I couldn't wait to get outta the Bronx. This is a lot more my speed."

She stopped and stooped down, picking up a small sea shell. Jeff took advantage of the opportunity to get another look at her ass.

"Close," she said, standing, and showing him a shell. "This is *murexsul ianlochi*. See the long spines? But see how they're irregular, and look like branches of coral? The one I am looking for is *murexsul zylmanae*. The spines are thinner and more delicate, which is why they're so rare."

Walking again, Jeff scanned the beach, hoping to find the shell she was looking for. He sensed that she was a little older than him, but not much. And real smart.

"You some kind of marine biologist or something?"

"I was once," she said, walking slowly, and looking all around.

They continued to walk toward the boat resting at anchor, gently rolling in the waves. Jeff could see that there were at least two people on the upper deck. "I hope I'm not being too forward," Jeff said, "but the cruise ship puts on a beach party here tonight. And it's not quite what you'd call a single's cruise."

"I don't know if my friends would like that," she said, glancing over her shoulder to look back down the beach.

"Ah, you have a boyfriend. I'm sorry."

"Oh, no," she said, stopping, and turning to look at him. "I *had* a boyfriend, but he's gone now."

Jeff noticed her eyes seem to grow cold and she again looked back down the beach where they'd walked from. On the boat, he could now see that there were three people. One was a small woman with long dark hair. If he didn't know better, he'd have sworn it was—

"Leilani?"

CHAPTER TWENTY-TWO

Standing at the rail on the top deck, Leilani looked toward the beach. The woman she only knew as Gabby was walking with Jeff, just a hundred yards away. He didn't seem like he was being forced, and he hadn't seemed to notice the boat yet. How the woman planned to get him out to it, she had no idea. Leilani couldn't believe the woman would be much of a match for him physically. He was big and heavily muscled.

She looked up at the tall man next to her. None of them had given her their names, but she'd heard them talking to one another, when the black guy had left the intercom on. The other two had called him Stretch.

"What if he doesn't want to swim out here?" she asked.

"He's not going to be invited," Malcolm said, joining them at the rail. "She's just going to knock him out and drag him to the boat."

"No way," Leilani said. "Jeff's pretty tough."

The couple on the beach stopped, and Gabby stepped in front of Jeff, looking all around as she said something to him. Jeff turned and looked directly at the boat. Leilani was certain that he could recognize her and tried to step back. But Stretch was right behind her and blocked any retreat.

Suddenly, Gabby moved. In the blink of an eye, she stepped forward, lowering her left shoulder and driving her right knee into Jeff's mid-section. Even from fifty feet away, Leilani heard the whoosh of air from his lungs.

Gabby stepped beside Jeff and delivered the edge of a closed fist to the back of his head. Jeff dropped to the sand, his hands not even attempting to break his fall, instead hanging useless at his sides.

"Whoa," Leilani breathed out, slowly. "Who are you people?"

"Besides being a chopper pilot," Malcolm said, "she was once a martial arts and combat fighting instructor for both the Army and Miami-Dade Police. That dude wasn't much of a challenge for her."

"You wanna go down and give her a hand?" Stretch said.

Malcolm nodded, then moved quickly down the ladder and opened the little door on the back of the boat. On the beach, Gabby had dragged Jeff to the water and now had an arm over his right shoulder and hooked under his left arm, pulling him through the surf.

"So the government fired you guys or whatever, and now you just go around shooting and beating up people you think broke a law?"

"No," Stretch said. "That's vigilantism. We just want to live our lives, like anyone else."

"So why are you doing this?"

"There are some people in this world," Stretch said, "people like us, who will always try to walk away from a fight. But when cornered these same peace-loving people are more than capable of stopping a fight real quick, using overwhelming force. Your former associates picked the wrong guy."

"Well, why are you helping me then?"

The tall man looked down at her, his face unreadable. "I'm not," he said, bluntly. Then pointed toward Gabby, now swimming, and pulling Jeff's inert body along. "I'm helping a friend. Someone who once helped to save my life. She sees something in you that I don't, and wants to give you a shot. If I were you, I'd take her up on it in about half a heartbeat."

Leilani didn't understand. Stretch had been the one who convinced Malcolm not to shoot her. "I thought you were the one who wanted to give me a chance."

He looked down at her again. "You're a thief; I don't associate with thieves. If it was up to me, I'd turn you over to the cops. But for whatever reason, she's decided that she wants to help you and give you another shot in life. The fact that you're part of the group that killed her boyfriend speaks volumes about that woman's character."

Leilani had no idea who Gabby was, but she could obviously take care of herself. The woman wanting to help her made no sense to Leilani. There wasn't anything in it for her.

"Need any help?" Stretch called out, as Malcolm reached down and pulled Jeff's inert body onto the platform.

"I got it," Malcolm replied, pulling Jeff by his arms through the little door.

With Jeff face down on the floor, Malcolm took something long and white from his pocket and looped it around Jeff's ankles. He inserted one end into the other and drew the band tight with a zipper sound. He then pulled Jeff's hands behind his back and did the same with his wrists.

Gabby was already swimming back toward the beach. Leilani could just see the trail of bubbles moving quickly toward shore.

"She's a pretty good swimmer," Leilani said.

"Former Olymp—" Stretch started to say. "Oh, what the hell, she'll tell you anyway."

"Tell me what?"

"Her name's not Gabby," Stretch said. "It's Charity Styles. She used to be an Olympic swimmer."

"Is Stretch *your* real name?" Leilani asked, watching Charity sprint across the beach again, disappearing into the foliage.

"Course not," he replied. "What kinda parents would name their kid Stretch? I could just as easily have been a midget. No offense."

Leilani smiled up at him. "You *do* like me. You're making jokes. I'm not a dwarf, I'm just real short. Most people where I come from are short."

"It's not a matter of like or dislike, Leilani," the tall man said. "I don't know you. All I know about you is that you stole money from a friend of mine. That puts you way down on the totem pole. Below even a total stranger."

"That's pretty harsh. You must not have many friends."

He looked down at her and one corner of his mouth came up in a half-grin. "No, I don't. But the few friends I do have, I know I can trust with my life."

"Is she one of them?" Leilani asked, as Malcolm climbed back up.

"All week and twice on Sunday," he replied, moving over and extending a hand to the other man.

Malcolm took Stretch's outstretched hand, stepping lightly up onto the fly bridge. "He's sleeping peacefully, but his head's gonna hurt when he wakes up. And he's gonna really freak out when he doesn't know where he is."

Stretch sat down behind the wheel and spun the seat around. He put his feet up on the rail and watched the beach. But his eyes kept straying toward the setting sun.

"What do we do now?" Leilani asked, dropping her tiny frame onto the bench.

"We watch the sun go down," Malcolm said. "And wait for Gabby to bring us the other guy."

"Stretch already told me her real name."

The two men exchanged glances. To her, it seemed as if there were words moving back and forth between their eyes.

"She'd tell you anyway," Malcolm said, shrugging his shoulders, and moving around to sit beside Stretch. "That is, if you take her up on her offer to help you go straight."

"And you guys aren't who you say you are either," Leilani said. "Every time you say one another's name, it sounds like the words are clumsy for you."

"No, we're not," Stretch said, offering nothing more.

Turning on the bench, Leilani looked west, toward the setting sun. Charity wasn't anywhere to be seen and both men seemed content to just sit and watch the sun go down.

"He's going to think I ratted him out," Leilani said after a few moments.

"That guy down there?" Stretch slowly nodded his head. "Probably will. He saw you up here with us."

"I tried to duck, but you stopped me."

"Yeah, I did, didn't I."

Glancing at the man, Leilani studied the side of his face closely. He seemed the epitome of cool and calm. His legs were crossed at the ankles, feet bare, long tanned legs, and powerful arms crossed on his chest, as he gazed off toward the setting sun. Even though he wore sunglasses, they weren't so dark that she couldn't see through them. His eyes were fixed on the horizon. Yet, she sensed that the impression he gave off was completely the opposite of reality. She felt as if she were sitting just a few feet from a deadly snake, coiled and ready to strike.

Why did he block me when I tried to hide? she wondered. He even admitted that it was intentional. Why? The realization hit her before the question was fully formed in her mind. He *wanted* Jeff to look up and see her there. He *wanted* the man to think that she'd ratted the group out. Even if all of them were arrested, Jeff would somehow get word to the others. She knew that Mister Pence had a lot of associates all over the world and would send someone to kill her. Stretch was reinforcing the woman's offer to help her start over, by making it more difficult not to.

"If you take Charity up on her offer," Stretch said, never taking his eyes off the sun as it slowly disappeared over the horizon, "she can make Leilani vanish completely. Like you never even existed. Start over anywhere, with a brand-new, bullet-proof identity." He slowly turned his head and removed his sunglasses. His eyes were dark blue and conveyed a great seriousness. She could see pain there, as well. "Or get you safely home to your mom and dad," he added.

Makuahine? Makuakane? Suddenly, early childhood memories flooded Leilani's mind. Memories that she'd suppressed because of the sadness and longing that came with them. Her father fished. Leilani, being the oldest, had helped unload his boat when he came in at sunset. Her days had been filled with lessons at school, and when she got home, she helped her mother tend the garden behind their house and helped take care of her two little brothers. Her brothers — they'd be grown men now.

For years, she'd buried the idea of ever seeing her family again. Pushing those memories down became a habit, so powerful that even when she and Brent were headed toward Florida the thought of going home had never even entered her mind.

"I can go home?"

"If that's what you want," Stretch said, turning his gaze back toward the sun. "She can help you do it."

Leilani stared at the side of his face, as he slipped the sunglasses back on. His hair was unruly, and the wind tossed it this way and that. He hadn't shaved in some time and both his beard and hair showed signs of turning gray. There were fine lines at the corners of the man's eyes, but they didn't make him look old. Her father had lines like that. They became deep furrows when he laughed, and he was always laughing. The reflection of the sun in his sunglasses winked out, and at the same time, a single tear traced its way down his cheek, disappearing immediately into his thick beard.

Hearing a splash, Leilani looked toward the beach. The badass lady helicopter pilot was standing over a man who was on his hands and knees in the surf. Leilani rose and went to the rail. Stretch merely turned his head, as if there had never been any doubt that this would happen.

Charity bent and grabbed the hair on the back of Doug's head and pulled it back, raising his face. Doug was looking right at Leilani, when Charity struck him on the top of his head with the bottom of her closed right fist. Just like Jeff earlier, Doug collapsed onto the sand, only to have a wave wash over him.

In seconds, Charity dragged Doug beyond the breakers, pulling him the same way she'd pulled Jeff. She had something clutched in her teeth, but Leilani couldn't tell what it was.

Halfway to the boat, Doug began to thrash around, splashing with his hands and feet. Charity moved her arm, from around one shoulder and under the other, to a strangle hold around Doug's chin. He continued to struggle for a few seconds, then stopped. Charity moved her grip back and resumed swimming for the platform.

"She killed him!" Leilani said, both hands going to her mouth. "Choked him to death."

"No," Malcolm said, rising, and moving toward the ladder. "You gotta maintain a choke hold for a couple minutes after a person blacks out before it kills them. He's just taking a snooze."

A phone on the console vibrated and Stretch turned and picked it up, looking down at the screen. Malcolm paused on the ladder expectantly. Stretch looked over at him and said, "A message from Livingston's computer tech."

CHAPTER
TWENTY-THREE

Clive kept looking around, obviously frustrated. Rayna and Fiona had joined him and Yvette at their table, but Doug and Jeff were still nowhere to be seen.

"They'll be along," Yvette said, touching his hand. "This is just a social thing. They're always punctual when it comes to work."

"They were still here when I took the ferry back," Fiona offered.

Clive turned toward her. "What were they doing?"

"Just as you said, looking for a possible recruit. I saw them at the Tiki bar before I left. Then they split up, Doug going to the dock, I guess to meet the ferry, and Jeff went down the beach, talking to a blond woman."

"And you didn't see them after that?" Yvette asked.

"I saw Doug," Fiona said. "I waited until everyone unloaded, before going over to the dock. He was walking away from there, talking to one of the other passengers."

"Another ferry is heading toward the dock," Rayna said. "Maybe they're on that one."

"They better be," Clive said.

Clive detested a person's inability to be punctual. When you were supposed to be somewhere at a certain time, you should be there. Tardiness showed a lack of respect and self-discipline.

A waiter, dressed in a crisp white linen shirt and matching shorts, approached the table and refilled their wine glasses. Others, dressed the same and working in pairs, were beginning to move large trays with big silver domes over them out to a large fire pit. A low wall surrounded the pit, well away from the flames. The trays were being lined up on the circular wall in preparation of serving dinner.

When the ferry tied up at the dock, only six people got off; three couples. Jeff and Doug were either still on the ship and not attending, or never left the island to get ready. Clive was becoming furious.

Fiona leaned toward Yvette, sitting next to Clive. "What's the new guy like?"

"He'll be ready by the time we board the next ship," Yvette replied.

Rayna conspiratorially leaned partway across Clive's lap, toward the other two women. "He's actually been pre-trained by someone. A total slave boy."

"Need I remind you ladies," Clive hissed. "There are ears all around us, all the time."

"Yes, there are, Mister Pence," a tall, shapely blonde said, stepping up to the four empty chairs on the far side of the table.

Clive's eyes went straight to the stranger. Her blue eyes were clear and non-threatening. Clive prided himself

on being able to read people's eyes. She stood with both hands on the back of a chair, as if waiting to be invited to sit. The dark green dress she wore was simple, and fit her well, clinging to the athletic curves of an elegantly long frame, and revealing just enough of her lean, tanned legs.

"Do I know you?" Clive asked, thinking there was no way he'd have forgotten meeting such an exquisite creature.

Slowly, the woman pulled the chair out and slid down onto it. She reached for the card tent in front of her and turned it around. It was the spot Leilani would have sat, had she not run off with Brent.

"For now," the blonde said, her voice quiet enough to not carry to the next table. "You can call me Leilani. And before we go any further, please look at Missus Pence and ask her to describe what she sees."

Clive started to rise, but then thought better of it. He turned to Yvette and she looked at him. Suddenly, she gasped and drew back.

"What is it?" Clive asked.

Yvette looked at the woman on the other side of the table, then back at Clive. "For just a moment, there was a red dot on your forehead."

"That would be a laser sight, Mister Pence," the woman said, leaning forward on her elbows. "It originates from the scope of a high-powered rifle no more than two hundred yards away. The man behind that rifle has killed men from five times that distance, so please don't make any sudden movements. Just because the light is no longer on, doesn't mean his crosshairs aren't fixed on your forehead."

Clive gulped. He had no idea who the woman was. He'd made enemies in the past, but had buried most of them.

Those he hadn't killed would have no way of knowing where or even who he was.

"What do you want?"

"You," she replied without hesitation. "Locked up behind bars for the rest of your life, getting butt-fucked at least once a day."

Clive paused, waiting for the woman to give the real reason for her intrusion, instead of some vulgar fantasy. She had to have been sent by someone he'd double-crossed in the past.

He studied her blank expression a moment. "Who hired you?"

"I'm not for sale," the woman replied.

"Someone had to put you up to this," Rayna said.

The stranger's blue eyes turned toward Rayna. "Miss Haywood, have you killed anyone recently?"

"Of course not!" she replied, a bit too indignantly.

"And you, Miss Russo?"

"How does she know who we are?" Fiona asked, turning toward Clive.

"Answer my question!" the blonde hissed, getting Fiona's full attention.

Fiona shrank back in her chair, as if the woman's eyes were daggers. "No," she replied meekly.

"I believe you," the stranger said, then turned back to Rayna, "but you're a liar."

Clive glanced around without turning his head. *Where were those idiots when they were needed?*

"Jeff and Doug won't be joining us," the woman said, as if reading his thoughts. "They've been detained."

"What do you mean?" Yvette asked, her eyes darting around nervously. "Are you with the police?"

Slowly, the blonde turned her eyes toward Yvette. "What I mean, Missus Montgomery, is that your days are numbered, too."

The shock on Yvette's face was palpable.

"Yes, I know who you are," the blonde said. "As does the LA County Sheriff's office. And the San Francisco Police before that."

Yvette's hands involuntarily moved to her mouth, gasping once more. The woman on the other side of the table smiled, as a waiter placed a plate in front of her. She thanked him, and the man moved around the table, serving the others. When he left, the woman was still smiling at Yvette.

"The two agencies seem to have received a tip," the blonde said. "And now they've linked you to three other dead husbands in Colorado, Nevada, and Oregon. Those agencies are now sharing information about five dead husbands."

"What is it you want from us?" Clive said.

The woman picked up a knife and fork and cut off a small piece of the fish on her plate, popping it into her mouth. Her eyes rolled back for a moment. "Mmm, you should try the grouper, it's really delicious."

"I asked you what you want," Clive said, clearly irritated.

She took another bite, then delicately touched a napkin to the corners of her mouth and swallowed. "I already told you what I want. The only reason I'm here is to extend an invitation if one is warranted." She turned her eyes on Fiona. "If you want to leave; want a chance at redemption and an ordinary life, now's the time to decide. You won't be arrested for anything. Just come over here and sit beside me."

"You stay where you are, Fiona."

"Need I remind you, Mister Pence," the woman said. "A sniper is watching your every move. If I raise my right hand, my associate will *end* your miserable life."

"I don't believe you," Clive said, becoming more certain that this was just a ruse to take one of his people away.

The woman slowly raised her left hand and pointed at the ground off to the side of their table. "I have no problem with ending this here and now," she said, "but it would be very messy and ruin dinner for all these nice people. I'll allow that you may need some proof."

Clive turned and looked where she was pointing. There was a loud crack, that seemed to come from all directions. A coconut laying on the ground simply blew apart as he watched it. People at other tables looked up, wondering what the sound was, but Clive was apparently the only one who saw where the shot landed.

"You don't have a lot of options here," the blonde said, then turned to Fiona. "He can't stop you. If you want out, come over here and join me. This is your last chance."

Slowly, Fiona rose from where she was sitting and went around the table. "I don't want to do this anymore."

"What about me?" Rayna asked.

"You're as dirty as they are," the stranger said. "You killed at least three men in Palm Beach, and you're going to have to answer for those crimes."

"I'll track you both down and kill you," Clive snarled.

"No," the woman said calmly, as she rose slowly to stand next to Fiona. "You may track me down, but only if I let you. Trust me, I know everything about you, and you're completely out of your league. Fiona and I are going to leave now. If you're smart, you'll sit right here and enjoy

the grouper. If any of you stands, you will die. I can't make it any simpler than that."

Taking Fiona by the arm, the woman turned and led her away.

Yvette's face was an unusual pale pink, as if she'd been in the sun for too long. Clive turned toward her. "What was all that about five dead husbands?" he asked, very suspiciously.

CHAPTER
TWENTY-FOUR

"Who are you?" Fiona asked, as the tall blond woman walked her briskly through the interior of the island, which was mostly loose, bare sand and an occasional palm tree.

"Keep moving," Charity said. "Leilani's with me and I'm going to help her out of this mess."

"But who are you?" Fiona asked again, then stumbled. "Damn these shoes."

"Take them off," Charity replied, pausing for a moment. "I can explain it all once we get a little farther down the beach. Now please hurry. I don't want anyone back there to get killed."

Once they reached the hard-packed sand on the far side of the island, they were able to move faster. Charity still wasn't sure what she was doing. Both Fiona and Leilani were part of the group who'd murdered Victor. Jesse had shown her Chyrel's email, and after talking to Leilani, they'd adjusted their plan once more.

"My name's Charity, and no, I'm not with any police."

"Where's Leilani?" Fiona asked.

Charity pointed toward the *Revenge*, about a hundred yards farther down the beach. "She's on the boat with friends of mine. We'll make sure you and she are safe, while my friends and I dispose of the Pences."

Fiona hurried to keep up. "What do you mean by *dispose of*? They both can be very violent."

"Not nearly as violent as I can be," Charity replied. "You'll just have to trust me on that. The Pences will be going away for a long time, possibly forever."

Together, the two women hurried down the beach to the waiting boat. "We'll have to get wet," Charity said, as she angled toward the surf, pulling her dress up over her head. She wore the swimsuit beneath it. "Don't worry, it's not over your head."

"I'm not exactly dressed for a swim," Fiona said.

"No other way out there," Charity replied.

Fiona hesitated only a moment, then unbuttoned her blouse and wiggled her skirt down over her hips. She quickly joined Charity, already moving toward the large yacht. Reaching knee deep water, the boat's engines roared to life.

Holding their clothes above their heads, the two of them reached the back of the boat in minutes. Tony was waiting on the swim platform to help them out of the water. Charity waited as Fiona climbed the ladder. Tony, ever the gentleman, quickly draped a large towel over her shoulders.

"You can get dressed inside," he said to Fiona. "Don't mind the dog. He won't hurt anyone."

Charity climbed up and moved past Fiona. "This way," she said, toweling off by the open salon hatch.

Leilani waited inside, feet up on the couch, watching Finn with a wary eye. Charity held the hatch open and told Finn to leave. The dog immediately did as he was told.

Once he was gone, Leilani jumped off the couch and hugged Fiona tightly. "I'm glad you're coming, too. These people are going to help us start over again."

"But how?" Fiona said, confused. "Mister Pence said he saw you and Brent leaving together on a boat. He sent someone to kill you."

Leilani glanced over at Charity. "These people got to us first. But Brent tried to pull a gun. He's dead."

"It's a long story," Charity said. "For now, let's get you out of those wet things. Follow me."

Charity led Fiona to the forward cabin, the sound of the anchor chain rattling in the forepeak ahead of it. "There's a shower there on the right, if you want it. Once you get dressed, come up to the fly bridge."

"What about the dog?" Leilani asked.

"Finn wouldn't hurt a thing," Charity said. "Well, except clams, that is." Noting the fear in the woman's eyes, she added, "I'll wait for you in the galley."

"Where's that?" Leilani asked.

"The kitchen," Fiona replied.

Charity nodded. "I need to put some coffee on anyway."

When she left, Charity closed the door behind her, leaving the two women to talk. Although she could hear their voices, she couldn't make out what they were saying. Fiona sounded anxious and Leilani seemed to be doing her best to console her.

After setting up the coffee maker, Charity got two insulated thermos bottles out of the cupboard, then went over to the intercom and punched the button for the bridge. "We're all set down here," she said. "Just go easy, these ladies don't have their sea legs yet and I'm pouring coffee."

"Roger that," Jesse's voice replied through the tinny sounding speaker. "We'll be at Henry's place in less than four hours. We'll need to refuel there, then another two hours to Little Stirrup."

"What time will the—"

"Not till oh eight hundred," Tony interrupted. "We can deliver the packages before dawn with hours to spare."

"Since I'm not going to be flying," Charity said, feeling more self-assured and hearing it in her own voice, "I'll take a turn at watch."

"You can have first watch," Jesse said, "along with our guests."

Always nudging without seeming to do so, Charity thought, grinning, and looking up at the ceiling.

"First watch," she replied. "Copy that."

Below her feet, Charity heard the solid clunk of the transmissions dropping into gear. The boat shuddered for a moment as the large propellers bit into the water. She felt the boat begin to move and the engine revs stepped up a notch.

Fiona came out of the cabin first. "Where are you taking us?"

Charity leaned against the counter and folded her arms. "Andros Island, about a hundred and forty miles west of here."

Fiona had put her blouse and skirt back on, but still had nothing on her feet. "And what do you plan to do to us there?"

"Nothing at all," Charity replied, anticipating the question. "The guy who owns this boat has a friend there. You can stay with him until we get back, or you can leave if you want. But if you're still there when we return, I'll arrange to have new identities made for both of you and we'll come up with some way for you to get wherever you want to go."

"Just like that," Fiona said. It was a statement, not a question. "And what do you get out of it?"

"Another night with little sleep," Charity replied, filling the first thermos. "And I'll be out whatever money I give you two so you can start over." That brought a quizzical look from both women. "On the plus side," she continued, "I'll have the satisfaction of knowing I put the five criminals who orchestrated Rene's murder behind bars. And I'll walk away having helped two comparative innocents find a new way. The last part is up to you two."

"How do we know you can do any of this?" Fiona asked.

The boat's engines slowly started to increase in pitch and Charity felt the surge in speed. "You don't know," she said. "We're getting underway and the three of us are taking first watch. The men only got a few hours' sleep last night. Let's finish this conversation up top, so they can get some rest."

Filling the second thermos, Charity handed one to each of the women, grabbed two plastic mugs, and nodded toward the rear for them to follow. Outside, she saw Finn lying in the corner of the cockpit. The big lab mix lifted his head crookedly, raising his ears.

"Stay put, Finn," Charity cautioned.

Tony was standing at the rail, and Charity handed the mugs and thermoses up to him. Leilani moved to the ladder first, practically leaping over the two fish boxes mounted in the deck, and then went up the ladder as fast as she could.

Tony directed the women to the forward seating area, just in front of the helm, cautioning them to keep at least one hand on a grab rail at all times. Leilani was more cautious than Fiona, who seemed to be more at ease on the big charter boat.

Once they were seated, Tony went down the ladder without saying a word, and Charity moved behind Jesse to the second seat.

"I have the course set on the autopilot," Jesse said. "The radar warning is set for ten miles."

"I promise I won't break anything," Charity said, as Jesse rose and stepped out from behind the helm. He tousled her hair, then disappeared down the ladder.

"Fiona," Charity called forward, "you seem to know your way around a boat. Why don't you come back here and help me out. You too, Leilani. The more eyes the better."

The two women moved to the back of the bridge, Leilani sitting at the end of the side bench nearest the helm. Once they were settled, Charity pushed the throttles slowly forward until the boat was going right at thirty-five, then backed down to hold that speed.

The unlikely trio rode in silence for a while, Charity doing what she figured Jesse would do, letting them have time to formulate what they wanted to say.

"Why are you doing this?" Fiona asked. "There's gotta be a payday in it for you somehow."

Charity mulled the question over for a moment, before speaking. "We're not all that dissimilar," she said. "My biological mother abandoned me and my dad when I was little. He died when I was seventeen."

"I bet you were never raped," Fiona mumbled.

Charity looked over at her, meeting her eyes with her own, searching for a soul that had to still be there. She knew enough about both women's backgrounds that she didn't have to ask them that question.

"Yeah," she said, softly. "I have."

Charity went on to tell them her story, beginning when her father and uncle died. She told them about her experience at the hands of Afghan terrorists, which seemed to strike a chord with both women. She explained to them who Jesse and Tony were, though she didn't use their real names, and told them of some of their missions together with Homeland Security. She kept it brief and didn't go into a lot of detail about the missions she was sent on solo. Some things were better not shared.

The two women asked questions and seemed to relax a little, seeming to accept Charity as a kindred spirit if nothing else. Fiona told her about her own life; about growing up in an orphanage and constantly being overlooked due to her age. She didn't remember much about her parents, they'd died when she was four. She'd been molested in foster care, grew up fast in the orphanage, and ran away when she was fourteen. She'd been living off the streets since then, doing whatever she needed to do to survive.

Both women's stories were tragic. They'd each been abused, one by her kidnappers and the other by those in the very system put in place to protect them.

If anyone deserves a second shot, Charity thought, *it's these two.*

They rode in silence for a while, each absorbing the information learned about the others. Thankfully, the sea was calm, just long low rollers that became visible for a brief second when the moon hit them at just the right angle, reflecting off each one's glassy shoulder. They stretched all the way to the horizon.

The wind covered most of the engine sound, and it was surprisingly quiet riding ten feet above the water.

"Any idea where you'd like to go?" Charity finally asked, after they'd talked for over an hour.

"You're serious?" Fiona said. "You can help us go any-where?"

"I can, and I will," Charity replied, feeling more self-as-sured. "The question is, can you change your lives to make the effort worthwhile?"

"I'll do anything to keep from going back to them," Fiona said, studying the instruments in front of her. "What do we have to do?"

"Do you sail?" Charity asked.

CHAPTER TWENTY-FIVE

The boat drove itself, needing no input from Charity, sitting at the wheel. Fiona had experience on boats, but nothing as large as the one she was currently on. The instruments weren't all that different from another boat she'd spent some time on. It had belonged to a man in San Diego and was much slower.

Barry had also promised her a new life, but Fiona eventually learned that the new life he'd promised included her being used as his punching bag. He'd never hit her in the face, and rarely left any bruises, but he'd broken a rib once. He enjoyed rough, unrestrained sex.

She'd been working the streets when Barry had found her. She had a few regular Johns who paid enough for her to make ends meet in a crummy little apartment. Barry had promised her a lot of things if she gave up that life. She'd had fun with him at first. She was only nineteen at the time and he'd been in his thirties, a moderately suc-

cessful attorney. But the man had a dark side that came out when they were out on his boat, far from shore.

The radar was showing a large landmass ahead, still eight miles away from the looks of it. "We're nearing shore," she said to Charity.

"Would you mind going down and waking Stretch?" Charity asked. "He's probably asleep on the pull-out sofa-bed in the salon."

"The big, hairy, white guy?"

"Yeah, tell him we're about ten minutes from the barrier reef."

Fiona rose and went down the ladder. The dog was no longer in the back of the boat. She figured the man had taken it inside. She pulled the door open and stepped up into the cabin, almost colliding with the tall man called Stretch.

"I, uh, was just coming to get you," she stammered.

Though she was average height at five-seven, he could probably rest his chin on the top of her head. And she hadn't missed the man's powerful-looking arms and chest.

"Yeah," he replied a bit gruffly, holding up a metal thermos, like it should have been obvious. "Just on my way up."

Stepping back out the door, Fiona heard a thumping noise from below the floor. The man ignored it, so she didn't think it was anything serious. She turned and looked up at him. "Is this your boat?"

"Uh huh," he grunted, stepping past her, and climbing the ladder. He held the handle of the thermos firmly between his teeth as he climbed. Fiona had a momentary vision of a pirate boarding a ship with a knife held in his mouth.

She followed him up the ladder. He was much older than her twenty-two years. *Probably older than Barry*, she thought. But where Barry was short and a little pudgy around the middle, with both a receding hairline *and* a bald spot on the back of his head, this man was tall, all sinew and muscle, and would probably be one of those men who'd still have a full head of gray hair when he reached his eighties. She wondered just how old he was.

"Move over," he ordered, handing Charity the thermos.

She quickly complied, rising and moving over to Fiona's seat. Fiona joined Leilani on the side bench. Every man Fiona had ever known had only been interested in one thing, but this man seemed above it all.

Charity removed the screw-on cup, then twisted the lid to the pouring position and filled the cup. Once the man was seated, she handed it to him, then turned to Fiona and Leilani. "Stretch can be grumpy until he's had a jolt of caffeine."

"No, I'm not," Stretch mumbled as he studied the radar, then took a long drink from the cup. He switched off the auto-pilot and turned the wheel slightly to the right while watching the chart plotter.

"What do you do for a living, Stretch?" Fiona asked.

"I drive this boat," he replied. "Charter fishing and diving mostly."

"Is Henry expecting us?" Charity asked.

"Yeah." Stretch checked his watch and flipped a switch on the dash. "We're right on time. He probably already hears us coming."

Fiona recognized the screen that lit up, even under the subdued lighting. He pulled back on the throttles and the

boat slowed. Far ahead, she heard waves splashing against rock.

Stretch bent and studied the chart plotter, turning the wheel slightly. Then he stood and looked out over the front of the boat, glancing occasionally at the sonar screen.

"You know your way through the reef?" Fiona asked.

"Got a coupla spots marked on the plotter," he replied, without looking over. "Then I just follow the forward scanning sonar. You know this reef?"

"No," Fiona replied. "I've never been here before. She said to tell you we were nearing a barrier reef."

"The third longest fringing barrier reef in the world," he replied.

"Who is Henry?" Leilani asked.

"An old guy I know. He was friends with my grandfather; that's how old. Owns a little charter business with a few cabanas for his guests. You'll be completely safe there. He'll see that you're comfortable and well fed, that I can guarantee."

By the light of the moon, Fiona could see a line of churning, white water stretching off to both sides of the boat. Once clear, Stretch pushed the throttles forward and sat back down. He concentrated on the chart plotter and sonar. Fiona leaned past Leilani and looked at the screens. He was following what looked like a shallow channel.

With the shoreline approaching, Stretch finally slowed the boat. It settled down in the water, and he steered toward an opening in the trees that the moonlight revealed just before they entered it. Obviously, it was the kind of place you could only find if you knew it was there. Through the trees, Fiona could see lights.

Stretch steered the big boat into a channel that looked like it dead-ended just ahead. As they approached the end. Fiona could see that it didn't end but turned to the left. Standing, Stretch used the throttles and somehow turned the boat much more sharply than she thought he should be able to. Again, it looked like a dead end, but the lights she'd seen earlier were closer, just beyond the trees on their right. The lights clearly showed the canal turning that way up ahead.

Rounding the second bend, the boat entered a large lagoon with a long dock. Several boats were tied up to it; two were big like the one she was on, but there were several other smaller boats. Beyond the dock was a row of small houses, the one on the left larger than the others.

As they idled slowly toward the dock, Fiona saw what looked like gas pumps, which Stretch turned toward. There was a slight, gray-haired man standing next to the pumps with a much younger black woman.

The black man came out of the cabin below. Leilani had told her earlier that his name was Malcolm, but Fiona didn't think that was his real name. He moved quickly to the front of the boat, where he threw a line to the old man. Then he moved to the back, putting fenders over the side, and threw another line to the black woman.

Stretch turned off the engines and turned to face her and Leilani. "That's Henry and Angelique," he said. "They'll put you up in two of those little cabins over there until we get back."

"We don't have anything, Mister," Leilani said.

Stretch dug into his pocket and reached out his hand to both women. "Here's a thousand each," he said. "Go ahead, take it."

Fiona took one of the two rolls he held out and looked at him, puzzled. "Are you people for real? None of this makes any sense."

"Take some of that money," he said, ignoring her question, "and get Angelique to take you into town in the morning for some clothes. Get enough to last you a week and a suitcase to carry it in — or you can have her take you to the airport and just disappear on your own. But when we get back, if you're still here, we can make disappearing a lot easier."

As the two climbed down, Malcolm was stretching a hose across the boat. The old man and the young black woman stood beside the boat, waiting.

When Stretch climbed down, he went straight to the old man on the dock and shook his hand. Fiona's sharp eyes caught something in Stretch's hand which he palmed into the old man's.

"I'm Henry," the man on the dock said, smiling. "You got nothing to be afraid of here. Hardly anyone even knows where here is."

Fiona was surprised at the black woman's bright blue eyes. Even in the subdued lights from the boat and a single bright light over the gas pumps, she could see that the woman was obviously of mixed ancestry.

"Come wit me," she said, smiling broadly. "We have plenty of room. All our cabins have two beds, would yuh be needin' one of dem or two?"

In her tight skirt, Fiona had to sit on the side of the boat and swing both legs over at the same time. She looked back to Leilani, a question in her eyes.

"We can share one," Leilani said.

"One or two," Angelique said, raising her hands, palms up. "Or three even, no matter. Dere ain't but two of dem occupied now anyway."

Fiona looked down the row of cabins, each one smaller than the boat they'd arrived on. There were eight of them, plus the larger house on the end.

"You live in the bigger house?" Fiona asked.

"Lord no, girl!" Angelique exclaimed. "I jes work for dis old fool, I ain't his house woman." She smiled, putting Fiona at ease. "I live in di second little one; di blue one wit coral shutters."

"We won't be any trouble," Fiona said.

"Don't you worry," Henry said. "This ain't the first time he's dropped girls off here that he'd plucked from danger."

Charity stepped down to the dock and shook hands with Henry, introducing herself to Angelique. Taking Fiona and Leilani by the arms, she led them away from the others. "We'll be back tomorrow," Charity said. "By then, all this will be behind you. I know it's difficult to swallow, but there really are good people in the world, and you're among some of the best I know."

"What happens tomorrow?" Leilani asked.

Charity looked back toward the others before answering. "We're kinda scattered right now. My boat's in Nassau and my helicopter is on Cat Island. When we're finished with this in the morning, we'll come back here and work it out. But while the legal system deals with them, I think you two should disappear. We'll hole up on my boat for a few weeks, somewhere that can't be found."

Fiona looked around. The setting was straight out of an old sitcom she used to watch, with a bunch of castaways on a deserted island. "You mean like this place?"

"By comparison, this will look like it has giant cartoon arrows in neon pointing down at it."

Fiona looked back toward the others. "What did the old man mean by it's not the first time Stretch has dropped girls off here?"

"I wasn't a part of it, but as I understand it, a woman and her granddaughter were kidnapped by Jamaicans and taken to Cat Island. Our team, Stretch included, rescued them and arrested the kidnapper."

"I thought you weren't cops," Leilani said.

"We're not, they were working with the FBI. That's who actually made the arrest."

Fiona felt the wad of cash in her hand. It was the most money she'd held in her whole life. But what this woman was offering was worth a lot more. She exchanged a glance with Leilani, then extended her hand to Charity.

"Thanks for doing this," she said. "I still think all of you are nuts, but thanks. We'll be here."

Charity smiled. "Tell Angelique you need clothes for sailing. She should know a place that will have what you need."

As Charity turned to shake Leilani's hand, the smaller woman stepped past her hand and hugged her. Fiona was moved by the display and wrapped her arms around them both.

After an awkward moment, they stepped back. Charity turned and went back to the others. Malcolm was handing the fuel hose back to Henry, and Stretch was waiting up on top, the engines already running.

In minutes, Charity boarded the boat and they'd untied the lines. The big boat slowly started to move away from the dock, then began to spin around without moving forward. Fiona thought that was a neat trick. Charity glanced back and waved, as the boat started toward the canal. Fiona and Leilani waved back.

"You ladies look about done in," Henry said.

Fiona turned toward him. Angelique was nowhere to be seen.

"She went to her place to fetch y'all something to sleep in," Henry explained. Then he glanced down at Leilani. "I'm afraid you'll be sleeping in something baggy. Are you all growed up?"

"I get that a lot," Leilani said. "I'm twenty-four, so I'm pretty sure I won't be getting any taller."

The old man chuckled and turned to walk down the dock. "Come on this way, then. We got you in cabin three, right next door to Angelique's place. The two cabins down at the far end are taken by a couple of my fishing guides. They'll be heading out early, so I doubt you'll see them in the morning. They're harmless guys, though; both of 'em grew up right here on the island."

Angelique came out of her cabin as they approached, carrying a small basket. "I got some clothes here," she said. "Nuff to get you through di night and to di store tomorrow."

Henry turned toward the bigger house. "I'm goin' to bed. Wake me if ya need anything."

"Come," Angelique said. "I show you to di cabin."

Walking into the little house, Fiona was surprised. It was bigger than a regular motel room, but not by much and only because it had a loft. The one big room was decorated to create a light, airy, island vibe, with natural driftwood wall-hangings instead of the usual paintings by some unknown artist.

238

"Di beds are up dere," Angelique said, pointing toward a ladder attached to the wall of the bathroom.

The front room was a simple living area, with a small sofa, two chairs, and a coffee table. Beyond it was an efficient little kitchen with a tiny table and two wooden chairs.

"I put clean linens on di bed when Mistuh Henry tell me dat Jesse was bringin' guests."

"Jesse?" Fiona asked.

"Di cap'n of dat boat yuh came in on," Angelique said, placing the box of clothes on the coffee table. "Anyway," she continued looking Fiona up and down, "we be 'bout di same size, clothes in here will fit yuh okay till tomorrow."

Turning to Leilani, Angelique said, "Dere was a woman and her granddaughter here some time ago. Di girl was only thirteen or so, but as tall as you, and she left some things. I'm afraid dey are kids clothes."

Leilani grinned. "I mostly shop in the kid's department anyway."

"We set till we get to di mall tomorrow, den."

"Mall?" Fiona asked.

"Di outdoor market place in town," Angelique replied, opening the refrigerator. "Dere is water here, and I just started my little grill on di front porch. I was gonna cook up a lobster and got more if yuh hungry."

"Lobster?" Fiona asked, incredulously. "God, I just realized how hungry I am."

"Oh, we got plenty. Sometimes we eat dem little bugs two times a day. I like to cook dem on di grill, still in dere shells. Mmm, dey good."

"Would it be too much trouble—" Leilani started to ask.

"No trouble at all," Angelique replied with a big smile. Fiona found that she liked this Bahamian woman. "Ole Mistuh Henry go to bed early, but I never go to sleep before midnight."

"How does he fit in with the others?" Leilani asked.

"Henry?" Angelique asked. "He and Cap'n Jesse's grandfather fought in World War Two together, in di Marines." She turned to go and stopped by the door. "I will get some more lobsters from my fridge. Y'all get cleaned up and come over to my porch in half an hour. I have some good homemade wine, to go wit di lobster."

After Angelique left, Fiona turned to Leilani. "This is all weirdin' me out. How did you stumble onto these people?"

Leilani walked over and sat on the sofa. "Brent and I found a lot of money on that boat; we were running. I'm sorry."

Fiona sat beside her only friend. "You don't have to be sorry. I'd have done the same thing. We both promised, remember? How much money?"

"We didn't count it all, but I'm guessing over three hundred thousand."

"Dollars?" Fiona asked, her eyes wide.

"Yeah, the guy was some sort of spy."

"So what happened?"

"We could almost see Miami," Leilani explained. "Brent had said he was going to kill the guy whose boat we were on and take it. He said he knew people in Miami. When he got the captain to stop, Brent hit him with the one-ball."

"Brent's an animal," Fiona said.

"Yeah, well, just after Brent threw the captain overboard, a helicopter hit us with a big spotlight and another boat came up. Malcolm and another man were on the boat, and Charity was flying the helicopter."

"She's a pilot?"

"Among other things," Leilani said. "They all used to work for the government. Brent had a gun we stole from the guy's boat and tried to pull it out. They both shot him. Then Malcolm put me on the helicopter while it just hung in the air a few feet in front of the boat."

"Whoa," Fiona breathed. "Brent's dead? That had to be scary."

Leilani went on to tell her friend about the ride to where they met Stretch, whose name they now knew was Jesse. She told her about how easily Charity had captured Jeff and Doug, knocking them both out, and taking them one at a time out to the boat.

"They were on the boat?" Fiona asked.

"Did you see those trap doors in the floor in the back of the boat?"

"Fish boxes," Fiona explained. "That's where they keep the fish they catch."

"Jeff and Doug were in the fish boxes."

CHAPTER
TWENTY-SIX

Once clear of the barrier reef, Charity and Jesse went below to get some sleep, leaving Tony on the bridge. The ride to Little Stirrup Cay would only take them two hours and once there, they'd all be able to get a little more sleep before the cruise ship arrived.

Alone in the guest cabin, Charity stripped down to her tee-shirt and panties, then lay on the bed and stared up at the darkened ceiling. The only light in the cabin was what moonlight spilled in from the porthole. A shower was definitely in order, but not a good idea while underway.

The ride was smooth. The boat was taking the long, slow rollers on the starboard bow, rolling only a few degrees as it pushed through each wave. McDermitt had chosen his vessel carefully. Even rough seas were no match for the powerful fishing machine. This was like a ride on a pond.

She remembered watching Jesse at the helm of Vic's boat. He'd seemed a natural there, the boat merely an extension of him. He had to take Vic's boat. She couldn't think of anyone else, and even though Vic and Jesse hadn't known each other well, she knew there was a mutual respect.

Closing her eyes, Charity put everything out of her mind. Sleeping while underway had never been a problem for her, and within minutes she was asleep.

A change in the pitch of the engines woke her. She looked at her watch and saw that she'd been asleep for two hours. It was still several more hours before sunrise. They'd planned to make their move an hour before first light.

Listening, she heard the anchor splash into the water. Then the boat backed down on it and the engines stopped. She hadn't heard anything from Jesse's forward cabin, and assumed Tony was anchoring the boat himself. When they'd worked together, Tony, Andrew, and some of the others had learned how to run all the systems on Jesse's boat.

A moment later, she heard the salon hatch open and close, then it was quiet. Rolling onto her side, Charity soon fell back to sleep.

It seemed like she'd only dozed a few minutes when the alarm function on her phone went off. The steel drum alert tone brought back a memory from just a few months earlier, when she and Victor had spent the night ashore on Jost Van Dyke. They'd gotten a little drunk, listened to a great steel band play at Foxy's, and spent the night in a hammock on the beach. She'd added the ring tone to her phone the following morning, making it her alarm. This was the first time she'd used the alarm in a long time.

She rose and dressed quickly, hearing stirring sounds coming from the forward cabin. When she opened her cabin door, she nearly ran into Jesse.

"Ready to do this?" he asked. "The cruise ship will be here in a little over two hours."

"Do you really think we can get in and out without being seen?"

The smell of coffee greeted them as she followed Jesse up to the galley. Tony was pouring mugs for the three of them.

"Should be easy enough," Jesse replied.

Tony handed him a mug. "The ferry crews won't be arriving until after sunrise," he said, passing another mug to Charity. "There's only thirty-two people who live on the island, so there shouldn't be much activity around the docks until maybe an hour before the ship arrives."

They drank their coffee quickly, then went out to the cockpit. Jesse locked the salon hatch as Tony climbed up to the bridge and stood on the port bench to reach the roof. A moment later, the tip of a stand-up paddle board appeared at the aft roof edge and Tony slowly lowered it. Jesse grabbed the board and moved it to the swim platform, standing it on its tail. Within minutes, they had three boards and paddles in place.

"You first," Jesse said to Tony.

Taking the first board, Tony placed it in the water next to the swim platform. Stepping on it, he moved back on the board, until he was well behind the usual paddling position, the nose of the twelve-foot-long board riding high. He nodded his readiness.

Jesse opened both fish boxes and bent down next to one, patting the man inside it on the cheek. "Wakey, wakey, turd fondler."

Jeff Maple lay on his side, his legs pulled up in a near fetal position inside the cramped box. Jesse pulled his feet out first, then, with Charity's help, they got him under the arms and hoisted him to a standing position. The man's eyes were open, and he looked both angry and frightened.

"Here's the deal," Jesse hissed at the bound man, his mouth taped shut, while holding him steady by his shirt front. "We're taking you for a ride on that." He pointed to where Tony was standing on the board, just off the platform. "You just have to lay on your belly and be sure not to move around. If you fall off the board, it's a sure bet that you'll drown. Nod if you understand what I just said."

Jeff glared at Jesse and shook his head violently.

"Yeah, I kinda figured you wouldn't like it," Jesse said, patting him roughly on the cheek again.

McDermitt's as good a man as they come, Charity thought. But when it came to criminals and bad people, he just didn't have much sympathy.

"Do what I say," he growled at the man, "and you won't get cracked over the head with a paddle."

He half-carried, half-dragged Jeff over to the transom door, dropping him unceremoniously onto the swim platform on his back. Jeff looked very uncomfortable lying on top of his bound hands. Jesse didn't seem to notice.

When Tony brought his board up alongside the platform, Jesse simply rolled Jeff onto it, face down. "If he moves, just crack his skull with the paddle."

Tony nodded, and moved the board a few feet away, as Jesse looked up at Charity. "You have everything?"

She removed a plastic freezer bag from the cargo pocket of her shorts. In it were Jeff's and Doug's cell phones, along with a folded sheet of paper. "All set," she said.

Jesse didn't need help with the smaller man. He just reached down and hoisted him to his feet. "Did you hear what I told your buddy?"

Doug Bullard nodded, eyes wide with fright.

"Good," he said, dragging him over to the platform and dropping him onto it in the same manner he had Jeff.

With Bullard in position, Jesse dropped the second board into the water and stepped onto it, maneuvering it alongside, obviously very accustomed to it. When he was in position, Charity rolled the man onto the board.

"Let's go," Jesse said, pushing away from the boat with his paddle.

Charity grabbed the third board and dropped it onto the water. She was no stranger to paddle boarding and stepped easily onto the board, paddle in hand. The three immediately started paddling, aiming the noses of the SUPs toward the rock jetty at the entrance to the ferry terminal.

Paddling hard, all three kept a watchful eye on the shore. The east end of the island was where all the activities took place, but the few residents lived a bit further west on the mile-long island.

Tony had anchored the *Revenge* just a hundred yards east of the entrance, closer to it than the other five boats in the anchorage. They made the opening in just a few minutes. Charity moved into the lead, being lighter, and rounded the turn into the basin. The ferries were tied up at the dock, directly ahead of them. Just to the left was a sand beach of sorts, though not very big. She angled toward it and paddled harder.

When the nose touched the sand, she stepped off the board and pulled it quickly up onto the little beach. Tony and Jesse were right behind her. Jesse dismounted first, and she helped pull his board, Doug still on it, up onto the sand. Then Jesse turned, and he and Tony pulled Tony's board up next to the others.

"You sure you can carry the big guy?" Tony whispered.

"No problem," Jesse replied, hoisting Jeff to his feet.

He struggled with his footing in the loose sand but got the man up onto his shoulder in a fireman's carry, then started up the low dune. Charity knew Jesse's age, but apparently he didn't — or chose to ignore it. She helped Tony get the other man up, then Tony lifted him onto his shoulders in the same way. Charity hurried ahead of them.

The dock was only twenty yards away, and they arrived unseen. There was a large storage box at the end of the dock and Jesse dumped Jeff onto it in a sitting position. Tony deposited Doug next to him.

Looking around, Charity saw a dock line that wasn't in use, coiled neatly by the first ferry boat. She brought it over, and Tony and Jesse shoved the two men back against a dock piling. In moments they were tied to the dock so that they couldn't even stand and hop away.

Charity took the bag from her cargo pocket and opened it. She removed the two phones and put one in each of the men's shirt pockets, then removed the folded sheet of paper and handed it to Jesse. He opened it and read it.

"Call the police, we've killed someone?" he asked, then looked back at the paper. "Proof on our phones?"

"Well, you said to get the attention of whoever found them."

Jesse went over to Doug and leaned down close to his face. "Do I have to hit you before I remove that tape, to keep you from yelling?"

The man shook his head.

"If you try," Jesse warned, "it'll only sound like a chirp before I knock your ass out. You read me?"

The man nodded.

Jesse yanked the tape off of Doug's mouth and quickly stuck the paper to the edge of the sticky side. Then he put it back in place, smoothing it out roughly.

Looking around and still not seeing or hearing anything, the three returned quickly to the beach and pushed the boards back into the water. In minutes they were back aboard the *Revenge*.

Jesse went up to the bridge, with Charity and Tony following. From the overhead compartment, he retrieved his night vision monocular and turned toward shore.

"Good spot, Tony," he said, passing the device to Charity. "We can see everything. Want to hang around?"

"For a few minutes, maybe," she replied, watching the dock.

It didn't take long before their delivery was spotted. One of the ferry crew came out onto the dock and seeing the two men, hurried over. He stopped a few feet away, then turned and ran back to the boat house.

"How far will the police have to come?" Charity asked, suddenly worried that the cruise ship might beat the authorities to the dock.

"At most, two hours," Jesse replied. "Unless there's a patrol boat nearby, Nassau is the nearest Bahamian Royal Police station."

Tony picked his phone up from the console and scrolled through his apps. When he looked up, he smiled. "*Delta Star* will arrive on time in two hours," he said.

"You think it's wise to just hang out here?" Charity asked.

"We're fine until the sun comes up, or when they take the duct tape off their mouths," Jesse said.

Tony was watching through the night-vision scope. "The guy's back," he said. "With friends."

"If they ungag them, we're out of here," Jesse said.

Tony laughed. "I don't think that's gonna be a problem."

He handed the scope over to Jesse who looked through it toward shore and chortled.

"What's going on?" Charity asked.

Jesse handed her the scope and she trained it on the dock area. In the gray-green display, she saw several islanders now standing around the two men on the boat box. One had a large machete, and all of them were standing well away from the two men.

Though the wait seemed to be long, it wasn't. A little more than an hour passed, then a sleek-looking Bahamian Police patrol boat with its lights on came roaring around the east end of the island, swinging wide around the *Revenge* and several other boats in the anchorage.

The patrol boat turned into the basin and slowed to an idle. In minutes, they were tied up alongside one of the ferry boats, the blue and red lights washing over the whole waterfront.

Charity recognized the man who was first on the dock. It was the police officer from the boatyard, Sergeant Bingham.

"That's the cop who responded when Vic's boat was robbed," she said. "He took me to the hospital, just before Vic died."

The sun was purpling the eastern sky. Jesse got a pair of binoculars and watched alongside her, the lightening sky and waterfront lighting providing enough light to see now.

"What if they look out here and see us watching?" Charity said quietly.

"Not a problem," Tony said. "Look around."

Charity glanced around the anchorage. The three boats closest to them all had people watching the shore activities, most with binoculars.

Through the night vision, Charity watched as Sergeant Bingham placed a small satchel in front of Jeff and Doug and opened it. He first put on a pair of latex gloves, then carefully removed the phone from Doug's pocket.

"Watch this," Tony said.

Charity glanced over at him. Tony had a second pair of binos and was grinning as he watched the dock.

Looking through the monocular again, she watched as Bingham pressed the power button on the phone. After a second, he suddenly stood and motioned one of the other policemen over. Both men watched the phone intently for several seconds.

"What'd you do?" Charity asked.

Tony chuckled. "I made a slide show that starts automatically, using crime photos from all the murders and robberies these people were involved in. That Leilani is some kind of savant, remembering all those dates and places."

Bingham turned to the dock workers and said something. One of the men ran off toward the boathouse. Bingham turned toward the two men on the boat box and took a card from his wallet, apparently reading them their rights. He paused at one point and pointed at them, saying something to one of his officers, before returning to reading the card.

"A by-the-book guy," Tony said. "I like that."

A small boat came around the ferries and pulled up alongside the patrol boat. The dock worker who'd run off climbed out and handed the line to one of the cops.

"This isn't good," Charity warned. "He hasn't even removed the tape. Why would he need a boat? If he comes out here, he's bound to recognize me."

Jesse lowered his binos and looked down toward the bow, then back at the tender. Bingham was already climbing aboard with two other officers.

"That patrol boat made the sixty miles from Nassau in just over an hour," Jesse said. "He's making an educated guess that whoever put them there might still be in the area. His boat can probably outrun us. I sure hope he's not as *by-the-book* as he seems."

In minutes, the tender came out of the rocky inlet to the ferry berth and angled toward the anchorage. The Revenge being the closest boat, it started straight toward them.

"What do we do?" Charity asked.

"Take it easy," Jesse said. "Just see what happens. What's his name?"

"Bingham is all I know," Charity said. "He gave me his card, but I don't know where it is."

"Tony?"

"Working on it," Tony replied, concentrating on his phone. Just as the boat slowed to come up to the swim platform, Tony said. "Clarence. Sergeant Clarence Bingham. He's a uniform detective, Jesse."

Bingham was standing in the bow of the tender. "May I speak with the captain?"

"Come aboard, Detective Bingham," Jesse called down.

The sergeant's eyes had been on Jesse and Tony. He hesitated a moment, hearing his name, and gazed at all of them before his eyes settled on Charity. He dropped lightly from the bow of the small tender onto the platform and tied the boat off. When he stepped through the open transom door, another officer started to board.

"Just you if you don't mind, Detective," Jesse said.

The man looked up. "I do not need permission, Captain."

"Yes, I know, and I'm not offering it. That's why I said *if you don't mind*. We may have information for you, but only for you."

Inwardly, Charity smiled. It wasn't exactly common knowledge, but throughout the Caribbean there were many policemen, as well as other government officials, who were underhanded and often solicited bribes from Americans. Jesse was counting on Sergeant Bingham being both a straight shooter and knowledgeable about the corruption in his own department.

Bingham stared at Charity for a moment. She looked back at him, keeping any emotion from her face.

Bingham held a hand up to the other officers. "Wait in the boat."

When he turned back toward them, Charity thought for a moment that he grinned at her. "May I come up dere?"

Jesse nodded, and Bingham climbed the ladder to the bridge. Tony stepped back between the port bench and console to make room.

"Miss Fleming, is it?" he asked, but Charity could see there was another question in his eyes.

"By now you know who Victor was," Charity said. "And there's a good chance that you may even know that's not my real name."

Bingham glanced around the bridge. "A beautiful boat, Captain. May we sit down a moment?"

Jesse waved a hand toward the bench, and Tony stepped back further. Once everyone was seated, Bingham actually smiled.

"Yes," he said, leaning forward with his elbows on his knees. "I know dat Rene Cook was Victor Pitt, formerly with your Central Intelligence. And yes, I know you are not who you said." The man's brow furrowed, as he gazed at her. "But dat is all I know, and dat tells me more dan I want to know."

"I am Charity Styles," she said. "I once worked for America's Homeland Security. As did these two men, Captain Jesse McDermitt, and Tony Jacobs. We're now employed by a private security firm."

"And Victor Pitt?"

"He freelanced for us on occasion," Jesse lied. Or at least Charity thought it a lie. Jesse had said that he'd met Victor once. Perhaps he had worked with the team some time over the last year.

Bingham looked down at the deck and sighed. When he looked up, his eyes locked on Charity's. "And when you entered my country—"

"I used my own passport," Charity replied.

Bingham glanced at Jesse, who nodded. "Same here."

"I see. So why did you present a false identity to me in Nassau?"

Charity smiled. "I guess you could say it was force of habit. We were attached to Homeland Security's Caribbean Counter terrorism Command."

Bingham looked over toward the docks. "So you think dese men are responsible for Mister Pitt's murder?"

Charity started to speak, but Jesse cut her off. "I have no doubt that forensic evidence was collected from all the crime scenes listed on the phone you now have, Detective. Most of those crimes took place on Bahamian soil. You received that information anonymously, along with those two men, *and* the names of their cohorts on a cruise ship which is about to arrive here. All this anonymous stuff can be used in court."

Bingham nodded. "Dat's true, but—"

McDermitt cut him off. "Bringing us in for whatever minor infractions we may or may not have committed would taint that evidence, making it inadmissible."

Charity could see why the man rarely worried about anything. In every situation she'd ever seen him in, McDermitt was the one in charge. It didn't matter if he was dealing with the Secretary of State or a Game Warden.

Even scruffy and unkempt, he knew, and everyone around him knew, that he was the one calling the shots. If Sergeant Bingham pressed, McDermitt would push back harder. His attitude emboldened her.

Bingham looked down at the deck and sighed again. "Yes, I believe you are right, Captain," he said, looking up at Jesse. "On both counts. And it *would* make my job easier."

Jesse grinned. "Ever receive a horse as a gift?"

Bingham thought it over a moment, then looked out to the east where the sun was just beginning to peek above the horizon. A cruise ship could be seen out there, heading slowly toward them.

"There are more on dat ship?"

"Three more," Charity said. "The leaders of the gang who committed the murders you told me about back in Nassau, and which you now have evidence connecting all five people." Charity paused. "And there's a possibility that they have another victim on board."

That got the sergeant's full attention.

"We have witnesses in protective custody," Tony said. "They can place all five people at the scene of at least six murders."

Bingham glanced over at Tony. "You still work for the American government?"

"No, sir," Tony replied, but didn't elaborate.

"Your police force," Charity began, "as well as those of other islands around the Caribbean do a good job, Detective Bingham. I've met some of your crime scene investigators; they're sharp people. I have no doubt there will be evidence that can put those two men and three others arriving on that ship, at all of those crime scenes, on the dates and times the crimes were committed. All the information is on those two cell phones."

Bingham stared at Charity for a long moment. Then his expression softened. "I am sorry for your loss, Miss Fleming. I will do all dat I can to see dat justice is done."

CHAPTER TWENTY-SEVEN

When they returned to Andros, Charity was anxious see if the two women were still there. She couldn't quite understand why she wanted to help them, except that there hadn't been anyone to help her when she'd lost her father. If it hadn't been for a sympathetic social worker, and the fact that she had already been offered a college scholarship, she might easily have wound up in foster care.

Fiona and Leilani were waiting at the dock. "You were right," Fiona called up to Jesse as Tony tied the boat up. "We could hear you more than fifteen minutes ago."

The two women boarded the *Revenge*, while Jesse took Finn ashore to find Henry. The girls each had two small canvas bags that looked to be stuffed full.

"What happened?" Leilani asked.

"Jeff and Doug were arrested," Charity said. "When we left, the police were waiting for *Delta Star* to drop anchor, so they could arrest the Pences and Rayna. Did you find everything you needed?"

"I think so," Leilani said. "There were a couple outfits I liked, but Angelique said they wouldn't be suitable for sailing. Just one thing; I don't know anything at all about sailboats."

"I've sailed a little," Fiona offered.

"Don't worry," Charity said. "My boat can sail herself if need be. It's not hard to learn."

Jesse returned with Henry, Finn loping ahead of them. They stopped by the boat's transom, and Jesse thanked him again.

"Any time," the old man said, then turned toward Charity. "When you get back here, just buzz the camp and I'll pick you up at the airport. I got some parts to pick up in Nassau and can carry you across."

"We better get going," Tony called from the bridge. "It'll be past noon before we reach Cat Island."

Fiona looked at Charity, confused. "I thought you said your boat was in Nassau."

"It is," Charity replied. "But my helicopter's over on Cat Island. I'll fly it back here, while you two remain aboard the boat and head toward Nassau. We'll meet up somewhere offshore later this evening."

"Y'all are welcome to just stay here," Henry offered, getting a look from Jesse.

"Thanks, Henry," Jesse said, "but I think it's better if these two disappear."

"Those people got that kinda reach?"

Fiona and Leilani exchanged glances. "Yeah," Fiona said. "With one phone call, the Pences could have someone hunting us, just for the sake of revenge."

"They'll make that call soon," Charity said. "It's best if we head down island, disappear to Saint Somewhere."

The old man grinned. "Just don't get too drunk to karaoke."

"You're a parrot head?" Fiona asked the old man.

Henry smiled warmly. "Since before Timothy B coined the phrase."

"I just recently joined the Phlock," Charity said.

They all laughed, except Jesse, who had a confused look on his face. "We're wasting daylight," he said, extending his hand to Henry.

"Semper Fi, Gunny," the old man said, taking the offered hand.

Jesse grunted back, "Yut," and tossed off the lines. Charity helped the women stow their bags, while Tony tended to the fenders and made ready for a fast crossing. Both men were on the bridge when the three women climbed up.

The boat slowly idled through the canal, and Jesse asked Charity what the flocking parrot thing was about.

"You really don't know?" she asked.

He looked even more perplexed. "I'm not even sure what *it is* that I don't know. Chyrel talks about parrots all the time."

Tony grinned. "A parrot head is a Jimmy Buffett fan."

"The guy that did *Come Monday*, back when Christ was a corporal?"

"He went on to write a few more songs since then," Charity explained. She knew the man preferred jazz, but she also knew that, hanging around in bars in the Keys, he was probably familiar with a few songs by the Caribbean balladeer. "Ever heard *Cheeseburger in Paradise* or *Margaritaville*?"

"All the time," he replied, making the final turn into open water. He punched the throttles up a little, as the boat moved farther away from shore. "I thought those were just island bar songs that everyone played."

The others laughed. "And what was that language you and Henry were speaking," Fiona asked. "Semper yut, gunny?"

Charity looked at Jesse and he nodded. "Time to come clean," she said, turning toward the girls sitting with her on the side bench. "Jesse and Tony are everything I told you they were. Before that, Jesse was a Marine sniper and Tony, a Navy SEAL. Gunny is short for gunnery sergeant, the rank Jesse retired as."

The two women exchanged glances and Leilani said, "I've been using my grandmother's name. I started using it, the day I was taken from my family. She died just a year before that."

"Smart thinking," Jesse said. "Now you can go home and be yourself without worry."

A slow smile came to the tiny woman's face. "I am Moana Kapena. I am Samoan."

Jesse pushed the throttles forward, and the bow rose, as the big boat gathered speed. Once on plane, he smiled at the little woman, and rose from his seat. He moved around behind it, while reaching across the seat to hold the boat steady. "Come over here, Moana Kapena."

The tiny woman exchanged looks with Charity, who nodded. She stood and stepped behind the helm.

"Take the wheel," Jesse said. "See that red dot on the chart plotter? That's a gap in the reef. Aim the little boat

icon on the screen at the dot and when we get close, you'll be able to see the reef."

"Are you nuts?" Moana asked, gripping the wheel in both hands.

"You don't know what your name means?"

Moana twisted her head around, looking back at Jesse. "I was a kid when I was taken. I didn't even know names had meanings."

Jesse put a hand on her shoulder. "You'll do fine, just follow your instincts. Kapena means captain and Moana means ocean. Your parents chose your destiny when you were born. The Samoan people were the first true mariners. They crossed oceans three thousand years before Columbus arrived here in these islands."

"Really?" Moana asked.

"Anything to do with boats and seas," Charity said, "Jesse's the man to ask."

Moana settled down at the wheel and concentrated on the chart plotter, occasionally standing and looking over the helm at the approaching reef.

Charity looked out over the bow and could see the color change of the water and the eddies where the rollers rose over the reef. Moana stopped looking at the plotter and concentrated on the reef ahead.

Jesse reached past her and pushed the throttles almost to full speed, just shy of the rpm where the superchargers began screaming. The *Revenge* surged forward, quickly reaching nearly full speed. Moana squealed in surprise.

"Aim for the center of the undisturbed waves," Jesse said, pointing ahead. "That's the cut in the reef. Anywhere you see foam or swirling water, there's coral just below the surface."

A few minutes later, the *Revenge* charged through the breach into the TOTO, or Tongue of the Ocean, a long, wide trench in the seafloor that was nearly a mile deep. The wind was up a little and seas beyond the reef were choppier. The waves presented no problem for the *Revenge*.

"See the compass there on top of the helm?" Jesse asked, pointing. Moana nodded. "Turn a little to the right, until the number one-thirty shows up."

When she had the boat going in the right direction, Jesse reached past her shoulder and flipped on the auto-pilot. "You can let go now, the boat will drive itself."

"That was cool!" Moana shouted, standing and jumping up to hug Jesse. She nearly knocked him off balance, but he managed to grab the back of the seat in time.

"You're a natural, kid," Jesse said, blushing slightly, as he put the girl down.

Charity caught the flush in his cheeks and the quick glance downward at Moana's tiny frame. Although the young woman was about the same age as his oldest daughter, Jesse knew he hadn't just been holding a kid.

The reality of what she was about to undertake hit her. These two women had been treated as nothing more than warm meat nearly their entire lives. How did one go about unbreaking a person, putting the pieces back together in the right order and getting them to realize that their life can have purpose and meaning beyond being someone's punching bag or sex toy? It would be doubly hard, since even a good and decent man like McDermitt could have lustful thoughts around them.

Charity glanced at her charges. Neither was wearing a bit of makeup and they were dressed in new clothes made for boating; loose and baggy. Still, it was obvious that they

were two very beautiful young women. In any port or anchorage in the Caribbean, they'd quickly become the center of attention.

"So how did it feel, being in control of over two thousand horsepower?" Tony asked Moana, breaking in on Charity's thoughts.

"Whoa!" Fiona said. "Really?"

Tony went on, talking about the engines and how Jesse had modified them. He rattled on about twin turbo this, and supercharger that. In some deep, subliminal way, he was flirting with the two women and probably didn't even realize it.

She knew Tony quite well; they'd worked side by side for over two years. On first meeting him, Charity had found him attractive. He was witty and charming and completely forthright and honest about everything. But she'd been anxious to prove that she could not only fit in but was fit for the job, so she'd shut down his advances.

Yes, Tony Jacobs was a good man, too. A married man. And she somehow knew that he'd never be unfaithful to his wife, no matter the circumstances. Yet here he was, casually flirting with a girl at least ten years younger than him.

If these two men, both honorable and caring people, could have even a momentary lapse in judgment, seeing these two girls in a sexual way, what chance did she have of teaching them that all men weren't like those they'd known in the past?

Yeah, Charity thought. *This is going to be a challenge.*

If you'd like to receive my twice a month newsletter for specials, book recommendations, and updates on coming books, please sign up on my website:

WWW.WAYNESTINNETT.COM

THE CHARITY STYLES
CARIBBEAN THRILLER SERIES
Merciless Charity
Ruthless Charity
Reckless Charity
Enduring Charity

THE JESSE MCDERMITT
CARIBBEAN ADVENTURE SERIES
Fallen Out
Fallen Palm
Fallen Hunter
Fallen Pride
Fallen Mangrove
Fallen King
Fallen Honor
Fallen Tide
Fallen Angel
Fallen Hero
Rising Storm
Rising Fury
Rising Force (Fall, 2018)

The Gaspar's Revenge Ship's Store is now open. There you can purchase all kinds of swag related to my books.
WWW.GASPARS-REVENGE.COM

Made in the USA
Middletown, DE
17 May 2018